6

MY GUARDIAN GRYPHON

SANCTUARY, TEXAS BOOK SIX

KRYSTAL SHANNAN

My Guardian Gryphon

Sanctuary, Texas Book 6

Copyright © 2016 KS Publishing

All rights reserved.

This book is a work of fiction and any resemblance to persons –living or dead –or places, events, or locales is purely accidental. The characters are reproductions of the author's imagination and used fictitiously. This book contains content that is not suitable for readers 17 and under.

Cover designs by Clarise Tan - CT COVER CREATIONS

All rights reserved.

Please be aware that this book cannot be reproduced, scanned, or distributed in any printed or electronic form without written permission from the author, Krystal Shannan, at krystalshannan@yahoo.com, or within the sharing guidelines at a legitimate library or bookseller. Please do not participate in or encourage piracy of copyrighted materials in violation of the author's rights. Purchase only authorized editions.

WARNING: The unauthorized reproduction, sharing, or distribution of this copyrighted work is illegal. Criminal copyright infringement, including infringement without monetary gain, is investigated by the FBI (http://www.fbi.gov/ipr/) and is punishable by up to five years in a federal prison and a fine of $250,000.

❁ Created with Vellum

ACKNOWLEDGMENTS

This book has been one of the hardest to write in the series so far, but I'm so excited to give you Alek and Gretchen's story. They touched my heart deeply and I hurt for both of them throughout the process of writing.

For my readers that have sexual assault triggers, I want you to know that I tried to handle Gretchen's experiences in this book in a way that respects the emotional trauma an assault brings with it. She is a survivor.

The world of Sanctuary has been home to me for a long time and even though I'm excited to write the next book, I'm sad that it's so close to its finale. The characters have become my friends over the course of the last two years and I hope they are yours as well. I hope you are enjoying this journey with me.

A huge thanks to all the people who help make these books come together. My cover artist Erin, my editors, Jena and Jacy, and Cheryl, my fantastic publishing assistant who makes my life so much easier - Annie you are wonder woman! I wouldn't be able to focus so totally on writing without your support behind the scenes.

To my brain trust and fabulous friends - ChickTales. Becca, Jodi, and KC - You are priceless. This book was a struggle and you all helped me shape and build it into the fantastic book it is today. Thank you.

Also, a huge shout out to my wonderful ARC readers in Krystal's Cavalry! You rock and I love you all and I hope that you know how much I appreciate the time you take out of your busy lives spend with my books. You show so much love in your reviews and I can't thank you enough.

And to my fans! You've been amazing and have loved Sanctuary and I can't thank you enough for coming with me on this adventure. There's so much more to come and I hope you will stick with me for each and every step. An extra special hug goes to my fan Julie Bloomquist Walker. Thank you for your title suggestion for Alek and Gretchen's book!

Last but never least, my amazing husband and daughter who put up with Mama being part cyborg and always being connected to either the laptop, the iPad, or my phone. I do everything for you and because of you both. I love you both so dearly. You are my life. Thank you for putting up with my crazy.

PRAISE FOR SANCTUARY, TEXAS

"Wonderfully imaginative. Vampires have never been so sexy or dangerous." ~Liliana Hart, NYT Bestselling Author of the Rena Drake Series

"I couldn't put it down, action packed and sexy!" - Amazon Reviewer

"steamy love scenes, danger, friendship, magic, vampires, werewolves, adorable pixies and more!" - Amazon Reviewer

"Shannan weaves a sexy, action-packed tale sure to keep you turning the pages late into the night." ~~Liliana Hart, NYT Bestselling Author of the Rena Drake Series

"The dialogue is intelligent, exceptionally well written and flows effortlessly. Ah, the characters....they are the main component, the heart and soul of this story. Each and every character is fascinating, captivating, intriguing, engaging and sexy as sin." - Judy Lewis

MY GUARDIAN GRYPHON

A beauty and her beast...

Gretchen has been falling for the Gryphon of Sanctuary a little more each hour she spends in the Castle library. He reads to her, he tells her stories of the real history he lived, and surely he notices her growing affection. Only he hasn't. Or won't. But every moment she doesn't confess her love brings her closer to the doom she fears: the Sisters of the House of Lamidae need her to have a human's baby. And Alek is anything but human...

Alek looks forward to finding Gretchen in the Castle library. Her smile calms his inner beast. Her happiness reminds him there is beauty in a world out to destroy his kind--Others. Supernaturals waiting for a way to leave Earth and return to their world. But Gretchen makes him want to stay.

But Gretchen is off-limits. The House of Lamidae has

a present destiny, and his duty is to protect them. Not fall in love.

CHAPTER 1

GRETCHEN

"What about this one," I asked, my voice filled with a hope he didn't notice. He never noticed. I could choose the most romantic story in the Blackmoor's enormous library, and he would still look at me like I was the eleven-year-old girl who'd asked him a random history question fifteen years ago.

His wide brow wrinkled over amber-colored eyes that shimmered with flecks of gold. He was a man women dreamed about. At least I dreamed about him.

Tall. Dark. Mysterious. Broad shoulders melted into a tapered waist and narrow hips. Muscles went on for miles, muscles that I wanted to touch and feel against my naked skin. My stomach clenched and rolled. Lower in my body, a steady hum and throb started, growing with the ache inside I felt every time we were together. It'd gotten worse with each passing year.

By the gods, Gretchen, get a hold of yourself.

"*Antony and Cleopatra?*" The inflection of his voice carried surprise, and the words were spaced out, like he'd had to stop and think between the names.

I glanced up from the time-aged book. Not surprised. Even from across the expansive room he could read the embossed gold title on the cover like it was only inches from his face—he had telescopes for eyes. He never missed anything.

Except what was right in front of him. I could probably wrap my naked body in a clear shower curtain and he'd still be oblivious.

"It's one of the most classical romances of that time period." I emphasized the word romance, hoping to lead his mind in that direction. I'd never give up. Even if it took my whole life to make him notice me.

"Cleopatra was a..." His voice sharpened, filled with an emotion I couldn't quite pin down. Irritation. Annoyance. Disbelief. "She was a smart woman, but she only loved herself. Both Caesar and Marc Antony fell for her wiles. Perhaps it did look like a love story from the outside, but from the inside, the only thing you could see was her cold, calculating heart." He sat on our favorite couch and watched me expectantly. I half-expected him to pat the seat cushion and call me over. But he didn't. He just sat there—waiting. Frustratingly patient and oblivious as ever.

Well, that didn't work. Stupid Cleopatra. Instead of associating her with romance, he's all bristled and annoyed. "So you're saying Shakespeare got the story wrong?" I flipped through the worn pages of the classic. The smell of aged, stale paper had long since become a staple. My life revolved around escaping my quarters in the basement level of the castle. The library had started out a childhood fascination with history—humans—and a way to escape the mundane tasks the Sisters were constantly participating in—gardening, meditating, learning how to copulate to encourage fertilization.

On and on and on.

I didn't get out of all the required studies, but I'd missed enough over the years that many of the Sisters were more than aware that I actively refused to participate in the destiny laid out for us thousands of years ago by the Lamassu—an ancient supernatural race more powerful than any other on Earth. A destiny that included giving myself to a stranger every weekend until I became pregnant. The House of Lamidae's sole purpose was to procreate to increase the power of our collective visions— visions that would lead us to the eight Protectors. Vampire warriors who Rose—the Lamassu Sentinel who'd been protecting our House for thousands of years—would use to fulfill the prophecy.

Bile rose in my throat, and I took a deep breath, willing it back down into my stomach where it belonged. I put a hand on the end of the bookshelf and exhaled. My stomach calmed, and the urge to vomit no longer waited anxiously behind my tongue.

"Are you unwell, Gretchen?" The concern in his voice gave light to my flickering hope. But I wanted more. More than just the concern of a friend.

"I'm fine," I answered, trying to purposefully sound more upbeat than I felt.

"You look a little green."

Seriously? I am not green. "I'm fine. Please read Cleopatra's story." Living in a town filled with ancient immortals had its perks. They'd experienced it. Breathed air with

3

many of the people in the books I'd read over the years. "How well did you know her?"

"Not personally, but I heard much about her from others in her employ. It was difficult to live in that time and not know *about* her."

"You're better than any book in this library. You know that, right?"

He blinked, raising his eyebrows. His lips parted for a moment before he closed them again. Closed off the emotion he'd let slip through the armor he permanently wore.

"We're lucky the Blackmoor's saved what they did during the American Riots. Most of the books here are the only copies left in North America. Oral testimony will never compare with the written word."

"I know. I know. Supernaturals are the only ones who raced to save history while the American people just eradicated everything—knowledge, individuality, expression. You've reminded me many times." When I'd first come across Alek Melos relaxing in a corner of Miles and Eli Blackmoor's library, I'd desired nothing more than the truth—an answer to a single question about what had torn apart the United States. I'd gotten so much more.

He'd told me which stories were real and which stories weren't. What events had led to the downfall of one of the most powerful countries on Earth? So strange to think there were other worlds. Well—at least two. Earth and Veil.

Still, my mind wondered if there could be even more. I'd asked him once and he'd shrugged, saying he hadn't heard of any others.

"If you don't like discussing Cleopatra, I can pick

something else." The stories used to be what drew me to the library day after day to learn everything I could from the quiet man I'd grown to care so deeply for. But now the stories were just the ancillary reason I went to the library. Now I desired something else completely.

I wanted to see Alek. Be next to him. Feel his touch. I wanted to belong to him. Something deep inside me sang every time we were in the same room. Joy filled me when we touched.

"It is a good tale. We should still read it."

"She committed suicide by snake. Was that real?" I walked across the room, enjoying the plushness of the Persian carpets covering the floor, and sank down onto the couch cushion next to Alek. The curtains on the floor-to-ceiling window behind us were drawn back with silken cords thicker than my wrists, and the afternoon light spilled in on my shoulders.

Alek's body, hard as the stone walls of this castle, burned hotter than the sunlight against the skin of my arm, but I leaned closer anyway. My mind automatically readied to receive the vision I always saw when I touched him, but I pushed it away this time.

Controlling my gift was something I'd mastered years ago. Some of the Sisters never learned to turn the switch on and off, but I had and took full advantage of not *seeing* things every time I touched someone or something. I pitied those of my sisters, who had to endure visions of past, present, and future any and every time they touched another being.

My past, present, and future was sitting right next to me. He just didn't know it yet, or if he did, he was doing a fine job of concealing it.

I crossed my legs on the silky brocade couch cushion and let my dress pool in the gap between them. The men who came to the castle for the *joinings* were always telling me my legs were long and beautiful, but I wanted Alek to notice them, not strangers there to ogle my body in hopes that I'd pick them for a *joining*.

Only Alek.

Only his hands would ever touch my body. That'd been my vow from the second I'd first had the vision of us together three years ago.

"She did," Alek answered. His rich, velvety bass tone drew me out of my bouncing thoughts. "She was to be captured. Taken prisoner. She was proud and cornered." His deep voice rumbled from the center of his chest, sending little fiery darts of joy straight to my nervous system. I loved listening to him speak.

These meetings in the library were the only thing that had kept me sane in this prison of stone through the last decade. Alek was my light. My hope. I still remembered the day I'd first met him, and it made me smile.

He pressed his lips together just slightly before speaking. "What are you thinking about?" His gaze bore into me, steady and strong, piercing straight through to my heart.

"The day I met you." I kept my tone soft, doing my best to hide the desire I knew would stream out of me like an overflowing bath if ever given the chance. "I remember wondering why people thought you were scary."

His eyes widened again. "You didn't find me frightening?" His mouth remained flat, but his dark brown eyes sparkled with amusement.

My destiny had been chosen for me the day I was born.

I wanted to tell him how much I hated it. How much more I wanted. I wanted to throw myself into his arms and tell him about my vision of us together. The perfect picture of the future that appeared to me every time I touched him.

"Never." I shook my head. "You were big and gruff, but you were kind. You took the time to answer the questions of a child who sought the truth. And you kept answering my questions. You keep teaching me, even now." I looked down to the carpet and breathed away the dampness in my eyes. I pressed my lips together and fought for control of my emotions. He made it look so easy, but it wasn't for me. My emotions leaked like sieve from inside to outside where everyone could see everything.

I'd forsaken all for the man who'd stolen my heart, and he didn't even know it. He had me. My whole heart. My mind. My everything would be his if only he...asked.

He cared for me. I knew he did.

I could feel it every time we spoke. Every time we touched. It could be so much more.

Everyone in the town watched out for me and the other Sisters of Lamidae. They protected us. Died for us. We were the chosen ones, the seers who needed to be shielded from everyone and everything. But Alek cared more. He had to. He spent so many hours with me—reading, talking, discussing things about his world I would never see. Because I would never be free from this castle.

"I'm glad our time together has been good. Reading with you is very... rewarding."

His words jarred me from my thoughts. *Rewarding?* I wanted to scream that I loved him. Wanted to ask him how he could just sit by and let me battle Rose and the

Sisters and everything around me. I wanted to ask him about that pause in his response, too. Had I missed something? Had he shown me affection in a way I'd missed?

But I didn't ask. I let it go.

The Sisters of Lamidae could see the future, and that was dangerous because people would use us to further their agendas—specifically Xerxes, Rose's brother-in-law, the only other Lamassu alive. He'd murdered his own brother and made it his mission in life to steal the Sisters from Rose. On and on the warnings rattled from the older Sisters. From Rose herself. We were too valuable to be allowed any rights, any freedom.

OUR ONLY DESTINY.

Have babies.

Build the numbers to strengthen the magick.

More magick meant better visions.

Better visions meant the prophecy would be fulfilled sooner and everyone would be safe from Xerxes foul intentions.

Fuck that.

We'd been on a mission to find the eight Protectors for thousands of years and still hadn't succeeded. Not that I could ever say any of that out loud. Everyone expected us to stay in line. Follow the rules. Fulfill our destiny.

It just wasn't working for me.

"You're going to catch a chill. Why aren't you wearing a cloak?" His tone was matter-of-fact, not even the slightest bit suspicious or interested in why I'd worn a dress that showed ample cleavage or why I'd purposefully bared most of my legs.

I spread the skirt of my dress over my legs to cover them.

He took the book from my hands and met my gaze with his beautiful brown eyes. I loved the way flecks of gold danced in them when he was irritated. It was probably part of the reason I continually tried to rile him for one reason or another. Just to see the glint of the Gryphon within. The whole shifting animal sharing a soul thing was pretty damned interesting. I'd never seen him shift before, but asking him at some point had crossed my mind.

I kept my voice light and fun, and I returned his invasive stare with a bright smile. "You're my personal heater. The last thing I need when I'm with you is a cloak." I couldn't help the laugh that rose inside me. I loved that he called a sweater or cover-up a cloak, so old-fashioned. I'd never seen anyone in Sanctuary wear an actual *cloak*, but I didn't get out much. Alek said people rarely wore them anymore.

Cloaks were from the old books we read, old stories of times so different from what existed now. At least that's what he told me. I had to take his word for it, having never set foot outside the castle walls.

Alek shook his head ever so slightly, amused again, but still no show of emotion.

I didn't get him to smile or laugh often, but it was worth it to try. His laugh made my insides melt and my stomach do a somersault. And his smile...*Damn*. There wasn't another man in town with a smile as perfect as Alek's. A smile that filled the void in my soul.

He opened the book and began reading the opening to Shakespeare's *Antony and Cleopatra*. His accent morphed after the first few lines. Listening to him read Shakespeare was heaven. The lilt of his voice as he read the words from the page was enchanting. Like a vision, it carried me away into the story, blocking out all reality. Blocking out the situation I had facing me again tonight.

Suitors.

Men came to the castle every weekend. Men approved and vetted and offering themselves to the Sisters of Lamidae in exchange for a night of mutual pleasure—called *joinings*. A night they would not remember after they left. It was all part of the contract.

They knew their memories would be wiped, and yet they still agreed. We were an experience they couldn't get anywhere else. A lot of the men came back multiple times, and the same Sister would take him to her bed week after week, month after month—a twisted way of pretending they had a relationship with their sperm donor.

Even though the men didn't remember.

We did.

It may have been a one-sided relationship, but it worked for many. Some Sisters didn't care and chose a new bed partner each time they were ready to conceive again. We were asked to have at least two children during our life-span, but many Sisters found refuge in having many children—at least the ones who could manage it. It filled their days with happiness and laughter to have baby after baby.

While others viewed it as I did—cursing a new generation into exile and a lonely existence. And then there were those who were never able to conceive. Through the years, more and more of the Sisters were plagued by infertility—or the men they chose were the culprits. No one really knew for sure.

Choosing a man to lie with over and over again until we had our minimum of two children was required. One might say it was ingrained in us by something so powerful that it consumed our every thought. We didn't just need to have children. We would lose our minds if we didn't. Several Sisters, who were never able to conceive, fell into a deep depression, ultimately taking their lives. A fine display of magick gone terribly wrong.

There always had to be a new generation of Sisters. Our power would deplete if our numbers got too low. They were too low right now.

It was our destiny. My destiny. One that I refused to accept, regardless of the burning agony deep in my gut that demanded I conceive.

But the child I wanted...the relationship I wanted...was a dream I'd never be allowed to make reality. Playing in the dungeon of the castle was permitted with the supernatural citizens of Sanctuary as long as no penetration was involved. Many of my Sisters enjoyed a little kink—or a lot, especially the ones who were hopelessly childless. Their fascination for play was just a way to distract them from the pain and depression that haunted them every month when their cycle started yet again—reminding them of their barrenness.

But *playing* was a pastime, not a path to children. We weren't allowed to have children with a supernatural. It was genetically impossible.

Or so Rose said.

It made logical sense in a way. Most supernatural species could only have children with their species. Though there were a few that could cross the genetic barrier—Lamassu being one—it was not common. At least from what I'd overheard through the years.

I leaned my cheek against Alek's strong arm. The rise and fall in his voice carried my imagination into the lyrical lines of Shakespeare. Everything fell away. All the worry and concern about tonight. None of it mattered. I wouldn't be forced to choose a suitor. Not today, perhaps not for many more months. I was only twenty-six, still plenty of childbearing years ahead of me, but the time was coming. I knew I wouldn't be able to avoid making a choice much longer.

A fight I would eventually lose. Depression gripped my soul, and I turned my focus back to the beautiful drama Alek was performing for me. I should be enjoying the moment, not dreading the coming night.

He reached the end of the first act and closed the book.

"I know this is just a story, but have you known anyone who loved the way Shakespeare describes?" I gazed up at him, and he rewarded me with a quick nod. No smile, though. Gods, I wanted a smile. *Please.* It'd been over a week since I'd coaxed one out of him.

"Miles, Eli, and Diana love with the same fierceness Shakespeare attributes to Antony and Cleopatra. Erick and Bailey. Killían and Eira. Charlie and her two mates, Travis and Garrett. There are many who I've met through the millennia who love and have loved in the way the great storyteller describes."

"Have you?" I asked bravely, wanting desperately to know. A part of me needed to know if he pined for a lost love or if the man was truly oblivious to every signal I'd attempted to hurl in his direction.

"No."

That's it? That's all he was giving me, a flat single-syllabled *no*? Not that I wasn't selfishly glad. I wanted his love for myself. I didn't want to compete with some ethereal memory of a woman who'd left him or died. "So you still have that to look forward to," I whispered without thinking.

The second the words had tumbled from my lips, terror tightened my lungs and I waited for a response that said I'd gone too far or crossed a line I shouldn't have.

He handed the book to me, then tilted his head, and kissed the top of mine. His lips were so soft and caring, perfection-embodied, but I didn't want the you're-a-sweet-child-who-I-like-to-tell-stories-to kiss. I wanted the kiss to be on my lips, and I wanted it to say you're-mine-and-I-can't-imagine-living-another-day-on-earth-without-you.

Alek was that for me already.

"I should go. The castle begins its rumbling for the start of the weekend's festivities." His tone had taken on the caretaker vibe, the one that dismissed me from his presence. But I wasn't ready to leave. Not yet. And I didn't give a flying fairy's ass about the so-called festivities tonight.

"We have plenty of time. I don't have to go." I circled my arm around his and snuggled closer to his side, reveling in the heat and hardness of his body. Thoughts of running my hand along his chest to feel the strength beneath the soft jersey t-shirt he wore flickered across the stage of my imagination, along with the vision of our bodies, naked and entwined on a bed.

I wanted more from the life I'd been born into. And one day I was going to get it. Happiness waited for me each time I touched him. Eight seconds of bliss. Eight seconds of Alek and me lying in a bed together, smiling and laughing and in love. In the vision, he would kiss my stomach and whisper endearments to the child I was carrying. Our child.

We would have a child. That's why I didn't fear the sadness and depression that typically found the childless Sisters.

I would have a child. His child.

He was my beast—my Gryphon warrior.

He had always been mine. And I would be his.

CHAPTER 2

ALEK

"I don't want to get you in trouble with the Oracle or your other sisters." I cupped Gretchen's face and stroked her porcelain white cheek with my thumb. Beautiful. Hair like a raven's wing and bright blue eyes that would make a sapphire jealous. I dropped my hand and pulled it away. The emotions warring in my mind would only confuse the situation.

And right now what I had with Gretchen worked. I didn't want to jeopardize the relationship we'd cultivated by making her uncomfortable in my presence. It wasn't like I could act on my attraction, either.

It wasn't allowed.

"You won't get me in trouble. We have plenty of time," Gretchen answered, squeezing my arm even tighter. "Keep reading." She pushed the book back into my hands.

Such a stubborn young woman, always stretching the rules—or breaking them. I hated breaking the rules.

Spending as much time with Gretchen as I did could be construed wrongly, but I'd returned to the Blackmoor's library nearly every day for the past fifteen years. Nothing short of being on a mission outside of the town had kept me from finding refuge in a peaceful few hours in Gretchen's company. Her bright blue eyes—so full of curiosity, a young mind eager to learn, full of joy and laughter. Her presence was like a bright flame in the dark cave of my self-imposed solitude, spreading warmth and light wherever she went. Warmth and light that I needed. Craved.

Besides my brother-in-arms, Jared, she was the only other person I considered a true friend in this town.

I opened the book again and started into act two. She deserved to be happy. If I could give her pleasure with a simple story, who was I to deny her joy?

Her heartbeat ebbed and flowed with the tension in the story, like the tide of the sea, pushing and pulling until the beach was smooth as satin. I kept reading, because she'd asked me to. It was all she ever asked of me, and I was grateful. Grateful that I always knew what to expect with Gretchen.

There were no surprises. No hidden agendas. Just peace and acceptance. It made keeping my emotions to myself that much easier.

She didn't fear me like many in the town. Didn't cringe every time I opened my mouth—scared that my Gryphon's cry would punish them.

When I'd first joined Rose's Sanctuary, I'd had a temper I didn't know how to control well. Anger had fueled everything Jared and I did through our lives on Earth. Rose had helped. The pixies had helped. Everyone had helped until that one day when I'd lost control on a Lycan male mistreating a female, not that he didn't deserve the punishment I'd doled out, but after that, everyone looked at me differently. Everyone except Jared and Rose. She still believed in me, and I owed her for that.

I read the Shakespeare through until the end of Act II and then closed the book. Gretchen's over-enunciated sigh of exasperation brought a smile to my heart, but I was careful not to let it show on my face. Not to let on just how much her very presence gave me joy. With Gretchen, I forgot how desperately lonely it was to be the only Gryphon on the face of the Earth. How lonely it was to take care of a town that feared you.

The town appreciated my presence, but there were still many who remembered what I'd done. What I could do if provoked. Those stories got larger each year, although they were whispered more quietly.

"I have to go." The clock on the wall chimed six o'clock.

"You'll read more tomorrow? I hate leaving it there. It was getting really good." Her tone carried a sharp slice of annoyance that I could only attribute to her not wanting to end our time together. I took the smallest bit of plea-sure in knowing my presence was desired, but letting my mind wander past that assumption would be dangerous. Therefore, I didn't let it happen.

Sometimes her moods changed so suddenly. I never knew what exactly triggered the changes, though they usually felt like my fault. That somehow I was disap-pointing her.

I hated that feeling.

"Of course," I responded, adding a hint of promise to

my voice to attempt to dissolve her sadness. I loathed leaving her in distress. Despised seeing and feeling the despair that washed over her every weekend. I'd asked her what made her sad, and she'd never answered. Just looked at me with this horrified expression that screamed you-should-know-without-asking. I didn't. Sometimes I wished I could read minds like the Lycans, but honestly, it would feel too much like a personal invasion of privacy.

"We will pick up tomorrow exactly where I left off."

The blue Texas sky was graying through the glass window to our right. Dusk was approaching. She needed to get back to the Sister's quarters below to eat and dress before the castle—the club—opened for the weekend. And I needed to leave. I preferred not to be around when visitors filled these stone walls and courtyards. Vetted or not, humans and kink put my beast on edge. It wasn't my scene. Ever.

I'd been asked to act in the capacity of hall monitor many times, but after refusing repeatedly, they'd finally gotten the message.

I held the book out toward her, but she shoved away from me and crossed her arms over her chest. A pout pulled at her lips, and her ever bright blue eyes shattered my expectation of ending this reading without feeling her unhappiness spill into my soul.

"I don't have to leave yet. There's still two hours before I have to be present and accounted for."

"You make it sound like a prison roll call." I regretted the words the instant they left my lips. They'd been callous and harsher than she deserved. If I'd felt like she was in a prison, I wouldn't have been able to handle it, but all the Sisters appeared happy and pleased with their life. The

Blackmoors took excellent care of them. They had free reign in the castle. Their only barrier was the outside walls, but even those of us on the outside rarely ventured outside the town. Perhaps our prison wasn't the size of one castle, but it still existed. The world outside Sanctuary—even in the Texas Republic—wasn't safe for any supernatural being. Not really. There were still people within the Republic who would sooner shoot us all than live peaceably with us.

Her head twitched to the side, and she jutted out her chin, defiance in both small movements. "It is and I hate it. I hate these *joinings*, and I hate it more that you don't even care." Her voice dropped on the last phrase, and she scrambled from the couch—as if burned by my touch.

Don't care? "Gretchen, I—"—*what could I say?* — "I care a great deal about you. Is someone making you feel uncomfortable?" My core temperature rose several degrees, and my beast stretched inside me, angry that something or someone was upsetting Gretchen, pressuring her in some way. "You have only to tell me, and I will make sure they never return to this town again. We may have six designated Protectors of the House of Lamidae, but *I* am the acting sheriff of Sanctuary."

She shook her head and pressed her lips into a tight angry line. "It's nothing." The two words slipped from between her lips barely louder than a whisper—both lies. "I'll see you tomorrow, right?"

"Yes, we will continue with *Antony and Cleopatra*." My jaw tightened. She was upset with me again. Over something I couldn't change. I would if I could. I wanted her to be happy. I'd do anything to keep a smile on her lovely face. I always returned from missions with a special gift or trinket. The surprise and joy on her face made it more than worthwhile, but I couldn't make her *not* a Sister. That was beyond my ability.

Beyond anyone's ability.

Her frame loosened, and her shoulder's slumped ever so slightly. Defeat shone in the blue depths of her eyes. She always spoke her mind. Nothing with Gretchen was ever a mystery.

"Is there something you need?" *Just give me a task. Tell me what I can fix.*

"No. I'm fine." She turned on her heel and walked out the door before I registered that she'd said the most dangerous words a female could utter.

She was far from *fine*, but there was absolutely nothing I could do about it if she didn't tell me what to fix, or what to change. Until she did, I would remain uneasy and my beast would pace until we saw her again tomorrow afternoon. Perhaps by then she would be able to ask for the help she needed with whatever problem was vexing her.

I placed the volume of Shakespeare on a bronze end table near the couch. No one would move it. Anyone using the Blackmoor library was expected to put away what they moved, but they all knew Gretchen and I made sure the books would be returned to their place when we were finished. We'd stuck to the same habits for years, but when Diana had arrived, I'd made sure to clear it with her also. She spent a great deal of time in the library as well, and I didn't want to annoy her—especially with all the pregnancy hormones racing through her body.

Diana's pregnancy was quite the topic of conversation in Sanctuary lately. Miles and Eli couldn't be more excited. With their first son from the Veil—Mikjáll—also taking up residence in Sanctuary, the town would soon be able to boast a population of seven Drakonae. Triplets were on the way.

As wonderful as having children would be... the idea of having children in a time where there were so many people and creatures out to kill us was terrifying—why would someone risk it? Plenty did. The Fated mate Lycans were constantly having children. Even Eira, one of the Protectors of the House of Lamidae—a vampire nonetheless—was pregnant by her Elvin mate. No one in the history of the world had heard of a vampire carrying a child, but no one had been in Eira and Killían's situation before, either.

"Alek."

I turned toward the familiar silky voice. "Lady Blackmoor," I answered, bowing my head in respect. She was not a queen in Sanctuary, but she'd been my queen before the Veil had fallen. My parents' queen. My grandparents' queen. Old habits were difficult to break, whether they were thousands of years old or only a few decades. It was hard enough not calling her *majesty* or *her grace*. She'd forbidden it. All the Blackmoors had.

Rose was Sentinel in this town—ruler. Her word was law, not the Drakonae.

"The library is empty now, if you were seeking privacy."

Her face lit with a pleased smile. She rubbed her rounding belly.

Pain slid through my gut like someone had taken a blade and stealthily shoved it between two of my ribs.

I would do anything to protect my queen, but I still couldn't believe she'd taken such a chance. Become vulnerable. Pregnant. Weak.

Why? There wasn't a throne to sit on here. There was

21

nothing more than there ever had been. Protect the Sisters of the House of Lamidae. Rose had recruited Jared and me over a millennia ago, and the battle to protect the Sisters from Xerxes and the human world hadn't stopped since.

"I see your longing and pain and worry. I assure you I'm quite capable of protecting myself while I'm pregnant as I am when I'm not with child."

Ever the mind-reader. I worked so hard to conceal my emotions. To not show anyone anything. Emotions meant vulnerability, and that was something I couldn't afford. "Forgive me, Lady Blackmoor."

She dipped her chin and smiled, assuring me of her favor.

Jared and I were both realists. Having a partner. A family. Such things were fantasy in this world. A lost cause, and neither of us had risked being so foolish. Our goals hadn't changed since the first day we'd arrived on Earth. Just like so many other supernaturals who'd lived through the millennia—we wanted to go home. I wanted to know if *I* was all that was left of my family. I wanted vengeance. Jared felt the same.

Love had no place in my life. A family certainly didn't, either...no matter how much the sight of her swollen belly raised tendrils of jealousy deep inside me.

The Drakonae had taken a chance, but they'd been given the choice.

In all my years, no one had ever meant enough to sway me from my first goal—getting home. Getting revenge on those who had chased me from it in the first place and made my parents fear so much that they and many of their friends had shoved their children through the portal, hoping Earth would be kinder than the Incanti fire that burned everything it touched.

But Earth hadn't.

"What were you and Gretchen reading today?"

Gretchen's name tugged the cobwebs of the past from my mind. "*Antony and Cleopatra*, milady."

"You'll have to tell me the story one day." Her voice carried across the room, pleasant and hopeful—not a hint of the stress plaguing everyone in town. She let a light sigh slip from her lips. "And you know I would prefer you to just call me Diana."

I shook my head firmly from side to side. "I would be happy to recount any human history, but calling you D—" I couldn't bring myself to say it even now. "It would not be proper. You have and always will be my queen." Though my family had not lived in the capital city of Orin, the town of Rekar had been loyal to the Blackmoor Royal House.

"We are equals in this little town." The tone of her voice held merely a wisp of a challenge. She knew what my answer would be. What it always was. We'd had this argument on more than one occasion.

"No one but your mates are your equals. I will forever be yours to command in this world, as my family served you in Rekar on the western banks of the Goddess Sea."

"What about Rose?" she asked, a bit of the dragon within shining through her icy blue gaze.

This was new. She'd never asked about my allegiance to the Sentinel of the town, the Lamassu who'd saved the Sisters to begin with and recruited supernaturals through the millennia to help her protect the women who carried the visions of the future. They were the key to getting back through the portal to Veil.

"I will always carry out Rose's orders to the best of my ability, but should you give the order, I would do everything in my power to see it through." I bowed my head again, waiting to be dismissed.

"Thank you, Alek. You are a good man."

"Not a good man, but a loyal soldier."

She stepped forward and took my hand before I could move away from her. A chill cooled the air around us, pulsating from her body like a commercial grade freezer turned up too high. Her fingers were cool against my skin, but not uncomfortable. "Never doubt you made it through the portal for a reason, Alek Melos. Just because you cannot see the grand design does not mean the gods have not woven a beautiful path for you through this life."

"You are too nice to an old warrior, milady. Please excuse me, I would like to leave before the castle awakens for the evening."

She pursed her lips, but didn't respond except to release my hand.

I bowed again and left the library through the door she'd used to enter. My feet echoed down the long stone hallway, empty but for the artwork the Blackmoors had studiously rescued through the years. A small reminder of the beauty this country had once valued and had cast aside due to their fear and ignorance.

So much had been lost because of the mistakes of a few. So many had died and many more would die before we found our way back through the portal to the world where we belonged.

By the time I reached the grand staircase leading down

to the main foyer, the castle was already filling with guests from town. Sisters were decked out in filmy white gowns that mimicked ancient Greek robes—loose, gauzy, and strategically laced with rope to accent the female body. These were not their usual cotton sundresses.

"Alek," a silky voice called from halfway up the right side of the grand staircases. "Are you staying for this evening's Luck of the Draw matching? You never stay." Kylie —one of the pixies who helped manage the club part of the castle—approached me one seductively slow step at a time.

Her dress, if it could be called that, was a light shade of green and utterly transparent, allowing me and anyone else to see her perfectly pink nipples and smoothly-shaved mound. Thin lines of red and pink and purple streaked through her white hair, reminding me of those children's pony toys from over a century ago. All the pixies wore bright colors in their naturally white hair, some dyed it completely, and others, like Kylie, wore multi-colored streaks.

I yanked my attention away from her familiar naked-ness. Strangely enough, I had absolutely no desire whisk her away to a bed. I just wanted out of this place tonight. Something in Gretchen's tone had put my beast and my mind into an unsettled state.

Air free of female pheromones and perfume and a chat with Jared was needed to return me to my normal state of controlled calm. Right now, I could feel every molecule of the atmosphere. It itched and burned like someone had scraped the top layer of skin from my body and dipped me in a vat of chili powder.

"I'm on my way out."

An understanding nod came from Kylie. "Another time, perhaps?"

"No," I answered, my tone more gruff than I'd meant for it to be. I liked Kylie. She was nice, fun to be around, and sexy as hell, but I'd had less and less interest in being with anyone over the last few years. In fact, I couldn't think of the last time my cock had felt more than the palm of my own hand.

I was nearly out the wide front door when Gretchen's name fell from a female's lips in the back of the foyer. Leaving was my goal. The last place I wanted to be when the humans arrived was the castle, but I also couldn't help the pause in my step. Anything to do with Gretchen was important to me. Perhaps they knew why she had been so angry with me earlier. Something was going on. Something she wouldn't come out and tell me.

"Gretchen's going to have to choose a man soon. I'm really getting sick of her excuses."

Choose a man. The instant image of Gretchen with a man between her legs nearly sent my afternoon meal spewing onto the polished marble floor of the foyer. She was still so young. I knew what the *joinings* were, but it'd never registered in my mind that Gretchen was participating. How old was she? I tried to count up the years in my head, but they ran together in a blur.

She'd never mentioned it when we read together. Though why would she? It was part of being a Sister. Procreating to continue the visions that would one day fulfill the prophecy. A prophecy Rose and the Sisters kept closely guarded, except to say that failure would mean the end of our dream of returning to Veil—something I very much wanted.

I swallowed down the bile in the back of my throat. Gretchen fulfilling her destiny shouldn't make my stomach turn. I had no claim on her. She was a Sister.

I could never have a claim on her.

But I didn't want anyone else to have a claim on her either, and that revelation threatened to put me on my ass right there in the middle of the Blackmoor's foyer. I wiped sweaty palms on my jeans and struggled to pull in a breath.

"Alek, are you alright?" Kylie called from the top of the staircase. She took a step down, and I waved a hand signaling her to stop.

"I'm fine," I growled, yanking open the front door and slipping out into the warm Texas air. The last thing I needed was an interrogation about why the personal business of a particular Sister's sex life—or lack of one—had put my entire body and mind and into a tailspin.

CHAPTER 3

XERXES

"*R*eport," I said, not bothering to glance up from the files on the ornate Resolute desk I'd made my own since overtaking the Washington Republic. Stacks and stacks of reports on towns who had pledged allegiance to me, and reports on the executions of those who hadn't. A few supernaturals had been rooted out of the woods here and there, wolves, mostly, and a few vampires who quickly fled the area—according to my Lycan captains.

Most other supernaturals were difficult to find. Pixies could literally disappear into trees, ponds, rivers, any type of nature—not that I expected to bring any of the pixie-dust-sprinkling-nature-loving-kumbaya-hippies into my camp, but their magick was helpful to have around. My men knew where to look for them.

It was a pipe dream to think I'd stumble across any overtly powerful supernaturals. Most had left the US after the Riots made living here a pain in the ass and somewhat deadly.

Then there was Rose.

My throat burned, bile filling the back. Rose had collected supernaturals for millennia. The most powerful beings still on this continent likely *all* lived in her fucking little town in Texas. A snort escaped from between my lips. It wouldn't be a *sanctuary* for much longer.

The Djinn were mine, though, and that's why I'd win in the end. They were the piece that stacked the deck in my favor. Always had. Rose hadn't managed to turn any of them against me, not in four thousand years. In fact, most of them hated her more than they hated me. *Quppa* prison boxes weren't something they took kindly to and she had hundreds, if not thousands of their people locked away in her fucking vault.

"Master." Cal, one of my Djinn bodyguards, stepped through the open Oval Office door. "Commander Martin and Commander Max have nearly completed the military executions in New York and Washington DC."

I raised my gaze to meet the lavender-eyed assassin. "You supervised both sites?" Cal was a slave, but his penchant for torture and death had lifted him high in my military ranks. Even though the newly-promoted Commander Martin and his pack had proven themselves in Ada weeks ago—burning down the Mason pack lodge and killing most of the pain-in-my-side Lycans who constantly interfered with my plans—I still preferred to have another set of eyes as witness to the obedience I expected.

Cal's eyes made sure everyone who was supposed to die did, and painfully. Death rarely needed to be swift.

Martin's brother, Max, had also proven worthy of a promotion. They and their two packs had risen to command my mixed human and Lycan forces, answering to no one except me and Cal.

"Yes, General Xerxes." The corners of his lips curved just slightly, but I didn't miss the mark of pleasure. He loved killing. Loved pain as much as I did. "Eighty percent of the human army in New York has been executed. Commander Martin did the same for the stationed armies here in Washington DC. Deaths for Washington and New York total in at sixteen thousand. The remaining four thousand are still being put through paces to see who is left standing." His tone rippled with excitement.

"Clean up?" I closed the file in front of me and set it on the stack to my right.

"Bodies are being staked at all cross-roads and in front of all military stations per your orders. Excess bodies are being burned systematically throughout the cities' waste management and cremation facilities."

"Excellent. I want our forces and the newly-acquired humans assault-ready by the end of the week. Be sure they are fed and clothed and in new uniforms. We will take down the SECR before they have a chance to formulate any type of plan and before the armies get hungry." I purposefully kept my voice even and calm. No one needed to know how pleased I was that my years of preparation would finally be coming to fruition, that I would finally be taking my rightful place in the public eye as a world leader to be feared. My rule would be all-encompassing, and the rest of the world would never see it coming.

"Should I fetch an up-to-date report on the move-ments of the SECR from Ms. Farrok?"

I scribbled a note on a small piece of stationary and held it up. "Deliver this to her. She needs to convince the SECR leaders to meet to develop a strategic defense. We will cripple them there, and the South will fall with no more of a scream than the Washington Republic."

Cal bowed his head, taking the note from my hand. Then backed away several steps, waiting like the loyal Djinn he'd proven himself to be.

"Dismissed."

"Thank you, General." He bowed again and turned on his booted heel. His steps echoed for only a few seconds before they vanished, and silence once again enveloped the Oval Office.

One piece at a time was falling into place. The Kitsune serum had worked. My soldiers were undetectable by human scanning technology. The Washington Republic had fallen to my hand weeks ago, and the South East Coast Republic— SECR—would be under my control in a matter of days. To top it off, the base I'd secretly built twenty miles outside Sanctuary was coming along nicely. The witches had kept it cloaked from detection by human or Others. Not even Rose herself knew I was about to come knocking on her door.

AN HOUR LATER, I finished going over the field reports from my two Lycan commanders. They'd located several hidden Lycan packs and had imprisoned them for death or draft. I needed more warriors, but I was quite particular about how they joined my forces.

"Cal."

"Yes, General Xerxes." The Djinn male stepped

through the semi-open oval office door and bowed his head.

"Do you have the current location of Commander Martin?" I stood from the grand desk and moved around it toward Cal.

"Yes, General."

I took his outstretched hand. Space folded around me, whooshing past like I'd been sucked through a vacuum. My heart skipped one beat, and I held my breath until we rematerialized. I'd been traveling this way for thousands of years, and it still surprised me a little.

The New York City skyline stretched out ahead of me, brilliant and bright and an example of extraordinary human ingenuity. The Washington Republic had capitalized on having technology above and beyond what most of the country possessed—except the small hub of very advanced research and development in California.

Most of the East Coast's bustling metropolises continued to function at the same capacity they always had. The smaller cities were the ones that had turned to ghost towns. The power plants required a great deal of upkeep, and only the cities with money to pay continued to receive a steady supply of utility services.

"Commander Martin's temporary base of operations is behind us."

I turned, taking in the view of hundreds of army green tents and military vehicles. The rolling landscape seemed to crawl with movement. All organized. There were no shouts of rebellion. No shots echoing through the quiet.

The humans never saw it coming.

Grabbing Cal's arm, I nodded. We blinked through another vortex, this time reappearing inside a large tent. A few snarls slipped from some of the men before I was recognized. Their demeanor shifted immediately from that point forward. Straight backs. Eyes on the ground. Silence.

"Commander Martin," I said, keeping my voice level and low. "Your reports are excellent. Where are the troops you're offering a chance to join ranks?"

The tall dark-skinned male stepped from the shadows. A cruel smile twisted his handsome face, reminding me why he'd been the perfect choice to lead half my army. He shared my bloodlust for pain and torture.

"The loyalty ceremony starts at the top of the hour. If you'll follow me, I have a place set up for you to observe, or participate," he answered, his tone pleasant and eager.

"How many accepted at the last one?"

"Twenty-two out of the hundred."

I exited the tent ahead of Martin, and we walked across the base toward a more permanent steel structure. The scent of blood clung to the air, and I breathed deeply, taking in the familiar fragrance of a conquered enemy.

"The next hundred for this afternoon have already been lined up. Cal let us know you might be coming through."

"Excellent. I look forward to seeing your progress."

"Thank you, General. It is my honor. If you will excuse me for a moment?" He paused, waiting for permission.

I nodded, and he gestured me toward a raised concrete platform before disappearing through a side door. Rows of men in steel shackles flowed from a door across the open area, herded by soldiers in black with ready rifles in their arms. The footsteps of the men thudded heavily—

knowing this might be their last walk on the Earth they called home.

One man on the end of the farthest row elbowed the nearest guard in the face and made a run for the door on the opposite side of the room. Suicide by guard? Surely he knew he wouldn't get off that easily. My army was conditioned to desire blood and pain and suffering. The Lycan's were taking their revenge against humans for centuries of being hunted, and their rage in turn furthered my rise to power.

"Halt or die, human." The guard he'd hit raised his rifle and took aim.

Cal shifted behind me, and I nodded. A moment later, he appeared in front of the fleeing man. The human lunged to the right, attempting to avoid Cal's block. The Lycan guard lowered his rifle and smiled, allowing my man to do as he pleased.

The Djinn blinked twice more. Then again. And again.

"What the fuck!" The desperation in the human's voice echoed through the building. The other captives standing quietly in rows watched, their expressions rotating between horror and fear. Most had probably never seen a Djinn in person, much less watched one move effortlessly from point to point within the same nanosecond.

The human finally gave up and sank to his knees. Cal materialized in front of the kneeling human, pulling a scimitar from the sash around his waist. "Say a prayer to your God, human. My master has granted me your life-force."

"Fuck you and the creature that bore you." The human spit into blank air.

Cal reappeared behind the man. He sliced through

both of the captive's Achilles tendons, moving so quickly he barely stained his blade.

The man screamed out, but didn't fall completely to the ground. He faced his death with pride. A shame he wouldn't be joining my ranks. Strength of will like that was difficult to come by.

Cal blinked again to face his victim, sliding his sword slowly into the soft part of the human's belly. Blood poured from the wound, and the soldier clutched at his stomach, holding back his entrails.

I leaned forward in my chair. The tangy, metallic scent of blood permeated the room. I drank in the pain of Cal's victim, reveling in the fear and horror vibrating from the rest of the waiting, watching prisoners. My pulse spiked, and I held my breath, waiting for my slave to end the human.

The human choked, coughing up blood. Cal drove his sword deeper, nearly running him completely through. Then my slave straightened, wrenching his sword upward through the man's chest cavity and slicing through rib bones like they were made of twigs. The steel and stones in the hilt of his scimitar glowed red. Cal drank in the man's life-force through his hands—the sword merely acting as a means of transference. For Djinn, blood was the ultimate high, but even pheromones—especially those released during periods of fear—were as satisfying to most Djinn as a phenomenal glass of wine was to me.

Everyone in the room was silent, even the Lycan guards watched with a still reverence. Death had a way of reminding even the hardest men they weren't invincible. Lycans lived several hundred years and could recover from wounds that would be fatal to humans, but they were far from possessing power like most other supernaturals who could live for eons—immortals in a way. Even I would eventually die, but it would be thousands of years before that happened naturally.

The gutted soldier's body fell forward with a thud. Blood ran freely, covering the gray concrete floor with a wide burgundy stain. Cal flitted through the room, appearing and disappearing through the lines of men still standing in formation...waiting, their destinies hanging more in their hands than they probably realized. Their lives depended on how much life they were willing and capable of extinguishing.

Cal appeared again at my side with his head bowed low. "Thank you, Master."

I nodded and then turned to Martin, mouthing the permission he'd been waiting for. His guards moved between the prisoners, unchaining fifty of the men. The remaining prisoners were secured to steel rings bolted to the floor. The fifty men who'd been freed rubbed their wrists and kept their gazes darting between the Lycan soldiers, Cal, and myself.

"You men are the next lucky group who have the honor of being given a chance to join General Xerxes' forces. If you feel that chance is wasted on you, please step forward now and kneel before your master."

"So you can murder us the way you did our—"

One nod from Martin and the man fell forward to the ground, his neck snapped before he'd been able to finish his sentence. The Lycan soldier who'd carried out the unspoken order stepped back from the body with a wry grin on his face.

Cold.

Calculating.

Cutthroat.

Perfection wrapped in six feet and two hundred and fifty pounds of angry Lycan muscle. Martin had trained his men well.

"Anyone else feel the same way?" Martin stepped forward with a thin silver briefcase.

None of the remaining men moved or breathed a word.

"Excellent. Let the games begin. The ten of you standing at the end will join Jasper's squad." Martin gestured toward the large Lycan male who'd killed the mouthy prisoner. The soldier opened the silver case and placed it on the floor. Gleaming black knives lined both sides of the case. Some of the unchained humans made a mad dash for the weapons, and the others simply fell to their knees, waiting for death to take them away from the nightmare.

A couple of the men immediately turned on each other, slashing and dodging and cursing. The prisoners completed the task set before them, murdering each other for a place among *us*. A chance to survive the hell that had swiftly surrounded and ruined their perfect lives.

When the shouts faded and the groans died away, ten men stood quietly in the center of the room, each holding one of the knives. Blood and sweat coated them like a shroud. They were the ones willing to shift loyalties. The ones who would die to protect their families no matter what. The ones who didn't care who they fought *for*. The ones content to kill for the sake of killing.

Those were the ones Martin wanted.

The ones I wanted.

I flicked my wrist, paralyzing everything and everyone

in the room. A knife was frozen in the air a mere four feet from my face. The man who'd thrown it was one of the standing ten.

Walking forward, I pulled the knife from its place and continued to approach him, feeling the focus of every paralyzed individual trained on me. I loosened my grip on the room, releasing all the men from the bonds of my magick.

No one spoke and no one moved. The man who'd attempted to assassinate me widened his eyes, but did not flee.

Fearless.

I could appreciate that, but trying to kill me was a debt I never failed to repay.

"What are you?"

"The god you tried to kill."

"You're no god, just another fucking Other."

"I am so much more than you could possibly comprehend, human. I've seen more history than your world can even fathom. Lived through more wars. Seen empires rise and fall." Dropping the knife, I raised my hands, letting my magick curl around him, enveloping him from head to foot. My vision tinted blue, and I knew by the reflection in his eyes that my eyes had turned white. I opened up my voice, allowing it to grow and fill the room. "I am your god. And I am sending you to hell."

The other nine men backed away, fear for their lives lighting a fire under their feet.

Claws grew from my fingers, and my body contracted and released. Muscles tightened and bulged. I roared. The change coursed through me like a lightning bolt, searing every cell with fire. The transformation took a few moments, shifting me from human to the size of a jumbo-jet with four sequoia-sized legs, talons the size of a man, wings that spanned the entire breadth of the hanger, and the head of a human mixed with features of a lion.

I snapped my teeth once, enjoying the terror I finally witnessed filling the eyes of the man who'd thrown the knife. He still didn't run. Instead, he fell to his knees, accepting his fate. I roared again, my power and form shaking the building to its foundation.

Lifting a paw, I pressed it down against the man's body, taking pleasure while listening to his bones snap like toothpicks. I continued ripping him apart with my claws until there was nothing left but the tattered remnants of flesh and bone.

I turned toward the fifty chained to the floor on my right. These men would know me as their god—all of them, humans and supernaturals alike. I would rule this entire country. Even if it meant killing every human on the face of its shores.

I would then move on to the rest of the continent before the rest of the Earth.

Taking a deep breath, I pulled the Lamassu back. My form shifted again. My wings tucked away, disappearing into my back. My legs and torso changed to human again, and I stood upright, waiting on my arms and hands to complete the shift.

My vision was still blue, and my voice bellowed through the hanger like I was wearing a personal megaphone. "Please, feel free to insult me again. I would take much pleasure in ripping you to pieces for your insolence or watching my man gut you with his blade."

I turned to face Martin. "Perhaps we should scrap this entire group and start fresh? I'm feeling hungry."

All fifty of the chained souls dropped to their knees, then prostrated themselves, pressing their faces against the grimy concrete floor.

Master. The name echoed softly through the hanger like dry leaves rustling in an autumn breeze. Even the Lycan soldiers were chanting along with the human prisoners.

Master.

Master.

Master.

CHAPTER 4

GRETCHEN

I looked up from the pages of my treasured copy of *Little Women*, a birthday present from Alek years ago. Rose Hilah herself and the Oracle—head Sister of the House—were both headed straight for me from the far side of the room.

Last night had gone about as expected. Men came. All the Sisters chose, except me. They all went off and had sex while I hid in the corner, doing my damnedest to blend into the potted plants along the gray stone wall of the foyer until I could sneak off to my room.

Hiding had worked for the past three years. That and faking illness. I was a master at always *not* being where I was supposed to be when the buses of volunteer human man-flesh arrived twice a month to *fulfill* the Sister's need to procreate.

"Gretchen," the Oracle spoke first. Her light tone

mixed with disapproval sent a chill of despair merrily skipping its way into the bottom of my stomach.

I put down my book and sat up a little straighter, hoping if I met them head-on the outcome might not be quite as terrible. Destiny or not, this was my life. "How can I help you?" I asked, hoping the shake in my voice wasn't as evident as it sounded from inside my head.

Rose took up residence in an armchair across from me while the Oracle sat down on the edge of the massive coffee table, her knees inches from mine. The fluorescent lights hummed, revealing to me how quiet the entire room had suddenly become. A brooding anxiousness filled my mind, and I rubbed my damp palms over the fabric of my skirt.

Everyone had left.

The Sisters who'd been working a puzzle in the corner. Gone.

The Sister who'd been playing the piano. Gone.

No one supported me. No one felt sorry for me. Most of them thought I was rebellious or selfish or just crazy.

"We were hoping we could help you. It has come to my attention that you are not participating in the *joinings*. Are you ill? Is something wrong? Did something happen that wasn't reported?"

A plethora of lies leapt to the tip of me tongue, but the one that came out was the one I told the most often. "I haven't been feeling well." It was true in the moment for sure. My stomach was doing acrobatic flips and threatening to send up everything I'd eaten thus far today in a spewing volcanic display.

"Why are you lying, Gretchen?" Rose asked, her tone

as even and as hard as the steel that plated the heavy door guarding the Sister's basement living quarters.

Of course the all-knowing-heartbeat-reading-Sentinel-of-Sanctuary would know I'd just lied. My racing pulse was probably like a giant red checkered flag waving around in the air. I might as well just get up and scream, *Hey, look at me. I'm lying through my teeth.* Why did I even try? Every supernatural in this town was a walking-talking-breathing-lie-detector.

"I didn't want any of them. They didn't appeal to me, and you can't force me to have sex." *Shit.* Had I just told Rose and the Oracle to shove it?

Yes, I had, and it'd felt damn good. I crossed my arms and leaned back against the couch cushion. They'd come into my space to make me feel bad for a choice that I deserved to make. No one had the right to make it for me.

Not even Rose.

The Oracle's shoulders slumped, and her brow furrowed. "Rose makes sure the men are vetted, handsome, and kind before they are even allowed onto the bus into Sanctuary. What is there not to like?"

"I just need more time. I can't just pick someone out of a lineup and force myself to have sex with them. There's no talking. No connection. It's not me."

"This is the safest way to fulfill the urgency welling deep within us to have a child. Don't you feel it, Gretchen?" The Oracle leaned forward to lay a reassuring hand on my knee. It burned and I wanted to slap her hand away. I wanted to run out of the room screaming that they had no right. That I already loved someone else and I had no desire to ever sleep with and bear a stranger's child, no matter how hard the supernatural urge in my gut cried out for a baby.

"I know it's a little awkward the first time, but these men are chosen because they are good to us."

"Then *you* sleep with them. I made my choice, and the answer last night was *no*."

I shook my head, thoughts of Alek bouncing around like the tennis ball I threw against the wall for hours each day, waiting for it to be time to go to the library and see him.

"I can't do it. Maybe I'm just not ready." Maybe if I wasn't already utterly-completely-totally-unconditionally in love with Alek. Maybe then I could've chosen. Probably would've.

But I couldn't now and hadn't been able to since the moment when I'd seen the possible future I could have with Alek. That we could have together.

He was so lonely and quiet. He needed me as much as I needed him.

Astrid—the Oracle—glanced to Rose, who nodded her head, a silent confirmation that I didn't want to have anything to do with the men coming in for the *joinings* and I wasn't going to be bullied into it. Not that my stubbornness would stop them from trying.

The only man I desired was Alek, but broaching that subject at this point would not benefit anyone. I desperately needed these two women to accept that I refused to sleep with a stranger, no matter how much my genetically-programed desperation for a child reared its ugly head. That was my problem to bear, not theirs.

"Why is it so important for us to have children?" I turned my head and met Rose's gaze head-on, deciding to try another tactic all together. "Why should we want so desperately to raise another generation in a prison of your making?" Maybe if I could piss Rose off, she'd leave me alone, like the unruly child who nagged until the parents just gave up.

A gasp slipped from the Oracle's mouth, but she didn't speak.

Rose's brown eyes narrowed, and I felt the warmth of her magick rise through the room, creeping around me like a corporeal fog, but I wasn't scared. We'd always been assured they wouldn't force us to be with a man. Now I was merely putting that unspoken statement to the test.

"You are the last hope for the supernaturals on Earth. You will be our way back home. Without the Sisters— without enough children to keep the visions complete— there is no hope for any of us to ever get home. To ever get off this human world."

"But *I* don't belong in Veil. *We* are human." I jabbed a finger at Astrid. "No matter the funky visions, we are still human. We belong here."

Rose stood from her chair, her eyes turned white. Her voice deepened, taking on an ominous phantom quality. "You are the Oracles of the House of Lamidae. Your sole purpose on Earth is to fulfill the prophesy that will open the Veil, and allow supernatural beings the chance to go home."

Each word thudded into the bottom of my stomach, one heavy declaration at a time.

All the urging and posturing in the world wouldn't make me forsake my hope that Alek would be the first one to ever lie with me. The first man to ever kiss or touch any intimate part of my body. Not even Rose Hilah, playing the Wicked Witch of the West and trying to scare me back onto the proverbial yellow-brick-road, would sway my decision.

"Why do you even care anymore? What's there for you?" *Damn.* I shouldn't have said that. I knew I shouldn't have, but once I got started, it was difficult for me to put a halt to my thoughts. "A stranger doesn't deserve the honor of being with me first. If I have to sleep with someone, it should be someone I care about."

"You do not get to have a typical life, Gretchen. You are special. You have a gift and responsibilities because of that gift."

"Why can't we just choose husbands? What could be the harm in a few men taking up residence in Sanctuary? You take in everything else. If it has fangs or fur or fantastical powers, it automatically gets a ticket to stay in Sanctuary. But me? I don't get a say because I'm just a vessel. I'm not a person who gets to decide her fate. Who gets to fight for what's right or wrong or make any kind of life choices." Drawing a deep breath, I focused the anger welling inside me on her once again brown eyes, on her dispassionate, expressionless face. "What makes me worth less than any other person in this town?"

"You are worth more." Her voice was steady and calm, but her gaze burned with an anger that made my insides squirm. "Everything we do in this town is to protect you. To make sure you can fulfill the destiny you were born to. What gives you the right to feel more important than any of the other Sisters here in this sanctuary? Only in a united group can you produce enough children to raise the magick back to a level where the last two Protectors can be found. Don't you want to have a child?"

Of course I wanted a child. We all did. We all had this abnormal obsession with procreation, but maybe it wasn't impossible to have one with Alek. Maybe they'd lied about that, too. If she was so worried about Xerxes stealing us to have children...

What if I could have Alek's child?

The thought struck suddenly like a crack of thunder. My palms ran slick while the inside of my mouth dehydrated to the consistency of bread flour. I banished the urge to blurt those thoughts aloud.

Rose's posture softened. "I do not do this for myself. I protect and care for all supernaturals who ask for shelter, be it from humans, or Xerxes himself." Her warm magick flicked across my skin, like fingertips looking for a good place to take hold. "The sacrifice you make is not for me alone, it is for entire races of people. There are hundreds —thousands of supernaturals who have no desire to remain on Earth. They are the children of murdered parents, the orphans of a war that made them homeless. The time is almost here. We are so close to completing the prophecy, yet you purposefully shirk the burden placed on your shoulders."

I shivered, casting a glance at the Oracle mother, but she offered no consolation or support. I'd vomited the mess, and I was on my own to clean it up.

"There is something making you discontent. Making you desire more than what is possible." Rose's tone was like velvet, sweet and sugary and a damn trap if I'd ever seen one. "Who is it you desire?"

I still hadn't gotten Alek to realize my affection or admit his own. I knew he cared about me. A man didn't show up in a library to read for hours on end every day of every week of every month for years on end if he didn't care. The Sisters gossiped that he was broody and rude, but he'd never been anything but kind and caring and protective toward me.

It was more than friendship, but I didn't have anything to say to Rose right now. I needed a plan of action and I needed Alek on my side. If I said something without any confirmation that he wanted to be with me, I'd lose my only chance with him.

"No one," I answered, breathing slowly, willing my heartbeat not to give me away.

"You cannot have children with any supernatural in town. It is impossible, and if you cannot have children with them, then you are not fulfilling your purpose."

"Maybe I don't want to *fulfill* my purpose, and if we can't be with other supernaturals, why are you so afraid of Xerxes getting us? Our histories say we've been running for thousands of years. What does it mat—"

"It matters because Lamassu are the exception to the rule. Genetically, you are compatible with our species and with humans."

There it was.

Another secret kept from us.

"Why?" I stood, moving to stand face to face with the Sentinel. Our protector. Our mother. Our jailer. Anger seethed beneath the surface of my skin, like molten lava waiting to burst free from the Earth's crust.

"Because that is the way you were made." The words were spoken so softly I strained to hear each one. The revelation sent a cold chill ricocheting down my spine. I couldn't feel my feet, or my legs. I sank back onto the leather couch behind me and snapped my stunned mouth shut.

Made?

Rose turned on her heel and walked out of the room, her footsteps strangely silent on the hard stone floor.

I glanced at the Oracle Mother, weird to call her that, since she was barely five years older than I was. "M-made?" The word sputtered from my mouth. "Like we were a batch of cookies she whipped up? Am I the only one that feels this is unfair?"

"It's time to grow up, Gretchen. We have a good life here. The Drakonae take care of us. Rose takes care of us. The whole town works to keeps Xerxes at bay so that we aren't subjected to—"

"We've found two protectors in less than a year."

"That was because our numbers were up, but then Arlea died. Cara had a stroke and passed away. Pythia passed as well. The loss of three adults was too much. My visions about the next Protector are sporadic at best, and rarely do I get any clarity in them."

"What if it takes centuries to find the last two, and what *really* happens to us after the prophecy is fulfilled?"

"We will be free, Gretchen. Free of these visions that plague us, no one will hunt us, and no one else will have to die for us. We will be safe from Xerxes. That is our hope for the future, Gretchen. That is the legacy we want for all our children, for ourselves. You're not the only one who would like to have a normal life...whatever that really means."

She stood from the chair and bowed her head. "Please. Even if you were to love a supernatural, your lifespan pales in comparison. Would you put yourself through the pain of loving someone only to lose them when you grow old and die?"

"I would enjoy every moment I got. That's what life is about. And life without love, the way we live it...I can't do this."

The Oracle's blue eyes hardened, and her voice tempered sharply. "We love, Gretchen. We love each other, and we love our children. Our lives are not without love." She made a growling huff of irritation at the end of her statement before leaving me alone in the room to stew in the guilt she and Rose had managed to stir to life.

I cared about my sisters. I knew they loved their children. And some of my sisters even created fantasy romance relationships around the men they chose to sleep with.

It wasn't enough for me. Maybe it was for them. Maybe they were truly content with the status quo, but I wanted more.

I wanted Alek...even if we couldn't have children.

Even if being with him was only a brief moment of bliss in his immortal lifetime.

It would be enough for me.

I could only hope it would be enough for him.

CHAPTER 5

ALEK

*M*y jaw caught Jared's fist, and a haphazard pattern of white stars skittered across my line of sight. The fucking Phoenix could really hit hard. I shook my head and rubbed my jaw, shaking off the blow.

"Fuck," I growled under my breath.

I rotated and swiveled, changing angles, raising my fists. Jared backed off, but my quick jab forward and then an uppercut caught a solid hit to his gut.

"Better," he said, his voice wheezing while a painful smile curved his face.

He took a step toward me on the soft blue mats, faking right then left then right again before striking home.

Fucking hell!

"I never get you this good, man. Something's got you off your game." Jared rolled his neck and raised his eyebrows. He backed off, rose out of his crouched fighting stance, and stared at me with that brotherly look that said he was about to put his foot in my business. "You need to get laid?"

I roared, barely reigning in my beast. Breathing deeply, I halted my body, flexing my hands to fists at my sides. If I changed inside our small back-office sparring area, my wings would tear up the ceiling and my claws would decimate our padded mats.

He held up his hands in surrender. "Hey, no need for that." His tone was light, but his eyes burned with his Phoenix fire, prepared to put me on the ground if I went that far. I might be in the worst mood I'd dealt with in centuries, but the threat of his fire made my beast take pause.

There was truth in his accusation. I actually couldn't remember the last time I'd been with a woman...it hadn't mattered and I hadn't gone looking, but now—now that I knew I'd been bottling up feelings for Gretchen...

Heaving a sigh, I let my shoulders slump forward. How did this happen? How had I let myself fall for the child who'd made me smile fifteen years ago? Who'd continued to warm the heart in my chest I'd considered long dead?

"There's no way out of the proverbial grave I've dug." I crossed the room and took a long swig from my water bottle. Sweat dripped from my forehead. The two-hour sparring session was supposed to clear my head. Instead, I was sore, and I found my thoughts even more focused on Gretchen. On what *caring* about her meant for my life.

"Really? Is it someone I know?"

I shrugged. He'd probably met Gretchen at one point. "It doesn't matter. She's not an option, no matter how many different ways I look at the situation."

Jared took a long drink from his bottle of water, giving

me an appraising eyeball-glare for the duration. "You can't go back to the library, man."

My stomach threatened to upchuck everything inside. *Fuck.* "How did you figure it out that fast?"

"I can't remember the last time you got some pussy, but you go see that damn girl in the Blackmoor's library every fucking day." He took a step closer. "You're going to piss off Rose. Where will that leave us?"

I didn't have an answer to that question. My normally strategic thought patterns had locked into a formation that refused to do anything but spiral around Gretchen. How beautiful and grown-up she was... *How had I not noticed that until just now?* How I wanted to flay any man who dared lay a hand on her.

My entire existence centered on spending time with her or taking care of the town or doing something Rose needed done. Somehow she had become more. More than just the girl I told about history. More than the girl I read books to.

So much more.

"I can't stop thinking about her. Since I left the library today, she's been on a loop in my brain."

"Why today? What changed?"

"There were people talking about her. About how she was going to have to pick a man for the *joining* this weekend. They were mad that she'd been avoiding it." I glanced up at Jared, hoping to hear the advice I wanted instead of the advice I needed.

"Why would she avoid her destiny? Is she interested in you?" He stalked closer. "Have you already taken her?"

I snarled again. "I've done nothing. I just realized I

didn't want her to choose another and... I don't know what to do next."

"Nothing, brother." He stepped closer and laid a gloved hand on my shoulder. "You can't act on this. They are the Sisters. We protect them, not fuck them, and think about it, she's human-ish. Even if you were granted permission to be with her, she'd grow old and die in a few short decades. Why put yourself through that?"

"She would be worth... she *is* worth every moment." The last fifteen years were fleeting in comparison to the life I'd already lived, but it didn't matter. Even if I only got another fifteen, I'd still show up every day to be with her.

"But you can't go against Rose. This would break the very foundation of the trust she's put into you. If she came at you, I'd fight. You know that. If she told you to leave, I'd leave with you."

"I know."

We'd been together since escaping the Veil. Our friendship had been forged in fire and steel and pain thousands of years ago. Like many others, we'd gone through the portal. But unlike the hundreds who'd crossed that day for the last time, we knew our families were dead, burned alive by Incanti fire. Their screams would forever haunt my sleep the same as they haunted Jared's. Both our families had served the Blackmoor royal line for generations. Once we'd heard Miles and Eli Blackmoor lived and served a Lamassu, we'd sought out Rose and joined.

"Do you feel something for her?" The tone of his voice was hesitant, but hopeful.

"It came on so slowly, I didn't notice it, but, yes, I do feel for her. My beast desires her as much as the rest of me. I don't understand why I snapped today."

"You don't think it was overhearing that men were coming to fuck and impregnate her?" His words sliced through my heart like one of the old broadswords on the wall of our workout space, filled with anger and power and chastising all in the same breath.

"Watch your tongue."

"I'm just being realistic."

"You're just pissed about—"

"Don't go there." His friend's eyes narrowed. "It's not even close to the same."

I opened my mouth to take another jab, but held it back. Just because I was in pain didn't mean my best friend —my brother—deserved to feel my wrath.

"Rose would never allow it. I know, you don't have to tell me," he said, his tone falling with each word, the finality of his defeat making my own situation appear even more hopeless.

I wanted to tell him he'd have a chance when all this fucked up shit between Xerxes and Rose was over. I wanted to assure myself we'd both have a chance, but my fatalistic realism knew better "Sorry, bro."

Nothing would ever end between those two Lamassu. They were two equal gods on Earth, fighting their right-eous war. They'd been at a stalemate for centuries. Rose had us and the dragons and so many Others on her side. Xerxes had Djinn and the Lycans who felt the need for revenge against humans. We would all die eventually and probably tear this planet apart in the process. Unless we could get home. Unless Rose could deliver on the promise of the House of Lamidae—a way to open the portal without one of the dagger keys.

Not many large packs remained outside of the Texas

Republic, but those that still functioned with an alpha pair were secretive and kept to themselves. Revenge or vengeance or whatever the traitors working with Xerxes felt they deserved was not the common view for the warrior-like race of wolf shifters.

The Djinn were beings humans would describe as similar to a genie. The lavender-eyed deceivers were an entirely different can of fucked-up-paranormal-vengeance-on-a-rampage. They hated Xerxes for enslaving them and Rose because she boxed thousands, possibly more over the centuries, locking them away like trinkets in her underground vault. Never to be seen or heard from again.

But my problem concerned none of them. My problem was a little girl who'd grown into a twenty-seven-year-old woman, and I hadn't even noticed it happen. But now that I had...I couldn't take back the realization that I did indeed want Gretchen of the House Lamidae so fucking much it hurt.

"We're a couple of lost causes," Jared said, waving me toward the back door. "I'm going to go grab a shower. See you at Rose's tomorrow for lunch. I think we could use some pixie-dust-infused comfort food."

"They don't put *actual* pixie dust in the food. The pixies don't even cook. The brownies do all the cooking."

"Do you have to be so literal?" He shook his head, disbelief flowing from him like a waterfall. "The pixies grow ninety percent of what we eat. From their magick," he said, emphasizing the last sentence. Did he imagine my skull too thick to absorb his meaning?

"Shut up." I growled. The last place I wanted to be was within earshot of Rose Hilah, but her food was the only restaurant in town, other than the bar run by the Lycans. I could cook, but it paled in comparison to what the brownies could whip up with their eyes closed. "I'll be there," I said, storming toward the front.

He was right. We were both lost causes...or should've been. As far as we could tell, we were the only ones of our kind left alive on Earth.

There were only a few supernaturals who could mix genetic code for sure and create offspring —Lamassu and Kitsune were the only ones I knew of, but that didn't mean there weren't more that could...I'd just never heard of it happening.

One could always hope. *Right?*

Not that I'd get the chance to find out with Gretchen. Rose would kill me or banish me before that happened.

I rushed out the front door and turned, colliding with Mikjáll—the Blackmoor's long-lost son, who'd come to Earth shortly after his mother escaped. A grunt came from both of us. "Sorry."

"It's fine."

"How's your Kitsune?"

His nostrils flared and his eyes widened. "Riza is not mine. We are not mated, nor does she wish to be."

I threw up my hands, heat flushing my neck. "My mistake. I've seen you with her, and I just assumed. She's always with you."

"She feels safe with me, but I have no desire for her as a mate. I lost the woman I loved. Xerxes murdered her, and my destiny will be to kill the Lamassu bastard."

"How's her sister doing?" I asked, purposefully changing the subject to cool the quickly rising temperature of the air surrounding us.

"She is healthy. The pregnancy is going smoothly, but she weeps for the child still in Xerxes' grasp."

"We still don't have word of where Xerxes moved the baby?"

The dragon prince shook his head. "Calliope would move heaven and earth to get that baby if she knew. She feels personally responsible for not getting her out when she got Sochi."

"It's not Calliope's fault."

"Try telling that to her."

A half-smile tugged at my lips. "I can imagine the black eyes and the long claws now. Did you attempt it?"

He nodded. "It was a short-lived conversation."

"I'll bet." I gestured toward the street behind him. "Want a drink? I was just about to go drown myself in a bottle of good scotch."

The Drakonae cocked his head to the side, but didn't ask the question I knew rested on the tip of his tongue. Instead, he nodded and fell into step beside me. We traveled the few blocks from the center of town to my front door in a matter of minutes.

We went inside, and I flipped on the lights. Walking directly to the bar top, I grabbed two glasses and joined him where he'd taken a seat at my kitchen table.

"A little bare." His tone bordered on incredulous. "Haven't you lived in Sanctuary since it was founded?"

"I don't need much. The table and chairs were a gift."

Beyond the dining room, I had a worn leather couch in the living room with a stereo system on a rickety table next to it. Other than the bed and dresser in my bedroom upstairs, there was no other furniture in the home.

"What is the electronic thing in there by your couch?"

58

"A stereo. Hang on." I poured us both another finger of scotch before crossing the room. I flipped on the stereo, pushed the button, and waited for the CD tray to open. I placed an Aerosmith CD in the tray and nudged it closed. "Humans may be weak and their lifespans short, but their appetite for creating art is immense."

The haunting notes and colors and lyrics of *Dream On* spilled from the stereo and vibrated through my house. Mikjáll followed me into the living room, carrying the bottle of scotch.

Sitting on the couch, we drank half the bottle, listening to the music play, one lilting, and memorable song after another. I particularly enjoyed this band and the heartfelt emotion it evoked in my hardened soul. The lyrics spoke of pain and loss and longing that connected with life even now—a hundred years after the band had their first release. Music like this didn't exist in Veil. Instrumental and ballads were all I remembered growing up, nothing electric based.

Hell, we didn't have electricity, either, but in a world filled with magick, there were alternatives.

"I like this." Mikjáll filled his glass again and downed another mouthful of the smooth alcohol. "The beer served at the bar in town is fine, but this—this is what I've needed for a while."

"Are there any of my people left in Veil?" The question just popped out. I'd wanted to ask him since he'd arrived in town, but the opportunity had never presented. Now we were alone. No one to overhear. No one to interrupt.

I needed to know. He'd lived there for centuries. If anyone knew whether mine or Jared's families were still alive, it would be him.

59

"You mean Gryphons?"

I nodded, raising my glass so he would fill it again.

"I know the twin cities of Rekar and Resar were burned to the ground and remain in ruins. All knowledge of the Gryphons and Phoenix dissolved with the flames that swallowed their homes."

Pain seized my chest, a vice intent on strangling my hope. It'd been foolish to hope any of my people had survived. Jared knew at least some of his kind would've survived. Phoenix could regenerate from ash. "The Phoenix couldn't stop the fires?"

"No, and the Incanti Drakonae boasted for many years about how they'd burned the Phoenix and Gryphons from their homes, though they are always on guard for an attack from those that would rise from the ashes."

"They didn't rise again immediately?"

"There were no sightings during my lifetime. No one has risen against the Incanti. Not a single being in Veil. The Incanti have spies everywhere and rule with an iron fist. There are no trials. No fair rule. You live and die by their word alone." He poured me another drink and raised his glass. "To the fallen. I'm sorry for your loss."

"And for yours, Drakonae, and may the Lamassu bastard burn in Dragonfire for eternity after we make a pincushion out of his heart with the swords Eira and Killían carry."

"I look forward to it."

CHAPTER 6

GRETCHEN

J slipped from my room the next morning, trying desperately to avoid being seen by any of the Sisters or the men who had stayed the night. Midmorning breakfast had already been served, but I wasn't hungry. The only thing that mattered to me was making it through one more night without choosing someone. Without being forced to choose someone. Not that they would physically force me. They wouldn't, but my life would become increasingly unbearable until I chose to follow through on my own.

"Morning, Gretchen," said May, her voice bright and shiny like sunlight reflecting on a dew drop. The child was barely eight years old, if that. I couldn't remember exactly. She was so happy, so content. Not burdened yet with the destiny that struggled to choke me, but since she'd learned to speak, she'd always been at peace. She was wise beyond her years, and Arlea knew her niece was truly the most

61

gifted in the castle—just too young to serve as the official Oracle.

"Morning, May," I said, keeping my tone level and cheery. The last thing I needed was her running to her mother and tattling anything about me. The Oracle of the House of Lamidae was May's aunt. Even May herself had experienced visions of a so-called Protector, and they'd come true. Eira had joined Sanctuary with Killían, and we were only two Protectors away from fulfilling the prophecy. From freeing ourselves completely.

Thankfully, May didn't press me for more interaction. She kept going down the hallway in one direction, and I continued in the other. My only goal was to get upstairs to the second level and into the library.

The library was safe. It was rare for anyone to go in on the weekend. The Blackmoor's closed it to the town when the club was active. The books were contraband, illegal to own. Not that any of the humans would remember seeing it if they did wander through. The vampires made sure they remembered nothing about Sanctuary, except their desire to return for more sex.

Even if someone did come in, no one would see me. It was easy to stay hidden until they left. The room was huge and filled with at least a dozen rows of bookshelves, not to mention a half-dozen reading nooks.

I'd stay there all day if need be. Alek and I didn't usually meet until after lunch, but I wanted nothing to do with anyone else today. Not the Sisters, not the Blackmoor's, nobody but Alek.

Very few of the Sisters were up and moving around after the *joining*s last night. Mostly I saw children, a few of the pregnant Sisters, and a couple of the more elderly who no longer participated in the sacred weekend coupling. If you asked me, the supernaturally overwhelming urge to procreate really sucked—a colloquialism I'd picked up from an old novel, but it sounded appropriate in this instance.

I skirted the edge of the rooms, slinking through the kitchen and pausing only long enough to grab an apple from the basket on the counter. No one stopped me. No one asked me why I wasn't curled up in my room with a man trying to get pregnant.

The whole process would start again this evening. Once again, I would be faced with having to hide my feelings and reasons for not wanting to participate. I was the Sister everyone talked about and was disappointed in, but it didn't matter to me how much they gossiped. I knew my future lay with Alek. I'd seen it, and I would never forget it. No matter how hard my body screamed for a baby, I wanted Alek's love and devotion more.

The castle was quiet. My soft footsteps echoed down the marble-floored halls. The stone walls carried sound the full length of the castle walks. If anyone was listening, they *would* hear me, but no one came. No one appeared to stop me from reaching my destination.

I pushed open the heavy glass French door and slipped through into the library. My senses were flooded with the musty scent of books, and it took a few moments for my eyes to adjust to the soft lamplight. The couch where he typically sat, waiting for my arrival, was empty. I was early though, very early.

Strolling toward the couch where the copy of *Antony and Cleopatra* lay undisturbed, I sat down and leaned back into the cushions, inhaling his lingering scent. Spice.

Musk. Male. My body quaked from the inside out. Nothing was more important to me than finding a way to be with Alek. I touched the book he'd held yesterday, closed my eyes, and slowed my breathing. The vision came —pulling me deeper into the trance I sought.

The air was foggy at first. Then clear. Alek and I were sprawled across a bed—perhaps his. I'd never seen his home. The sheets were twined around us, and I could feel the heat of his body on my skin like I was right there next to him instead of watching like a spirit yanked from its corporeal form. He kissed my neck. My lips. My cheeks. Soft and tender. Every touch was purposeful and loving. I was his. He was mine. We belonged to each other. We were happy. Joy permeated every moment of the vision.

I pulled my hand away from the book, drew in a deep breath, and then opened my eyes. The vision of us together had come to me almost seven years ago, a few days before I would've participated in my first *joining*.

From that moment forward, I'd done everything to avoid that fate. Even when I'd been attracted to the male visitors—desired them—strangers in my bed weren't my destiny. No matter how loudly my body ached for a baby, I would not succumb to something less than what destiny herself had taken the time to show me over and over and over.

I grabbed one of the couch throw pillows and hugged it to my chest, taking another deep breath of Alek's comforting scent. The human males that visited the castle didn't have a distinct trace like many of the supernatural ones. I could always tell who was around, whether they were Lycan or Vampire or Drakonae. Even Jared, Alek's friend, had a very unique and pleasant fragrance. The female supernaturals had unique smells, too. The pixies that frequented the club part of castle smelled like the vanilla sugar scrub I used every day in the bath.

"Gretchen?" Diana's crisp voice filtered into the dimly-lit library like a stream of sunlight.

"Yes, ma'am." I opened my eyes quickly and stood from the small couch before turning toward the beautiful blond woman Alek and Jared both referred to as their queen—*snøen mor*. I'd asked him once what the words meant. He told me it was a title of honor bestowed on her for feeding the hungry children of her kingdom. That it meant Snow Mother.

Diana's belly was rounded, and her alabaster skin glowed pink, unusual since she typically leaned toward a more bluish hue. Unlike her mates, Miles and Eli, who were fire-breather Drakonae and heated up a room just by entering, Diana was an ice-breather. And had quite the opposite effect on the air around her—cooling the humid Texas air in an instant and often making it snow in the middle of a sunny day, much to the delight of the children in the town.

"You look well, Lady Blackmoor," I said, using the title her husbands had requested all the Sisters use to address their mate.

"It's been so warm lately. These babies are like carrying glowing hearthstones inside me." Her comment about the babies distracted me from my dreams. Alek would be here soon. The clock on the wall to my right read just past noon—I'd slept for several hours.

"Have you had anyone try to *see* them?" I asked, running my sweaty palms along the skirt of my white linen dress. If I could keep her talking about the babies, perhaps

I could avoid the conversation concerning why I was napping in her library.

"Please feel free if you like, but don't tell me what you see. Several of the Sisters have *seen* them as you say, but I only ask that you keep it a secret. I want to be surprised." Her bright, hope-filled tone carried into her wide smile.

I approached slowly, reaching a hand toward her stomach. Trying to get a vision from a single baby was difficult, but Diana was pregnant with triplets. My fingers touched her round belly, and I jumped in surprise. Spots were warm and spots were cold.

"Your skin... Even through your dress." I couldn't hide the astonishment in my voice.

Amusement sparkled in her ice-blue eyes. "I'm quite sure at least one of them is an ice-breather like me."

A second later a vision filled my mind.

Joy and pain mixed with anger. Some emotions belonged to Diana, and some belonged to the babies. Visions of death and new life mixed with love and romance. Two male Drakonae, eyes blazing with flame, stood out in front of a crowd of hundreds of warriors of all different races. Another, a female with silver-white hair, stood apart from the two leaders. Another man stood behind the female— a large figure hidden in shadow. He wasn't a Drakonae. Something else.

I couldn't see his face, but the female wasn't afraid, not like the others around her. The landscape was covered in ice, so different from the landscape surrounding Sanctuary. Even the sky had been a different shade of blue—otherworldly.

"Did you see them?"

I nodded and met her gaze. My mouth opened to

speak, but the firm look in her eyes made it snap shut again.

"It is better not to know our future, Gretchen. Life would be too difficult if you were always striving for a vision or fighting against it. The gift you Sisters bear is a heavy one indeed. I prefer the freedom of *not* knowing."

"It can show us future. What to look for. What to look forward to," I said, brightening my tone while sorrow threatened to pull me beneath its dark shadow. Her words rang horribly true. My vision of Alek and me together had consumed me since it'd first come years ago. Every move, every decision since that point had been to try and *make* the vision a reality. I knew my choices thus far had not changed our future, because the vision kept returning, but I lived in constant fear that one day I would ruin that perfect scene I'd carried in my heart for so long. The fear that I would never feel loved or whole as I did in Alek's arms in that one moment.

"But your visions are not the whole tapestry. They show small threads and knots in the fabric of time. What the Lamassu cursed your people with so many years ago was not a gift of visions for you, but a means to an end for them."

Cursed? "How can you say that? We are the hope for every supernatural being not of Earth." That was what we'd been taught since we were children. What Rose reminded us of every time she spoke to the Sisters. "We are the key to re-opening the portal to Veil. We are *your* salvation."

"Perhaps." Diana laid her palm to my cheek. "I have lived so many more years than you, child. Things are not usually what they seem on the surface."

"You just don't know Rose. She's protected us for thousands of years. She saved my ancestors from Xerxes and continues that crusade to this day. We seek the Protectors who will fulfill the prophecy." I spouted off the stuff the Oracle and Rose were always repeating. It was what everything centered on.

"I do agree that Xerxes is an imminent threat, and I am new in Sanctuary," she continued, her voice calm and even. "Perhaps I just don't fully grasp the mission of your Sentinel yet."

I nodded, accepting her explanation. She hadn't been in Sanctuary long. She hadn't been on the Earth long, either. It could easily explain her hesitation to believe...to trust in the goal we all worked toward.

"Jared asked me to tell you that Alek won't be coming by today," she said, dropping her hand from my cheek.

"Oh, thank you." I managed to keep my voice flat, emotionless, void of the disappointment flooding my body. I wanted to scream and cry and go hide in the farthest corner of the library. Why was Alek avoiding me? "That was kind of him. I think I'll still stay and read a while, though."

"Of course." She turned and walked for the French doors at the far end of the large room, pausing just before turning the corner and looking back over her shoulder. "Be careful, child."

Be careful? Of what? Every conversation I'd had with Diana Blackmoor had been strange. She was strange. Like she'd stated herself, she didn't understand this world. She hadn't lived here long enough to know Rose and trust her.

Without us, the prophecy could never be fulfilled. We could never be human and free from the visions that plagued us. We could never have sons. Never have a normal life.

I'd heard whispers of others who had refused to participate in the *joinings*, but none who'd held out as long as myself. Rose and the all the elders maintained we couldn't have children with supernaturals—except a Lamassu, which is why we were kept hidden from Xerxes...but if Diana thought there was more going on than Rose let on... plus, there was my vision, what else was Rose hiding? Or lying about?

All other thoughts of Rose's possible deception were erased. My hope—my belief— smothered my doubts about the prophecy. I would be free one day, and I would have a real relationship outside of these stone walls. The prophecy could go on without me.

I walked down one of the aisles, letting my fingertips run along the edge of the books, finally stopping on one oversized old volume I didn't remember ever looking at. The cover was worn fabric and the lettering, like most older books, was embossed with gold leaf. Fancy script and swirls decorated the front and spine. I traced the title —*Legends of Arthur and Avalon.*

King Arthur? I'd read stories about his knights and the round table of Camelot. They were adventurous stories of love and devotion. The knights fought bravely for their king and defended their land from invaders.

I walked back to the favored loveseat and curled into the cushions on one side, opening the large book. The paper was yellow with age, but in good shape. It didn't flake as I turned the first page. The musty smell of history hit my nose, and I breathed in deeply, reading the opening line. *In the year of our Lord, five hundred thirty-nine, Arthur*

Pendragon fought and died for his kingdom. But the end of his story was merely the beginning of another...

The chapter went on to describe how magick was used in the many successful battles Arthur fought and then how magick left his side before he died. His knights took his fallen body from the battlefield and disappeared from the world into a fortress called Avalon, a fortress no man could find again after leaving.

A smile curved my lips. Sounded familiar to me. No mortal man ever *remembered* seeing this castle, either.

CHAPTER 7

XERXES

"Yes, General," Cal said, entering the Oval Office.

"To the lab," I said, walking toward him from behind the desk. He touched my shoulder and hurtled us into the vortex of space the Djinn used to teleport from place to place.

We materialized again in the new lab I'd set up inside the building formerly known as the Pentagon. Each level had been spelled by witches along with a twist of my own magick to allow only permitted personnel through the shields. Not even that fucking siren, Calliope, would be able to stroll through and take my people unaware again.

I'd made few mistakes over the course of my lifetime, but leaving the mansion at Whitemarsh without wards had been a costly one. Losing the Kitsune Riza and Sochi, and the baby Sochi carried in her womb, had enormously slowed my overall timeline. It would be a decade and a half before Lila, Sochi's first child, was able to bear a child of her own.

And today was the day we would harvest the last usable blood sample from her.

I left Cal in the main hallway and continued through the maze of doors and magickal barriers to the rooms set aside for Lila and her nurses. The pleased giggle of a baby's laugh greeted my ears once I passed through the very last barrier—soundproofed even to a supernatural level. I opened the door and stepped into the pale room filled with a few brightly colored blankets, toys, and a swing. Things her nurses insisted the baby needed for proper development.

I raised my hand, using my magick to lift Lila from where she lay on a blanket in front of a nurse. The woman was silent and bowed prostrate on the floor. The baby, however, continued to giggle. The corners of my mouth turned up, mirroring the tiny grin on her face. Her eyes sparkled with life and joy, completely unaware of how scared she should be and of what some might call a terrible situation. I was, after all, considered a monster.

And I was.

But I could still take care of a baby, especially one that would be very valuable to me in the future. She was provided with anything the nurses requested and now had four nurses who rotated in shifts around the clock to care for her. She was never alone.

Her brown eyes reminded me of the child I'd lost. The one stolen from me, who'd put everything that'd happened over the last four thousand years into motion. I'd simply been a man in love with a woman, excited to start a family. We'd known it was forbidden—love between a Lamassu and a Sister of House Lamidae—but it hadn't stopped us. Our baby had been beautiful. Perfect.

And then it wasn't. My family betrayed me, and I vowed to make them all pay for what they'd stolen, and I had, except for Naram and Rose. They evaded the massacre and took the Sister's with them. Rose had killed the woman I loved and my child. In return, I'd taken her husband and made it look like I'd killed him. For four thousand years, she'd had to live with the belief and that I'd killed my brother.

I'd given her the option to let me have Cera and the baby, but she'd stabbed them through the heart with a Dragonfire blade, telling me what I wanted was impossible, that I would ruin the entire prophecy by taking Cera away from the rest of the Sisters.

Fuck the prophecy.

I traced a fingertip along Lila's chubby cheek. "You are the only being on the planet that does not fear me. Yet." There would come a day. I knew it was inevitable. I'd lost whatever conscience I possessed along the way to seek revenge against my people. Against Rose. Against my brother. Though I hadn't killed him, he'd practically been reduced to a beast over the course of the passing millennia.

This baby would fear me, too. The whole Earth would one day tremble at just the mention of my name. Once the Earth bowed to me, it would be time to return to the Veil and take the thrones away from the Drakonae. Lamassu had reigned from the great stone thrones of Orin since the dawn of time, and history would repeat itself. I would make sure of it.

"Take her to the lab for the final procedure." I floated

the baby across the room and placed her gently on the floor in front of her prostrate nurse.

"Yes, Master."

I left the makeshift nursery and rejoined Cal in the main hall.

"General?" His tone even and slow, waiting for direction.

"The tomb."

Cal bowed then extended a hand.

I took it, and we jumped. A second later, we were inside a tomb beneath what had been the most powerful city on the face of the Earth. Babylon had fallen when I betrayed my kind to the Horde, but it'd taken many secrets with it.

Chains rustled in the back of the shadow-filled room. No natural light had touched the stones surrounding me since they'd been fit together thousands of years ago. I slipped a flashlight from my pocket and clicked the button on the handle. A beam of bright light flooded the massive room. This tomb held the bodies of many kings.

It also held my brother.

A huff of air stirred the room, and I cast the light in the direction of the sound.

"Kill me, brother." His voice rasped, filled with pain and void of any hope.

It was rare that I saw him in anything other than his Lamassu form. Today was no different—not that it mattered. His white eyes still glowed with the same hatred they'd had since the day I'd informed him that I'd ripped out his wife's heart with my claws and eaten it while she took her last breath at my feet.

Naram's lion-like claws clicked on the stone floor with

74

each limping step across the room. His body had been the size of a 747 jumbo jet when I first locked him down here in this massive cavern. He hadn't even been able to unfold his eagle-like wings completely.

Now with his magick and essence waning from near-starvation, his shifted form had lessened.

Less power. Less Lamassu.

When he stepped into the beam of light, I saw a wretched beast barely the size of a horse. His wings drooped at his sides, dragging the ground. Wings that used to span the entire breadth of the ancient temple.

"Kill me," he repeated. His human-lion head rose to face me straight on. Every muscle in his body strained and shook with effort.

"I came to feed you. Your time is close, brother, but is not here yet," I answered, speaking in the ancient tongue of the Babylonians with the same ease as I had four thousand years ago.

He shifted in front of me, morphing within seconds from the bedraggled beast to a weak, useless, dirty man. His shirt barely held together at the seams. Long ratted filthy hair hid part of his face. Pale skin gleamed in the illuminated light, and his hollow eyes had sunken so far into his face he reminded me of a mummified corpse.

"Kill me. You allowed every other of our kind to rest." The chains on his wrists and ankles clanked with each hobbled step he took toward me.

"You know why you're here, Naram."

He leaned against one of the massive pillars holding up the room and slid down it to the floor with a sigh. "She's dead because of you, not because of anything I did and you know it."

"Lies! You and Rose took her from me." I hissed. They'd killed Cera and my child, taken her in the night and stabbed her in the heart. The dragon fire weapon had been in Rose's hand when I entered the room, fresh blood still dripping from the blade. "Leave the bag." I turned to Cal, and he immediately dropped the canvas backpack to the floor with a thud and stepped toward me.

"She killed herself and the baby. You raped Cera." Even in his weakened state, his voice thundered through the enormous room, anger and something else—pity—laced his voice. "You ruin all you touch, brother."

"I suppose Earth's ruin is imminent then. Everything you thought I would accomplish has come true, brother. I will soon be the monster you feared all those years ago."

"If you had the Sisters, Xerxes, you'd never waste time taunting me again. So someone has them, and they are protecting them. You'll never get back to Orin." He sucked in a haggard breath and closed his bright white eyes to the beam of my flashlight.

"Rose's bitches are not the only way to the Veil." *Fuck.*

Naram chuckled, actually laughed, a hollow pathetic sound that echoed through the room and my soul.

Exasperation clawed at my chest like an annoying child begging to be picked up.

Then his gaze changed, suddenly becoming more focused. "You didn't kill her. Did you? You sick son of a whore. All this time, she's been evading you. That's my girl." His tone had switched from anguished to a strong sneer of defiance.

"Rose will see you again, brother, at least the pieces I choose to send." Once Rose and Naram were dead, I would be the only Lamassu left alive, and I would be unstoppable.

Dragons. Gryphons. Phoenix. It didn't matter in the least. I'd pick them off one by one until they were alone and running for cover. Without Rose at their side, they would be nothing. She was the strategist behind everything they'd done, every plan of mine they'd thwarted.

Soon, nothing they did would matter.

Each day my army grew. Each day they showed the humans who was superior. Soon humans would hide in the shadows and the Earth would be ours.

Once I'd accomplished a pandemic of terror, I'd take Earth.

Then I'd take the Veil. That damn fucking dagger was in Sanctuary. It was the only place it could be hiding from the spell my witches continually cast to locate it. Rose had the Sisters and my key, but not for much longer.

"You will fail, brother. She will find a way—"

I kicked the canvas bag full of bread and dried meat toward him before squaring my shoulders. It didn't matter what he thought, what he said. "I'm the one taking over the world one country at a time, Naram. You're the one slowly wishing for death beneath a city that's been extinct for thousands of years."

"Thousands?" His eyebrows raised in surprise before his head dropped low. "I knew it'd been a long time. But—"

"Over four thousand years," I scoffed. "And your stupid prophecy still hasn't been fulfilled."

He glanced up at me again and snarled, but didn't speak. The expression he wore screamed his frustration.

A smile tugged at the corners of my mouth. "It

shouldn't be taking this long...should it? What do you know that Rose doesn't?"

No answer. Naram turned and walked away from me, disappearing into the shadows again.

"What do you know?" I asked again.

"Kill me or leave me alone.

Anger burned inside my chest. I could stand there and yell at him. Beat him. Threaten him. It wouldn't make the slightest difference. Whatever piece of the puzzle Naram was keeping to himself would go with him to his grave. He'd never tell me.

Some things never changed. I'd won all those years ago. I'd taken everything from him, and yet there were still things my brother carried that I could never know. Things apparently even his fucking wife didn't know.

CHAPTER 8

ALEK

*R*ose's Cafe was extra busy today. The scent of sugar and cinnamon filled the air like a cloud. The Brownies had put their famous sticky buns back on the menu, and Sanctuary's pregnant mothers were flocking to the booths. Eira, Sanctuary's freshest vampire Protector, sat with Diana Blackmoor, both their bellies swollen with child. Their mates walked through the door a moment later, ringing the little brass bell wildly. The two Drakonae and the Elvin slid into the seats next to their respective mates, laughing and joking with each other about never getting to taste one of the elusive sticky-buns.

It is just a bit of fucking bread. Who really gives a shit? A pang of jealousy spun a web across my heart, tugging hard until I forced my gaze away from them. I didn't really begrudge them bread. What really hurt was knowing that I'd never partake of the sacred gift they'd been given— fatherhood. That I'd never have a mate-bond like my parents had shared. That I didn't even fully know what it meant to be a Gryphon.

My friendship with the Blackmoor Drakonae brothers spanned thousands of years, but since they'd recovered their mate Diana, Jared and I both had pulled away. At least Jared had a sliver of hope for a mate, since the Djinn woman from Savannah had lived through touching his flame.

I, Alek Melos, was the only Gryphon on Earth. No hope for me. There had been several dozen of us in the beginning when we'd first come through from Veil, but once we'd split up, that'd been it. I never saw any of them again. Not once throughout all the thousands of years I'd lived in this world.

For the longest time, I'd believed the Sisters of Lamidae were the key to getting back home, to finding out if any of my people had survived the fire of the Incanti. Maybe I would find a mate one day if ever I was able to return. Maybe someone there still knew what it meant to be a Gryphon.

But that dream had strangled itself a millennia ago. Four thousand years and only six Protectors had been found. Who knew how many more years would pass before the last two would be located and brought to Sanctuary? The Sisters said the seventh was out there—alive, but so far, none had been able to say where the seventh was. Whether it was a man or woman. Nothing. Nada. Zip. Zilch. Not to mention we still needed a fucking eighth.

Now I found myself attracted to a girl I'd spent nearly every afternoon with since she was a child, except she wasn't a child anymore. She was a grown woman—a beautiful grown woman, one who I couldn't trust myself to be around without betraying just how much I desired her.

I hadn't been back to the Blackmoor's library since last week. She probably hated me now for avoiding her. The companionship and camaraderie we'd build over the past fifteen years ruined because of my inability to control my lust.

It'd been like switch had flipped inside my mind. Instead of seeing the sweet innocent girl she had been, I saw a grown woman with curves that made me hard and lips that brought carnal thoughts to my mind. I wanted to taste her. Every fucking inch. I wanted her, wanted to claim her.

Hell, I didn't even know what that meant, but a small voice deep inside kept whispering that she was meant for me.

Returning to the old routine now wasn't an option. The thought of seeing Gretchen again and smelling her scent was like sunshine for my dark heart. No matter my mood. No matter what demons from my past clawed to the surface, seeing her made everything better, and I'd lost that.

Thrown it away.

"Hey, Earth to Alek," Jared said, his tone annoyed and amused at the same time. "Stop thinking about her."

"Shut up."

"We've been brothers since Fate threw us through that portal together."

I turned to face my friend and snarled under my breath. "Fate did nothing. My father sent us through. Fate stole our chance to help our families."

Jared glanced at the table. "I have wished for a chance

to take vengeance for a long time, but that wasn't what Fate intended for us."

"I know you believe that we were always meant to fight Rose Hilah's righteous war, but I don't. I stayed with you because you are my brother, the only family I have on this Earth, but don't for one second think I believe any of Rose's bullshit prophecy crap anymore."

"Anymore? You're just angry and horny and won't take my advice about finding someone else to satisfy your dick," he said, keeping his voice low. Not that it mattered. Everyone and everything in this fucking diner could've heard a needle drop at a rock concert if they focused hard enough.

Anger burned in my gut, bubbling and frothing at Jared's mention of my taking relief in another woman's bed. The idea made me ill, just as ill as the thought of Gretchen sharing her body with any other male.

Mine. My Gryphon screamed inside my head, and I winced.

But that was the problem; she wasn't *mine,* and I couldn't see a way around the rules laid out by Rose. I was the one that solved problems in this town, not created them, but this...if I wanted Gretchen, I had to take her and leave.

Run.

The Drakonae would kill me before I set foot over the castle threshold with one of their precious Sisters.

"Hey, Alek." Raven, one of the pixies who helped run the café, sauntered up with a bright smile that should've chased away my anger. "Hey, Jared. How's the town holding together?"

"Morning, Raven." He smiled back at the purple-haired sprite, and I attempted to fake my way through being fine.

"Morning."

"Man, you sound like you just drank spoiled milk. What's got you all twisted up, honey?" She scooted closer to me and slipped an arm around my shoulder, giving me a squeeze meant to comfort. The hairs on my arm rose, and a light shiver ran up both of them.

"What did you do?" I jerked away, grabbed her by the waist, and removed her from the bench next to me. Standing, I rose to my full height of seven foot two.

"Nothing much." Her voice came out in a husky breath laced with mischief.

Liar. All the pixies were meddlers, always had been.

"Just gave you a little pixie-upper. We can't have the town sheriff down in the dumps with Djinn knocking at our gates every few days and *his* personal rat-bastard Lycans stirring up trouble. People in this town depend on you two be in tip-top shape." She looked up at me, her hands propped on her little waist and smiled a smile that said too-bad-mister-you've-got-to-deal-with-your-shit-right-now-no-ifs-ands-or-buts-about-it.

My hands fisted at my sides, and I held in the growl rumbling in my chest. The pixie magick coursed through me like a firestorm, focusing my brain and my body on the one thing—the one person—who would truly lift my spirit. I'd been avoiding speaking or talking to her, and now the damn pixie had eliminated my resolve to stay away. *Fuck.*

I rolled my neck and grimaced, refusing to cuss out the fairy who'd stuck her nose way too far into my business.

83

"Raven, seriously, you can't do shit like this." Jared stood next to me. "Bro, you okay?"

"He needed it. The pixie dust was for helping solve a problem. It will be fine."

"It won't be fucking fine." Jared's snarl attracted the attention of most of the dining hall.

I didn't need more of an audience. "I have to go."

Jared lasered his gaze in on me with a look that screamed don't-you-dare, but it was too late, I was already walking past him toward the door. Ducking my head, I slipped out under the annoying tinkle of that damn bell and cut across the circle. The castle loomed before me.

Maybe, just maybe she'd give me a chance to explain. Somehow I had to get things back to normal—whatever that really meant. I knew I could never be with her, but I needed her in my life. Even if it was just reading books and talking every afternoon like we had for the past fifteen years. Her presence. Her touch. Her scent. Her friendship.

It could be enough.

It had to be enough.

The entrance to the castle loomed ahead, large and strong and defiant, reminding me what I was about to do was stupid. I was crazy to think I could maintain status quo with Gretchen—if she would even agree to see me again, but it was all I had to look forward to, other than babysitting this town from the occasional Lycan brawl.

"Alek." Jared's voice boomed from across the street.

I ignored him and placed a hand on the middle panel of the heavy eight-foot door, waited for the spell to lift, shoved it open, and stepped into the castle foyer. The beam was only put into place at night. During the day, a magickal spell locked the door from anyone who wasn't on the approved entry list.

If someone did try to enter without permission, the spell would give them a zap of magickal energy they'd have a hard time recovering from. One of Xerxes' Lycans had snuck into town and tried it a week ago. Besides burning over fifty percent of his body, it'd completely knocked him unconscious. Rose had tried to interrogate him, but he'd been too far gone. Mikjáll turning him to ash had been a kindness.

My heavy boots thumped across the polished marble floors. Grabbing the ornate railing of one side of the double staircase, I took the steps two at a time. The closer I got, the more powerful the pull.

Gods, I missed her. Until I'd kept away for a week, I'd not realized just how much I'd already bonded to her. I didn't know a lot about my Gryphon magick, Jared and I had both been teenagers when my father had shoved us through the open portal and said more of the family would follow behind us.

We'd waited at the entrance for nearly a week before hunger had forced us to hunt. Even then we returned to the ring of stones every day for months. No adults ever came through.

Jared and I weren't the only ones waiting or the only ones grieving, but we'd been the only ones that stuck together. The rest of the random supernatural teenagers from the cities of Rekar and Resar—saved from slaughter—vanished to the four corners of the world. I never saw them again.

I turned a corner, not surprised that the second-floor hallway was quiet. The Drakonae were all in the cafe, except Mikjáll. I hadn't seen him and his Kitsune rescues lately. Riza and her baby were always at his side. Sochi, Riza's sister, had remained a little more aloof from the town.

The younger Kitsune was also pregnant and grieving through the separation from her first child, who still remained in Xerxes' clutches. Rose was devising a plan to get the baby back, but so far we'd been unable to gather intelligence on where he'd moved his base of operations. Until a location was determined, there was nothing to be done. Our only salvation was in knowing that he needed the baby alive.

I stopped for a moment to admire van Gogh's *The Starry Night*. How those sneaky Blackmoor's had gotten their hands on it before the Riots tore through New York was beyond me, but they had.

It and many of its companions from the Modern Art Museum had found their way into a hall of this castle fortress. The stone floors were covered in Persian carpets, and the walls were draped in tapestries that looked like they'd been lifted from Camelot itself, and more paintings. They had so many paintings. It was like walking through a palace. So much history. So much wealth.

We'd all accumulated much through the millennia, but the Drakonae had a special penchant for art and history.

I pushed open one of the library's French doors and slipped quietly inside. A soft heartbeat thudded in the back of the room, steady and familiar. My footsteps were silent on the carpets lining the floor. Reaching the end of the first row of shelves, I peered around the corner and spied Gretchen curled up on a love seat in one of the reading alcoves.

Black lashes lay against her creamy white skin. A few strands of her silky black hair trailed across a cheek. I squatted on my heels beside her and used the tip of my finger to tuck it behind her ear. Then my gaze dropped to the gap at the top of her dress, where just enough cleavage showed to make my blood rise a few degrees. The dress she wore was thin and white, and how, by the gods, had I been so blind to her beauty? She'd spent hours almost every afternoon at my side.

Her heartbeat sped up, and her breathing hitched. Blue eyes appeared, bright and wide and filled with surprise. I'd scared her. My face was barely a foot from hers, and I was staring at her like a lion ready to pounce.

Instead, she pounced on me, wrapping her arms around my neck and pressing her velvety soft lips against mine. Shock paralyzed my body for a split second before instinct drew my arms around her torso, tugging her from the loveseat flush to my chest. My balance wavered, and I tipped from my heels, landing on my ass with a thud. Still our mouths explored each other's.

I dared to inhale as her fragrant scent twisted and spun around me, promising everything I'd ever desired—at least the illusion of it.

Her fingers slipped from my neck up into my hair, and a moan laced with need and frustration and a hint of simmering anger rose to the surface.

CHAPTER 9

GRETCHEN

*L*iquid head coursed through my body, originating from where Alek's tongue danced with mine all the way to the tips of my fingers and toes. Excitement. Hunger. Contentment. Everything. All the emotions piled into my heart at the same time.

I tangled my fingers in his hair and held on with what little control I had left. It was a dream, had to be, but I wanted it to last as long as humanly possible.

Alek wouldn't be kissing me in reality. He didn't even look at me like he knew I was a full-grown, twenty-seven-year-old woman, but this—this kiss was the stuff of my dreams, my fantasies. All I'd imagined paled in comparison to this one experience. This was what it would be like to really be kissed by Alek, held by him, to hold him. I'd cling to this for as long as the illusion would last.

He tasted exactly as I'd thought—a hint of the hazelnut coffee he drank every day and raw hungry male.

By the gods, he was better than the special wine the Black-moor's pulled out for holiday meals.

"Why can't you be real?" I asked, my words garbled through our entwined mouths.

Alek pulled me tighter, and my breasts pressed against his chest, nipples coming to needy points through the thin fabric of my dress. The material, usually soft against my skin, scraped and tugged with each movement. I wanted to feel his skin against mine. His heat.

I slipped my hand beneath the hem of his t-shirt and moaned again. Muscles rippled beneath my fingertips. He was perfection. Hard. Sleek. Hungry for me.

And then my illusion shattered. My dream pulled his mouth from mine, grabbed my hand from where it explored the enticing lines leading my hand to explore lower and lower on his stomach, and stared me straight in the eye.

"I am real. You are awake."

I blinked, tugging my hand, but he didn't release it. His other arm, still wrapped halfway around my body, hadn't loosened, either. I was nearly straddling him. One knee rested on the floor, the inside of that thigh grazing the outside of his. Then somewhere on the way off the love seat my other knee had nestled itself between his legs. The top of that thigh pressed into his very distinct, very aroused manhood.

Oh gods. Heat raced across my skin, up my neck, across my face. What had I done? I'd mauled him, thinking I was merely dreaming. Almost a week had passed with no word. I didn't dare ask anyone about him after Diana had delivered that first message, but there'd been no mission, no attack that had put us into hiding this week.

I wanted to scream and yell and ask why he'd just abandoned me without a word, but at the same time, I wanted to grab his face with my hands and just keep kissing him. I wanted to straddle him for real. I wanted to feel all that energy coursing between us explode into more. Instead, tears came.

Tears poured down my cheeks. The astronomical emotional loss of what was about to happen slammed into my soul. He'd finally returned to the library, and I'd ruined our friendship. He'd never come around again after this. He was Rose's soldier. I could see it in his gaze. Fierce, but apologetic. This wasn't going to go the way I'd fantasized.

"Gretchen, please." He lifted me from his lap and gently placed me on the cushions of the loveseat. "Don't cry."

"You're leaving me for good this time," I said, my voice barely more than a hoarse whisper. "Why did you come back at all?"

A heavy sigh slipped from between his perfect lips. Soft and kind and glorious lips that had returned my affections only moments ago.

"I hated the way I left things. I had to explain."

Explain? Pain lanced through my side, like he'd driven a sword through my gut. "I love you, Alek Melos." There, it was out now. I'd cut out my heart and offered it right up. Maybe I just wanted to hurt him like he was about to hurt me. At least my words might make him feel guilt. He'd kissed me back, held me tight, and wanted me with all the fierceness he was now using to pull away.

But he was a man, and men took what they could get— or so I'd been told, but I expected more from Alek. I knew that's not what he'd been thinking when he returned my kiss.

He was a giant of a man, but straightforward. He'd never lied to me before or disappeared without sending word. He'd been there for me for so many years. More tears fell. I tried to imagine what my life would be like from here on out without him. How would I continue in my caged existence without his bright light in my dark corner of the world? I didn't fit in the House of Lamidae. The life they all lived so happily choked me a little more each day.

"I didn't realize—" His eyes drifted to the walnut floorboards.

"What? That you were more to me than just a friend who reads stories and discusses history?"

"I didn't realize I'd fallen in love with you, Gretchen. Not until I avoided you this week."

Avoided me? Purposefully...wait? "You love me?" I wiped the burning tears from my cheeks and sniffed. Hope blossomed in my chest, unfurling like the roses in the courtyard garden. Maybe my fantasy wasn't about to sink to the bottom of the ocean and collect barnacles like the Titanic.

"I do, but this...this can't be, Gretchen." He inhaled a deep breath. "We can't be together. It would never work. Rose would sooner cast me out of Sanctuary than allow *this*." He gestured to each of us in turn. "We are impossible."

"If there's one thing I've learned in my short life, Alek, it's that nothing surrounding the supernatural is impossible. You're a Gryphon, a mythical being that shouldn't exist on Earth, but you do. I'm a woman who can see the future, our future. I shouldn't be able to do that, but I can.

Impossible is normal in our lives, or hadn't you figured that out yet?"

"I swore an oath to protect the House of Lamidae from all who would seek to take you from your destiny." His voice broke halfway through, and he dropped his bright gaze to the floor. "I will not be the reason all our efforts fail. If all the Protectors had been found, if the prophecy was fulfilled, perhaps then—"

"Perhaps by then another thousand years will have passed and I'll be dead and gone." My tone was bitter, anger seeping into each word. He wanted me. He was in love with me. But Rose's damned crusade was more important than us having a chance for one lifetime of happiness. "Who's to say the prophecy can't be fulfilled with one less Sister? We've lived and died for millennia, and the prophecy has yet to be fulfilled. Never ending. Always hanging over us like a shroud."

Even as I spoke the words, dread filled my gut. I didn't know exactly what made our visions come and go through the years, but I had an inkling from listening to the older Sisters talk that each and every one of us was very important.

"No supernatural is allowed to be with a Sister. If our DNA was compatible, I would be no better than a Lamassu, trying to create a more powerful race. The visions are contained within the House of Lamidae for a reason."

"I don't care."

"Yes, you do."

"No, I don't. Nothing ever felt right to me until I met you. And then you left me."

He rose from the floor, and all seven feet of his sadness

and regret loomed depressingly over me like a thunder-storm about to pour. It couldn't be that simple. There was more to life than the black-and-white destiny the Oracle, and Rose spouted day in and day out.

There was more to life than searching for a way to have a baby and continue my line. If I never had a child, I could live with that. *Right?* The emotional pain of the thought tore through my heart, but if it meant I could be with Alek, I would bear the pain for as many years as Fate would gift us together. I knew I only had one lifetime, and I wanted to spend every waking moment of it in his arms. In his life.

I looked up, meeting his gaze once more, halting his backward retreat. "What if it was allowed?"

He shook his head, a mask of pain shadowed his face. "It is not."

"But what if it was?" I pleaded for a tiny sliver of hope, something I could cling to. Something that might bring him back to me again.

"If it was allowed, Gretchen, I would take you in my arms again and never let you go. I would treasure you for as long as the Fates would allow. You would be *mine*."

The last word twisted the sword in my gut. It wasn't fair. He was mine. I was his. We were supposed to be together. I'd seen it over and over and over.

He took another step backward.

"Alek, please." My voice cracked through the plea. I'd never begged for anything my entire life. But I would beg for him. I would crawl on my hands and knees. I'd do anything if it meant a chance for us.

He shook his head, slowly deciding our Fate for both of us. He wasn't going to fight. He wasn't going to beg or plead. I knew he wouldn't. Alek was stoic and proud. He always did the right thing. Always followed the rules. Life was black-and-white for him. Why had I thought he'd change for me?

But I'd hoped he would.

Somehow, I had convinced myself that he'd drop everything he'd ever known, sweep me away from this stone prison and unwanted destiny, and save me.

"It is against the rules, Gretchen."

"What rules, and who said specifically we couldn't be together if we wanted to?"

His eyes darkened, sending shadows to dampen my hope. "It is common knowledge that Rose does not allow supernaturals to *be* with the Sisters. Why do you think so much trouble is gone to...to bring in...?"

He couldn't say it, so I did it for him. "Studs?"

"Gretchen." His tone highlighted his extreme discomfort with the topic.

"That's what they are. We're just cows. Here to breed and procreate and have visions that will fix something, but even we don't really know *how* the prophecy will play out." I stood, planting my hands on my hips, and sneered. "How about that for your black-and-white rules? The seers have never seen past a time when we were here. In this town. In this prison."

"This is far from a prison. You are well taken—"

"We are stock, bred and birthed, and kept bowing to the almighty Rose's every whim." The anger in my voice turned venomous. Years of bottled-up frustration continued to pour out. "I'm nothing but a tool for her, and apparently, I'm nothing more than a distraction for you.

We have a connection. I've felt it every day for the last fifteen years. Every time we've touched…I saw more."

He took a step forward and reached to touch my arm, but I jerked away and walked behind the loveseat. I didn't want to touch him now. What if I'd ruined it? What if the vision changed, or was just gone?

This wasn't how it was supposed to have gone. "You were my future, my hope, but Rose's big bad sheriff won't—"

He turned on his heel and walked out before I could finish. His shoulders slumped in defeat. Nothing. No words of anger. No argument. I didn't set out to hurt him, but I had. My chest tightened, and my heart burned beneath my sternum. The giant Gryphon of Sanctuary had taken my pain and verbal lashes and left without a single solitary cry.

"I didn't mean that. I'm sorry." The words echoed through the empty library. I knew he'd heard me. He could hear as well or better than any other supernatural I'd encountered. They could all hear a whisper through a wall of stone if they wanted. No privacy. Ever. "Alek." I dropped my face into my hands, and tears poured again, burning trails of regret down my cheeks. "Please come back."

What had I done?

How could I fix it?

There had to be a way. I refused to believe that I was so integral to the world's destiny that it would begrudge me *actual* love, a real life. Perhaps even a real family.

CHAPTER 10

ALEK

*B*y the gods, why had I let myself continue kissing her? *Because she tasted like heaven and sunshine wrapped into the most decadent of desserts.* Her lips had stolen my breath. I'd pulled Gretchen closer, taking her mouth like we'd been lovers for centuries.

The scent of her arousal had been like an aphrodisiac, robbing me of my common sense. Her breasts, firm against my chest, had sent my mind into a place where I thought—just for a moment—that a life with her might be possible. Only for a second had I wanted to roll her on the floor, strip her of that thin linen shift, taste her sweetness, and make her mine.

Fuck.

Right there on the floor of the library.

Fuck.

She deserved better than that. I was better than that. I

wasn't some teenage, hormone-driven lunatic who couldn't keep his pants on.

My body still vibrated with a desire that threatened my usually unwavering logic. My Gryphon struggled within me, desperate to get back to her. It didn't make sense. She wasn't my kind. She was a human, and a Sister. One of the women I'd sworn to protect from exactly what I was fantasizing of doing.

I couldn't bond with her the way my parents had bonded. I didn't know how. The rituals and ceremonies I'd watched others perform were vague memories from a childhood long past, wisps of shadows that teased and tested my patience. I was a man—a beast—without a people. Without any knowledge of my race except what my hormonal, teenage mind had retained from all those thousands of years ago.

I could shift. I could fight. I could scream a sound that made men tremble from miles away. Those were things I'd learned growing up with Jared, doing the best we could to survive in a strange world filled with people who would ostracize or kill us if they discovered our secrets.

Still, I knew there was more to being a Gryphon. That I had deduced through trial and error. Magick wound itself around my heart like coils of ivy, and every so often I'd feel it surge within me, driving me to fly, something I'd only done a few times over the millennia. Nowhere on Earth was safe for a winged monster. I wasn't as big as a dragon. One well-placed rifle shot could knock me from the sky.

I stalked through the castle, away from her, away from her tears. It was better this way, easier for both of us. I refused to be the reason Rose's precious prophecy was put on hold or, worse, destroyed. Even if I had moved past needing to get home, my friends had not.

The hallways passed in a blur, as did the staircase and the front door.

Sunlight beat down on my back. I crossed the street, headed for Avenue B, the street between the produce market and a row of townhouses where my home stood. Jared should still be at the office.

I needed a few minutes to myself before my nosy-neighbor-of-a-brother came stalking over to tell me what a mistake I'd made by seeing Gretchen again.

My feet pounded along the sidewalk, gaze glued to a fixed point across the street—the door to the Fire Station/Sheriff's Office that Jared and I shared. We monitored the town, knew everyone. Nothing happened in our town without one or both of us finding out.

Just don't come out.

My leg collided with a small person, and I leaned forward. A flash of iridescent blue hair filled my line of sight. I caught her before she fell into a pile of crates stacked in front of the market.

"Ouch!" a small female voice squeaked.

"I'm so sorry." My voice sounded beaten and hopeless. There was no way Jared wouldn't notice this mood. Getting *over* Gretchen was going to take centuries—if getting over her was possible at all.

I righted the tiny woman and took an apologetic step back, recognizing the pixie who ran the produce market, Bella. One of the only pixies who never changed her hair color. Since I'd met her over a hundred years ago, she'd always had the same silvery-blue-iridescent mane.

Honestly, it still reminded me of those children's pony toys, but it suited her—ethereal.

"I wasn't paying attention. I didn't see you."

"Well, you're what, like seven feet tall? I suppose someone so near the ground doesn't register quickly."

I shook my head. "I apologize." I tried to step around Bella and continue down the sidewalk, but she put a hand on my chest and moved to block my way, cocking her head to the side and angling her gaze all the way up to meet mine.

Magick coursed from her hand, not physically stopping me, but it soothed my frayed nerves. Her bright, moss-green eyes flashed with interest, and her alabaster skin glowed a soft yellow like she was a night light plugged into a wall socket.

"Our big scary sheriff has given his heart to another. I wondered if someone would ever be able to reach through the armor you'd constructed around your heart and win over your loyalty."

How the fuck?

She clucked her tongue. "Don't be such a sour apple. I won't tell anyone. Pixies are very good at keeping secrets."

"I don't need a secret kept or your discretion. Just leave me be and let me pass." Not that she truly posed a problem. I could've easily removed her from my path, but manhandling a woman wasn't on the approved action-list inside my brain. Bella was not one easily deterred, though, and I truly wished she would just drop it.

And she did.

Her hand fell from my chest. The magick coursing between us dissipated. The glow in her skin faded, and she stepped to the side, leaving the entire sidewalk open for me to continue. "Go then. Just remember, if you ever need help, I'm here."

"There's nothing anyone can do for me." I gave her a curt nod and walked past.

"Love is always worth the fight. There's nothing in the universe quite like finding the person you're meant to be with. Don't give up on that."

I refused to look back. Refused to encourage her meddling. I didn't need her or her pixie dust making a bigger mess than I'd already stirred up. Gretchen wasn't for me. She could never be for me, her destiny—whether she liked it or not—was tied up with Rose's crusade. Fate had already threaded that string, long before she'd been born.

Movement across the street caught my attention, and I focused.

"The Sisters must have more children," Rose's hushed words carried to my ears from where she stood next to the large passenger bus Harrison Bateman drove.

I didn't stop walking, but I didn't stop listening, either. It wasn't often that Rose revealed details surrounding the House of Lamidae. Harrison was probably one of the only people who knew a little more about the needs surrounding their circumstances.

"Astrid is a new Oracle, unsure of herself, and the House numbers are down. She's already told me they've had visions of another Protector, but that they are unclear and too vague to be of use. If just a few more could get with child, the collective power would be restored."

"It's not their fault. I've spoken with the pixies. Bella

agrees that the humans are the ones with the fertility issues."

"You have to go farther, more rural. Try to find men who haven't participated in the vaccine programs that started right after the Riots and offer them more money, whatever it takes."

"I've tried. It's hard enough to find decent men who don't have families already and then to agree to the contracts—even with gold payment as incentive. I'd have already tried Mexico and Canada, but that option disappeared years ago after—"

"I know, after the Republics dismantled the Federal government." The Sentinel sighed—the tone of her voice heavy and hopeless. "I'm depending on you. Please keep looking. We're so close. After all this time, we only need to find two more Protectors to be ready to complete the spell."

"There are still a few pockets of people who avoided some of the mandatory vaccinations from 2060, before they realized how damaging they were. I'll try there on my next run. The gold helped this last time, though I hate that aspect."

"In the end, this is the only way we get home, Harrison. Your family can start fresh in the Veil, away from the hatred and prejudice. All of Sanctuary will be able to escape the madness Xerxes is ushering toward us. Many from around the globe will want to join the exodus."

"I know."

I turned the corner onto my street, my heart sinking into the frothing pit of my stomach. The very thing that would free Gretchen from her duty was the only thing I didn't want her to do.

Imagining her with some other man, some stranger...

An alarm went off across town—a magical horn set up by the pixies, Sanctuary's very own alarm system. Poles with alarm triggers had been set at every cross street.

I increased my pace from a slow walk to a full-on-devil-might-be-on-my-heels run. Doors slammed around me. Men and women alike poured from the houses up and down the streets, joining me on the run toward the sounding siren.

A blur with a streak of blond whooshed past—possibly Erick—followed by several other nearly invisible figures. Vampires were capable of moving so quickly they literally blended into the background.

A cry of anguish from down the street spurred me faster, and my beast came forth. Unlike the Lycan's, my magick enabled me to shift without losing my clothing in the process. I lunged forward, allowing the Gryphon inside to take shape. My wings unfurled, and I propelled myself into the air within moments, my human form melting into the body of a lion, and my shoulders and head into that of an eagle.

The crying continued, and I circled over the street, crossing where a crowd had gathered. All six Protectors, along with dozens of Lycan's and others, huddled around an unrecognizable bloodied body. I used my eagle's vision to scan the surrounding roads and rooftops for any signs of intruders. Even the smallest movement of a leaf on the ground would trigger my enhanced sense of sight. Being seen wasn't a concern for me at this moment. Fuck whoever might be watching from a distance. Or satellite. I was the only Gryphon on Earth. My actions would only expose myself.

Two streets over, I saw them. It could've been two Sanctuary citizens, but they were running away from the alarm horn when the entirety of the town was running toward it. The pixies had made sure the alarm would never be used against us. No one from inside the town could trigger it. Everyone had been *programed* in, so to speak, even the children.

I swooped lower, letting loose a cry that sent both men pitching forward, falling to the ground in pain. Diving faster, I almost had them, but I pounded into an empty street instead. I screamed again in frustration, shattering the glass in several nearby houses with the force of the decibels.

I folded my wings and shifted back into human form. "Fucking Djinn."

"Alek," Jared's voice called from down the street.

I whirled to face my friend and shook my head.

His shoulders fell, and he nodded before turning to go back toward the scene of —whatever had happened. Murderers. Who had they killed?

I walked the street, following quickly behind Jared. He wove through the two blocks back to where everyone was standing. Rose was in the center of the group. Even though I couldn't see her, I could feel the pulses from her magick radiating from within the crowd.

Eira, Sanctuary's newest appointed sixth Protector, stood at the edge of the crowd with her mate, Killían North, rubbing her slightly rounded belly. The vampire-Elvin match had created a miracle between them. To my knowledge, no vampire had ever existed both alive and undead simultaneously. Eira's heart beat yet she still needed blood to survive, but the baby within her demanded normal human food for sustenance.

I walked to their side and stood between them and Jared.

"I don't suppose your super-sonic scream flattened anyone I can flay with my sword?" Killían asked, leaning closer to my arm. The Elvin was tall, but I still had a good six or seven inches on him.

"Nope, the spineless Lycan escaped with his Djinn."

"Figures." Killían's voice edged with disappointment. "I haven't had a chance to—"

"Killían," Eira said, her tone firmly saying hold-your-tongue-or-else, a skill only a wife and mate could success-fully master and wield. Still, her jewel-blue eyes held barely-contained fury. She was new to the town, but possessive as hell. She'd been recruited into the town—or manipulated—depending upon perspective, but she was family now and she considered every single person in the town somewhat her responsibility. A noble trait but an exhausting one. Her mate, though not a designated Protec-tor, had taken up the same ownership of Sanctuary and its inhabitants that many of us—myself included—shared.

Jared nudged my other arm. "Did you recognize the Djinn?"

"It wasn't her. They were both male."

A despondent sigh slipped from his chest. "She's still alive."

I believed him. He said he hadn't had long enough to form a connection link with her, but I knew he had some-thing. Phoenix were telepathic and telekinetic. I'd seen him manipulate everything from the furniture in the room to snuffing out a house fire. He hadn't given up hope, which meant he absolutely believed she was alive. Possibly even could feel that she was alive.

We were quite the pair. His soul desperately searching for a Djinn woman everyone in town wouldn't hesitate to kill and me...emotionally flogging myself for even considering the possibility that Gretchen and I could to be together.

The crowd dissipated and I watched, sorrow twisting in my gut for those lost today. They wouldn't be the last, no matter how hard we fought. Several Lycans lifted the mangled body from the asphalt. Finn held the man's legs and Brogan the upper body.

"You said earlier one of the intruders was Lycan?" Erick turned to face me directly.

I nodded. "Two males. One Lycan. One Djinn."

"It was quick thinking for you to shift and survey. We were all so surprised by the death *inside* our town borders we forgot to behave like the soldiers we are."

"This is not the first time they've come into town, but it is the first time we didn't know about it beforehand. Did the barrier fall?"

"No," a familiar male voice rose above the quiet sobs and words of comfort being passed through the crowd. "They found a way to cut a hole right through it. The barrier is still at full strength. No one should've been able to blink or even walk through it. One of the Lycans in town offered to test it for us, and it tossed him flat on his back and singed most of the hair right off his body."

"We just have to adjust the spell, Harrison. Come." Rose gestured to the resident head witch of Sanctuary. He and his daughters used to live part-time in Ada and part-time in Sanctuary, but with all the threats and the Mason

Pack's lodge being destroyed, he'd moved them both down to Sanctuary permanently. Rose had quickly put them to work assembling a spell that would not only inhibit a Djinn from blinking through it, but also from crossing it at all. From what I'd heard, she'd infused her own magick into the spell to strengthen it.

Harrison followed her away from the crowd, and everyone else began breaking apart, returning to whatever duty was calling them next.

But the only place calling to me was the damn castle, where the woman I loved was trapped, not only by walls but by destiny itself.

CHAPTER 11

GRETCHEN

*I*t was Friday again, and again I was hiding out in the library, as far away from the rest of the Sisters as I could get.

"Gretchen?" Astrid's voice drifted through the ajar French door.

Apparently, it isn't far enough. I held my breath and willed her to just keep walking. She couldn't see me from the doorway. I was on my favorite couch in the farthest nook of the enormous room, the one that still held Alek's scent. The one where he'd kissed me. Another week had passed and I wanted to run through the castle, screaming his name until he appeared. In my dreams, I'd gone to the parapet walk and waited for him near an open window. He'd come to me in his Gryphon form, and we'd flown away from the castle. Away from Sanctuary. Away from Rose's oppression.

A tear rolled down my cheek. I wanted to lay all of this

on Rose. She had protected us, and many people in this town had died to keep us safe. Here I was bitching instead. Alek was one who'd been with her for centuries—probably longer. I was asking him to be disloyal to someone he respected and held in high esteem.

I was a horrible person. Selfish.

Astrid's footsteps thumped closer and closer. A moment later, her head appeared around the last row of shelves. "Gretchen." She hurried the last few steps and sat down beside me. "Sweetheart, what's wrong?"

"I can't do this. I lo—" My chest tightened and I froze. What if they were angry at Alek? What if Rose punished him or sent him away. What was I doing?

Astrid's arm went around me and she tensed. A rush of air fled her lungs, and I knew she was having a vision. Her fingers tightened around my arm until the pressure was painful. I held in the hiss I wanted to release and just waited. Hopefully, it wouldn't be a long vision.

When her fingers released, I watched her and waited. Her eyes opened and her worried gaze mirrored the sense of dread wrapping around my stomach. "You haven't slept with him yet, have you?"

My heart stopped in my chest. Slept with who? What had she seen?

"Gretchen." Her fingers tightened again, digging painfully into the flesh of my forearm. "Tell me you haven't slept with him."

I shook my head, still unable to speak. Fear blossomed in my breast, spreading like a dark cloud over my soul.

She audibly sighed with relief. "You can't let this happen, Gretchen. We are not allowed to copulate with supernatural men. Our powers would transfer to the child if we were genetically compatible. They would forever be tied to this life. At least humans age and die in the span of a century, but paranormals would exist in this—"

"Hell?" I snapped. As if just because we had a typical human lifespan, it was easier to survive this sentence. At least an immortal would live with the hope of seeing the end of this torment. We lived and died knowing the end wouldn't happen in our lifespan. The visions hadn't shown anything more than that. Astrid had seen the seventh Protector in a few visions, but they'd been blurry and unclear—a sign that our numbers were weakened. More Sisters equaled more magick equaled better visions.

"We have a good life. This is far from the hell it could be if it weren't for Rose."

"They made us this way. How can you defend her?"

"Regardless of how we arrived at this moment, Rose protects and cares for us, and if I want my children and grandchildren and great-grandchildren to be free, then we have to keep our numbers solid. If we don't, the visions will remain unclear. You know as well as I why my visions and some of the other Sisters are covered in shadow."

"I can't."

"Then you would curse more of our Sisters' children to the same fate, instead of pulling your weight and helping us to finish this. We've added two Protectors in the last year because Vella, Keri, and Mata have all had two children each in the last three years. Their favored *joining* choices have returned to them year after year."

"It's not that easy for all of us. Reagan has only conceived once in ten years, and some of the Sisters have never conceived."

"You've never tried, Gretchen. What if you're one who can bless the House with many children?"

"I can't—"

"You're being selfish." Astrid's angry tone bit into my already tender emotions like the sting of a whiplash. "You can't be with him, and I'll make sure of it." She got up quickly from the sofa and marched away from me and out of the library.

I sank to my knees on the floor. Sobs overtook my body. My tears burned with the knowledge that I'd not only ruined my life, but I'd ruined Alek's as well.

"Astrid!" I screamed, getting up and chasing after the Oracle. "Astrid, please!" I turned the corner and ran down the hallway, nearly colliding with one of the Blackmoor Drakonae brothers.

Miles caught me by the shoulders and leaned down to meet my gaze. "What's wrong, little one?"

"She's going to tell Rose, and Rose will hurt Alek. I can't let her. I love him. I'll never see him again. We didn't do anything. He shouldn't be punished because of something in a vision that hasn't happened." *Oh, gods!* My hand clapped over my mouth like it had a mind of its own. How could I have blurted that out? Could I really make it worse? Of course I could. I could tell one of the dragons that the Sisters *oh by the way I've fallen in love with the Gryphon who lives in town.* That's definitely what I should do.

I wanted to evaporate into the air and disappear on the breeze flowing down the hall from the open window ahead.

"Alek Melos?"

"I don't want to sleep with a stranger at the *joining.* I

was hiding in the library, but the Oracle found me. When she touched the couch where Alek and I used to read together, she saw it."

"Saw what?" His tone was calm and comforting. I trusted him. I didn't know why, but I did.

"She saw the vision I've had of Alek and me...together." My voice was barely more than a whisper, but he'd heard every syllable. I waited for the lecture to come, but all I saw in his brown eyes was compassion and flecks of orange that looked like flames dancing in his irises.

"No one will force you to participate in the *joinings*. It has never been forced in the past, and it will not happen in the future, little one. On that, you have my promise, but I also know the limitations placed on the House of Lamidae are there for a reason."

"I know." The words fell from my lips, and my hope shattered like a crystal vase smashed against a stone floor. At least I had his promise that I could live the rest of my lonely human life without being afraid I'd be forced into something I didn't desire.

"Your Oracle is in the courtyard. I can hear her speaking to Rose on the com connected to the Cafe."

My vision blurred, and a new wave of tears burst from my eyes, rolling down my cheeks and leaving hot streaks of pain in their wake. "Please stop her." I couldn't live with myself if he were hurt or cast out of Sanctuary. At least if I knew he was safe and in Sanctuary, I could survive alone with my fantasy of how my life could've been in a different world.

Miles clucked his tongue and pulled me close, enveloping me in a very warm but comforting embrace. "Shh, little one, we will talk to Rose. Your Oracle is elected to represent the House, but she can't dictate your life or Alek's. Rest assured, the old battle-scarred Gryphon can hold his own."

Everything was ruined. Not only had Alek rejected me personally, but now Rose would make sure he never forgot who had ruined his life. "He's going to hate me." I pulled away from Miles, my body still shaking and tears streaming down my face.

"I doubt that. Alek's hatred is reserved for those who separated him from his family." Miles waved toward the other end of the hall. I'd never been in that direction— toward the dragon's personal chambers. "I'm going to leave you in my office while I go find everyone necessary to clear up this mess."

"I don't see how it will be fixed..."—I spoke, my words drawing out like honey dripping from a spoon—"by talking."

A chuckle rolled out from Miles' chest. "You never know until you try. I need you to feel comfortable in your home. Astrid's not the first to harass you about the *joinings*."

"How do—"

He pointed to his ears. "Good hearing." A smile warmed his usually-intimidating face, and I couldn't help but smile back. "Have a seat. Couch is comfy. Help yourself to any of the books. I'll be back in a few minutes."

"Thank you."

"My pleasure, little one." He gave a half-bow and exited the grand office, leaving me to explore his personal space. An oversized mahogany captain's desk guarded a wall of bookshelves overflowing with well-worn books I'd never seen but I didn't care about that right now. Right now that same sick feeling crept into the pit of my stomach as I'd had when Alek left me in the library a week ago.

I climbed into the window seat and stared out over the wall at the town. A few people crisscrossed through the streets. Several stood in front of Rose's Cafe across the circle, laughing and carrying on with each other. Just last week, I'd overheard Eli and Miles discussing the death of a Lycan who'd been murdered in the street.

Another life taken while I and my Sisters remained safe and secure behind a wall of stone and solitude. A few minutes later, I saw Miles and Eli both cross the street and enter the Cafe, ducking their heads to fit through the door.

Time stood still while I waited for them to re-emerge. I caught myself tapping a rhythm on the window, stopped, and closed my eyes, playing through the scenarios of what would be said when Rose got here. I'd never been so glad to have the Blackmoor Drakonae brothers on my side.

"Father, I need to—" Mikjáll Blackmoor burst into the office, snapping his mouth shut when he saw me.

I pulled my legs up to my chest and curled into the corner of the window as tightly as I could manage. "He's in the cafe. They are, I mean—"

Mikjáll's features softened from their surprised state, and he nodded. "Thank you, miss. Are you well? Can I help you?"

I scoffed and shook my head. "Unless you can make me a dragon. That might solve one of my problems." If I was a supernatural—something, anything besides a Sister of Lamidae—Alek would've given *us* a chance. He wouldn't have put me back on the shelf in the library, like a book he knew he'd never have time to read again.

"I'm afraid I can't manage that request, but I'm sure my fathers will make sure whatever plagues you is taken care of. They take their guardianship of you ladies very seriously."

"What do you think of Sanctuary?" Perhaps I could distract my mind from its self-terrorizing thoughts. I'd never had the chance to speak to the Blackmoor's son before. He'd only been in Sanctuary a short time, arriving shortly after Diana, their mate and his mother, had returned. Both had escaped the Veil.

And from what I'd discerned from Diana, neither was keen to remain in Sanctuary longer than necessary. Diana said she wished she could raise her babies in the snowy mountains of her homeland. She wanted them to know the freedom of flight, to not be ashamed or afraid or hide what they were from the world.

"I think it is a world very different from my home."

"It is not your home now?"

He shook his head. "We will go home soon."

"What makes you say that? There is no way through the portal without fulfilling the prophecy."

"Things are not always as they seem."

Again with the vagueness. He and his mother both acted like the prophecy wasn't the end-game for all of this. The town. The House of Lamidae. The war with Xerxes.

"I'm sick of that."

His eyes widened, and the corners of his mouth turned upward, the start of a handsome smile.

"I wish people would just say what they mean."

"People say that, but it rarely helps diffuse situations."

"There wouldn't be situations if people were up-front from the beginning."

"Says the woman who sees visions of the past, present, and future. How much do you and your Sisters see that is never shared?"

I took a deep breath and nodded. He had me there. We experienced dozens of visions every week and kept them to ourselves, because they didn't relate to finding the next Protectors. "We don't keep anything relevant from Sanctuary."

"You say that, and you might very well believe it." He pursed his lips—no doubt trying to decide whether or not to finish his statement. "But...what you have, however you may have come by the magick you and your Sisters possess, it is leverage. Never forget that. *You* are not something that can be recreated. It took the entire high council of the Lamassu to cast the spell to create the Sisters of the House of Lamidae."

"How do you know that?" I'd never heard anything about the creation of the House.

"My fathers," he answered, shrugging it away as if it weren't a big deal.

But it was. I knew nothing about our origins. No one did, unless they were lying. And I'd certainly never considered that the visions we held back might be relevant to other things...just not our end goal. I glanced out the window at the small innocuous town that few outside even knew existed at all. My mind drifted back to his mother's words spoken to me last week.

Things are not always as they seem.

I was beginning to believe her.

When I looked over again, Mikjáll had disappeared from the room.

115

CHAPTER 12

XERXES

"Master." Cal stepped up to the table where I was eating my afternoon meal. "Commander Martin and his captain are here with a report from Sanctuary."

"Good." I took a sip of the rich merlot and nodded. "Show them in."

He bowed and backed away from the table, leaving me once again in solitude. I enjoyed the silence. After as many years as I'd lived and breathed, silence was a rare commodity. The people on Earth always screamed and cried over something. Not that I didn't enjoy the screaming and crying, but I preferred to be the one who'd caused it. The one who made their chests tighten and their hearts stop. The one they all feared.

Heavy boots clomped through the entrance ahead of me. Martin and his man came to a stop, feet apart, hands clasped behind their backs. These wolves were good at following protocol. Their faces were hard. Eyes cold. Calculating...but obedient. Very obedient. Like well-trained attack dogs.

"I see no gifts."

"No, General Xerxes, sir. We encountered a barrier spell that alerted the residents of Sanctuary to our presence. The witch you assigned to my forces was able to cut through it, but an alarm sounded. We killed one Lycan before we made it back to out."

His tone was hesitant, worried that I'd take the news badly, but it wasn't anything I hadn't anticipated.

"It wasn't the hole that set off the alarm. It was the Djinn. Rose and Calliope and probably several other ancient supernaturals the bitch has added to her town are able to sense magick. Every time a Djinn jumps, they give off a unique magickal signal," I answered, deepening my voice with displeasure. Even if it wasn't his fault, no need for him to feel that I was pleased with his lackluster report.

"Can that signal be masked?" Martin spoke again, his tone hopeful this time.

I shook my head. *Smart dog, though.* "A witch could potentially hide the Djinn signature, but only if she was already in position at the final destination with the spell in place. Too much trouble to be effective."

Martin nodded. "We detected no sign of the key dagger, General, when we dumped the magick locating potion inside the town's barrier. It didn't react. No floating cloud to follow, but we can try again as soon as you command. My men are ready."

"How many men?"

"Six hundred. Two hundred and fifty are Lycan, and the

rest are human turncoats from part of the Washington Republic's army. We would need a large force of Djinn to move us quietly into the Texas Republic, far enough away from Sanctuary that we would still maintain the element of surprise. Currently, we have about fifty men in the compound twenty miles south of Sanctuary."

"You need to capture one of the Bateman witches. They are the only ones that will be able to undo the spells blocking Djinn teleportation on the castle and other buildings in the town. Until the Djinn can jump in and out of the buildings unimpeded, the forces in Sanctuary will still be too much. That castle may not look like anything special, but it was built to withstand heavy fire, and it's likely the entire lower levels are secured bomb shelters."

"Yes, General, sir." Martin and his captain both saluted.

"Once the teleportation blocking spells are broken, we can begin mobilizing the larger force to take down the pain in my ass that is Rose Hilah and her band of fucking bothersome supernaturals. The Sisters will be mine. Sanctuary will be gone. I'll have my revenge on Rose and Naram once and for all."

I waved a hand, dismissing the wolves.

"Cal, bring me Manda."

"Yes, Master." Cal disappeared into the air. Barely five seconds passed before he reappeared with Manda in tow.

"Get your fucking hands off me, you traitorous asshole."

The fury in her tone hardened my dick instantly. It'd been months since I'd seen a hint of her strong personality shining through. This was a most pleasant surprise. I hadn't had the pleasure of her body in nearly two weeks. Overthrowing a government took a lot of time.

"How dare you grab me out of my office? What if someone comes in look—" Her voice faded to silence, and her gaze rose to meet mine. The fury and strength dissipated like a sunny afternoon rainstorm. Her lip quivered, and she took a step backward.

"Thank you, Cal. Leave us."

My servant hurried from the room, leaving a trembling Manda in the cleared center of the oval office.

"Strip."

"Please. How will I explain my absence? You've put me in a position to help you overthrow the SECR from within. I can't be the most effective if—"

I used my magick to turn the pulley system and lower the steel frame from the ceiling. Then I pulled the wooden a-frame from the wall on the far side of the room. Chains clinked above her head, and a whimper slipped from between her lips.

"Strip now or I'll do it for you. Then you can explain to your colleagues why you're naked in your office."

Her shaking fingers worked at the buttons on her white blouse. It came away quickly, revealing her ripe breasts held high in a beige lacy bra. The rings through her nipples prodded at the fabric, and I licked my lips. Just the thought of the metallic taste of the rings coupled with the pain caused when I pulled on them made my pants even tighter.

The bra came off. Then her high heeled shoes, skirt, and panties. The rings in her labia glinted in the bright light flooding through the open window. Each one had been placed strategically to incur the most discomfort and lasting pain. The enchantment on them clipped her wings, preventing her from using teleportation to escape these little sessions.

"I'll let you pick today." I walked forward, gesturing to the various restraints around her. "Overhead chains or the bench?"

Fear spread in her lavender eyes like water on a flat surface, covering evenly until there wasn't a single inch of her that didn't fear what was coming.

Just the way I liked it.

"Kneel." I stepped closer, unbuckling my pants, eager to feel her skilled mouth on my dick. I hadn't had time to go back to the palace to visit my girls, but a session with Manda was even better.

Manda was strong. Just strong enough that I'd not been able to completely break her. Strong enough that she hadn't given up hope of defeating me yet, either. Her submission layered with her hatred was a heady combination, and not one I'd been able to duplicate as of yet. Another reason she was still alive.

CHAPTER 13

ALEK

"Alek," Miles' voice carried through the busy cafe. "Just the Gryphon I was looking for."

I snorted and set my mug of coffee down on the bar top and turned to face one of the burly, bearded Drakonae brothers. "Have you seen others?"

Miles grinned, shaking his head, but his joking mood didn't last long, like something was bothering him. A warning glance flitted to me and then to the kitchen door. "I have someone in my office that is very worried about you."

"No one worries about me." I listened beyond the door he was watching and felt Rose's magick before I heard the Lamassu's footsteps.

"Alek. Miles." Rose appeared through the kitchen door with one of those shit's-about-to-get-real looks. "I need to speak with both of you, and Eli if he's available."

"Figured since Astrid was just talking to you on the com." Miles lowered himself onto the stool next to me.

My eyebrows rose. Had someone seen us in the library? I was quite sure no one had been nearby.

"Eli is preoccupied." Miles' voice was even and serious. "He's helping the Lycan's organize the patrol schedule for next week."

"That is fine." Rose waved toward the door.

"I think we can solve this without him. Can you both come over to my office for a few minutes? There's someone there who needs to get something off her chest, and I do believe you both owe her an ear, at the least."

I stood from the stool and purposefully chose not to comment again. There wasn't a chance in Hades that this scenario played out in my favor. Gretchen was miserable. I was miserable. I'd stayed away from the castle to keep from drawing attention to it. Now the Oracle was somehow involved. *How the fuck?* The air in my lungs ceased moving.

Miles narrowed his eyes. "You better be headed to my place and not off to hide."

"I don't hide," I snarled, feeling my beast rear its head from within, making my voice reverberate through the dining hall. My Gryphon hated that I'd rejected Gretchen. Hated me. It'd done nothing but sulk and growl and whine inside me since the moment I'd pulled my lips from hers, but there was nothing to be done about it. I couldn't be with her. This *conversation* was ridiculous, but if it would make Gretchen or Rose feel better, I would participate.

Nothing would close the black hole leaving Gretchen in the library that day had ripped open.

"Good." Rose's voice snapped like the crack of a whip.

"Let us go talk to the little Sister who denies her destiny." Her gaze fell on me next. Magick whipped around my body, frothing and churning like the waves of a stormy ocean.

The entire cafe had silenced, all eyes focused on us, but I didn't care.

I glared back, angry. Burning on the inside because I'd done the *right* thing—or at least what I thought had been right—and now she was pissed. Rose only got pissed when something interfered with her grand design. And the Sisters were at the very center of that design.

She tilted her head just slightly to the side, waiting for me to speak. Waiting for me to hang myself on an emotionally reckless response. If she thought that tactic was going to work on someone more than four thousand years old, she was senile.

I wanted Gretchen, but if I was dead, it would make that dream null and void. Unbeknownst to many in Sanctuary, Rose had no issue removing obstacles from the path to her goals. Through the millennia, I'd seen more than one man she'd called soldier and friend banished or killed because he'd changed or botched her well-laid plans.

Lamassu weren't just *called* the most powerful beings on Earth—they were. And more.

"Let's go talk," I said, keeping my tone flat. We left the cafe and strolled casually across the town circle as if the tension between the three of us wasn't thicker than peanut butter in an arctic blizzard.

The closer we got to the castle, the more I could feel her presence. Her unhappiness. Her despair, and it struck me like a sucker punch to the gut.

I made a one-eighty. "Be right back." I caught Miles glance. "Wait for me in the foyer."

He nodded, and I took off back across the street and into the cafe.

"Hey, big guy. What's up?" Raven asked, weaving between the tables to my side. "Forget something?" She held up a to-go coffee cup and gave me an encouraging smile.

I took the offering, relishing the scent of the nutty roasted hazelnut aroma. "Thanks, but could I trouble you for a cup of hot chocolate as well?"

"You're so sweet to that girl. Gimme a sec." She bounded off, returning shortly with another covered paper coffee cup. "If it wasn't crazy, I'd totally think you were trying to win her over. You're always bringing her treats."

My throat cinched closed, her words much too close for comfort. "Crazy," I said, barely able to keep my voice from cracking.

I'd faced thousands of enemies through the years. All types. Weapons of mass destructions. Crazy lunatics.

I always won.

Never believed different, but the upcoming conversation with Rose and Gretchen was the first time I'd ever felt...fear. Things would be easier if I could just fight it out, but Rose wouldn't fight me with a sword. If she wanted me dead, she'd just snap my neck and stab me through the heart. There would be no words. No negotiation.

I knew her.

I knew what to expect.

"What are you and Gretchen reading right now?"

Raven's question jerked me out of the mire my mind was concocting.

"*Antony and Cleopatra*," I said, my voice managing a robotic quality.

"Very good play."

"It was and thanks for the drinks." I lifted the cups in a salute and used my shoulder to push open the cafe door, escaping from Raven's cheerful optimism and eye-opening realistic summation of how I spent my free time.

Did everyone in the town know I spent most afternoons tucked away in the Blackmoor library with one of the Sisters? How had I been utterly oblivious to my own infatuation? If someone had pointed it out sooner, perhaps I could've stopped it before it progressed to the point it was at now.

But I didn't want to forget Gretchen, and I wouldn't trade a single afternoon I'd spent in her company. She'd made my tired, bitter soul feel young and alive again.

I kicked the bottom of the large oak and iron door leading into the front space of the castle. Miles opened it, and I stepped inside beside him. Rose stood a few feet away, closer to the double grand staircases leading to the Blackmoor's personal quarters.

He glanced at the coffee cups and grunted his approval.

The library was on the second level as well, but instead of keeping it to themselves after the library in town burned in a Djinn attack, they'd generously left it unlocked and available to anyone who wanted to use it.

Miles was the book hoarder out of the two Blackmoor brothers. Eli preferred artwork and had filled the castle with hundreds of classic pieces. Both had been collecting since the castle was built. Between them, they probably had one of the most varied collections left in North America after the Riots.

The door thudded shut behind me and I directed my attention to Rose. "You will not be cruel to Gretchen. Whatever lashes you feel the need to inflict, direct them at me."

One of her eyebrows rose slightly, but nothing else in her expression changed.

I marched past her and up the stairs. She followed a few paces behind me, and Miles brought up the rear.

Halfway down the hall, I pulled open Miles' office door and allowed Rose to enter ahead of me. I might not be in her good graces right now. I might be pissed as hell that we were going to have this useless conversation, but I still respected her. She was a fair and strategic leader. She'd lost everything in her war to protect the House of Lamidae. I could sympathize. I'd heard her say on more than one occasion that her goal was to protect the Sisters, fulfill the prophecy, and give the supernaturals trapped on Earth a chance to return to Veil after all these thousands of years.

For that alone, she deserved my respect.

Even my loyalty.

But for once in my life, my head and my heart were torn.

"Rose, what a surprise. What can I do for you?" Diana's crisp cool tones carried through the doorway—Miles and Eli's mate had a way of speaking that radiated a confidence and strength that rivaled Rose's.

"We are here to speak with Gretchen. Would you give us the room?"

A growl rumbled in Miles' chest. "Diana can stay if she wishes. She's just as much a part of this as I am."

"Very well. I was merely thinking of Gretchen. The room is already quite crowded."

I stepped inside and moved past everyone, using my body to block Rose's view of Gretchen where she sat in the window seat next to Diana. I mouthed a *thank you* to Diana who responded with the slightest nod before standing and stepping forward just slightly.

"We should all give Alek and Gretchen a moment before whatever this is begins." The Drakonae queen gave a small gesture toward the door and waited. Miles moved first, his heavy footsteps retreated to the hallway. I didn't turn, but I could feel the churning, angry magick emanating from Rose—pissed that Diana was ordering her out of the room.

"There's nothing Alek and Gretchen need to discuss privately. This entire state of affairs came from them having privacy in *your* library without my knowledge."

"And their current *state of affairs* will not change with a few more minutes to speak with each other." Diana bit out her words like a whip lashing on soft flesh.

I kept my eyes trained on Gretchen, whose small body was tucked into the corner of the window seat, out of reach, her gaze trained on something outside the window. Not even once had she turned to acknowledge any of us entering the room.

Setting the coffee cup of hot chocolate close enough to Gretchen's hand to pick up when she so chose, I took the space on the window seat Diana had occupied a few moments earlier. Rose flashed me an irritated glance around Diana's round body. The heartbeats of her triplets beat loud and strong. I focused on the curved belly one of her hands rubbed slowly in a circular motion.

"Very well," Rose said, a polite smile plastered across her face while adamant displeasure echoed deeply in the tone of her voice. Rose walked to join Miles in the hallway.

Diana followed, stopping to flash me a proud smirk before closing the door behind them all, leaving Gretchen and me in an awkward silence.

"I'm sorry," I said, keeping my voice low. The others could hear from the hallway, but it at least gave the illusion that I was trying to keep my words between the two of us.

She didn't move. Her breathing continued at the same pace. Her cheek remained pressed against the glass of the window like a small child enthralled with...something, anything. It just wasn't me, and by the gods, I wanted her enthralled with me. I wanted to touch her. Touch her and feel my magick swell and ignite between us. It was unlike anything I'd ever experienced before and reminded me of the things my father said he used to feel when he was near my mother.

Possessive, protective, and painfully aware when she was unhappy.

"I wish things could be different, Gretchen. Sometimes Fate is unkind."

She jerked her head and looked right at me. Her broken yet fierce gaze gored me through and through. "Fuck Fate. You walked out."

Her words held so much anger and pain and hopelessness. Had I done that to her? I wanted the spunky fun-loving woman who always needed to know everything about everything back.

"Gretchen, I only did that to make it easier on both of us. We shouldn't have kissed. We can't be together. I was wrong to lead you to think otherwise by returning your affection."

"So you have no affection for me?" Her voice was weaker, thinner this time.

"I didn't say that."

"Take your hot chocolate, and come back when you actually have something concrete to say, Alek."

"I don't want you to be miserable for the rest of your life. I have no idea if we're genetically compatible. I can't give you what you want. What we both want."

"What's that?"

"Children."

"What if I just want you?" Her eyes widened, and she leaned backward, toward the windowpane again.

"You'd be lying to yourself and to me. I've heard you talk about your kids, about naming them, playing with them. You wouldn't be happy with just me. Perhaps you would convince yourself of that for a while, but soon resentment would fester. Then there's the entire issue of going against the Sentinel's rules. And you can't say *fuck her rules,* because we both know they are necessary or they wouldn't exist. She's not heartless."

"Oh, no? What kind of race enchants a group of women, knowing it will take thousands of years and generations to fulfill a single prophecy, but meanwhile they have to live in hiding and with the fear of being stolen by a madman?"

The door behind us flew open, and Rose stomped in, preceded by a wave of magickal energy that nearly put my ass on the floor.

"You can be together on one condition, Gretchen."

Rose's voice held an edge of promise mixed with manipulation. I'd heard this tone before.

"You would let us?" Hope bloomed in Gretchen's tone, like a field of blossoms on an early summer day. "Be together?"

"You participate in the *joinings*. Get pregnant, and during the pregnancy you can *be* with Alek. That is my compromise, and the only one you're going to get. Alek is wrong. He could give you what you want, but it is not allowed. A supernatural baby born with the abilities of the Sisters would be catastrophic to this world. That kind of power would corrupt even the kindest of hearts."

My heart both broke and soared at Rose's words. *He could give you what you want.* I could have a child with Gretchen. The rest didn't matter. Rose was worrying about something nearly impossible. A child born in a loving family wouldn't turn evil. Supernaturals existed all over this world with unbelievable powers, and they didn't slaughter everyone in their path.

Gretchen jumped up from the window seat and took a step toward Rose. "You lied to me."

Rose barely reacted, looking down at Gretchen's fuming face. "It was necessary."

"Necessary," Gretchen bit out, grinding her teeth. "Now look what else is *necessary*. I just have to do the *one* thing I don't want to do. Let a stranger fuck me—*then* I can be with Alek. So there's no chance of my baby being his. How can you give me a choice like that?"

"That is the only choice you will be given. The second you are pregnant, I won't stand in your or Alek's way. The magick in the House will remain at a deficit until more children are conceived and born. However, if you choose to continue not participating in the *joinings,* Alek will be banned from the castle. Permanently."

A snarl ripped from my chest. My hands fisted, and I struggled to contain my outrage.

Rose moved her harsh gaze from Gretchen to me. "Astrid's visions are blurry, unclear. The House must be at a certain power level to have usable visions. Gretchen must conceive to add to the collective reservoir of power. Only then will the Oracle be able to pinpoint where the next Protector will be found."

Fuck.

I could have Gretchen...but only if she was pregnant by another fucking man. And I'd never be allowed to have a family with Gretchen, ever.

Fuck. Fuck. Fuck.

CHAPTER 14

GRETCHEN

I stared at Rose, not able to believe what I'd just heard.

You can be with Alek.

But I had to get pregnant first. *Gods*, he'd never want me after that...

"That isn't a choice." My voice croaked like I'd swallowed a toad.

"Oh, but it is. It solves everyone's problems," she said, her tone sticky and sweet like honey for a fly trap. "The House gains strength and you two get to enjoy this short-lived affair." Rose turned her hard glare to Alek. "Once her baby is born, you will not be allowed to be together until she is pregnant again. You will only be allowed to see each other unsupervised if she is carrying a child. No more unsupervised visits to the library. Do you understand?"

Alek nodded, and I sucked in a quick breath. I had to

have sex with a stranger, get pregnant, and then we'd be allowed to see each other.

"There are those here that would and could give you a family, Alek. Those that wouldn't die a few decades later."

Others? My heart constricted, caught between what I'd assumed to be true and now what I knew to be true. Would he choose to be with someone else? Would Rose's lure work?

"Gretchen is the one my heart and soul hungers for. You can't force this on her."

His words were a balm to my bloody soul. He wanted me. Just me.

The arguing continued, their voices booming through the room, each trying to speak louder than the last. Alek hated that I was going to be forced into the *joinings*, but it was just for a baby. Not for love. It was just to speed up the process of fulfilling the prophecy. Wouldn't it be worth it? *I could manage, right?* Bile rose in my throat at the thought of any other man touching my body, being inside me. My stomach clenched and my hands slicked.

Miles and Diana joined the argument on my behalf, but Rose continued to reply that it was all my choice. Every detail, nothing was being forced. She'd simply given me the parameters for which I could ultimately have what I wanted.

Alek.

At the same time, I'd also heard what she said about Alek's Gryphon. That we could have children, but wouldn't be allowed to pursue that dream, and that even if somehow we had a child after the prophecy was fulfilled, I would still be human, with a human lifespan.

I don't care. He was worth the sacrifice. I would spend

every waking hour of my entire life with him...if he would still want me after.

"Nothing any of us say means anything unless Gretchen wants this to happen." Diana's voice cut through the chaos, effectively silencing the room. "Gretchen, would you like to speak?"

I met Diana's chilly gaze across the room where she stood leaning against Miles. "I need to speak with Alek alone. Would you all leave us for a few moments?" The calmness of my voice surprised even me. I was going to go along with her cruel rules. Fuck, I'd go along with just about anything to have Alek in my life. The question in my mind was whether or not Alek would want me in his.

Rose nodded, agreeing with my request, and quickly left the room along with Miles and Diana. I sank back down onto the window seat, and he turned to face me, his rugged face as handsome as the first day I saw him in the library years ago. Hard lines. Straight mouth. Brown eyes that hinted at the pain and suffering he'd witnessed through his long life. And then there was the kindness, the beautiful sincerity about the way he looked at me. My mother had been the only other person who'd ever looked at me that way.

She'd caught the same fever several years ago that had stolen eleven women and children from the House. That illness had crippled the magick of the House. It had hit so suddenly and with such fury not even pixie dust had been able to bring them back.

Since that incident, Harrison had increased his magickal health screen to include illnesses other than STDs on the men coming into Sanctuary. Several of the men who came for the *joinings* that weekend were among the deceased, and one of them had been the carrier.

No one else in the town had been affected.

We were the only humans.

"What are you thinking about?"

"When Mom died."

"Why?"

I looked down at my clasped hands. "It was the first time I had the vision of us. Right after I lost her, you came to see me. You brought me hot chocolate every day while she was sick and then for nearly two weeks after she passed. You hugged me after her burial ceremony, and I saw...us. Just for a second that first time. The vision lengthened as the years passed." My voice rose and fell as the memories replayed in my head. "But it was enough to know, even back then, that you were destined to be very special to me."

"You were always that inquisitive little girl I met in the library one day who just couldn't stop asking questions— until you weren't. And then I didn't know what to do. For the first time in my life, I didn't have the answer. I still don't."

"I didn't mean to bring you into this. If Astrid hadn't seen the vision when she grabbed me, I would've kept it to myself for the rest of my life. I know you already made your choice." My voice fell with each word was like a nail in the door on having a life with Alek, any kind of life. Tears burned on my cheeks again.

His hand cupped my face and lifted my tear-filled gaze to meet his. A current of magick flowed from his hand into my body. His eyes were bright and compassionate, yet glowed with the same hunger I'd seen just before I'd kissed him.

I wanted to kiss him again. Just to have one more memory to carry with me through the misery that would be my life without Alek.

"I want you, Gretchen. More than I've ever wanted anyone in my entire life. My Gryphon wants you. He's pissed at me for walking out of the library when I did."

My heart expanded, and shivers flitted up and down my spine. *He wants me.* "But—" There was a "but" coming. I could feel it in the pit of my churning stomach.

"I don't know if I can handle you being with another man. I would do anything for you, Gretchen, anything, but sharing is not in my wheelhouse."

"We could be together."

"Not for real. We'd only have stolen moments here and there after you got pregnant. What if pregnancy is hard on you? What if you're nauseous most of the time?"

"What if I'm not? That's nine months where we can spend every free moment together."

"How long will it take you to get pregnant?"

My gaze fell to the floor again, hope for us shattering into a thousand pieces. My mother had only had one child, and my grandmother had only born my mother. Multiple children didn't run strong in my line. I remembered my mother speaking about how difficult I'd been to carry. *Damn it.* What if he were right? What if this was a convoluted pipe dream, a manipulation of the circumstances to ensure that Rose got her way without really having to tell us no?

"And then what? What about after you have the baby?

Do I lose you then instead of now?" His bitter tone chipped at my already broken heart.

"I'm trying to find a way." The words came out in a half-sob-half-wail. "Please, Alek. I would leave with you right this second if you would take me away from here, away from all of it."

"I wish I could, Gretchen. By the gods, I would leave with you in a heartbeat if I thought it was safe."

The door swung back open, and Rose stormed inside, slamming it behind her before the Drakonae could enter. It locked without a touch from her hand, and even under Miles' pounding, it refused to budge. "Not a single Sister has left this castle in over a hundred years, and not a single one ever will. If you leave, you'd be vulnerable. If something happened to you, the entire House would suffer for it. Are you really that selfish?"

"I love him," I said, trying to keep my voice from shaking.

Rose was angry. Her typically soft, compassionate brown eyes were flecked with white, and her skin was starting to glow. She kept one hand focused on the locked office door—keeping out the dragons—while the rest of her magick filled the room until the air itself seemed statically charged.

"Is your love worth the deaths of hundreds, perhaps thousands more innocent people? People who need to leave this Earth and return home. People who've fought their entire lives without the support of a place like Sanctuary. Is that worth you throwing away the dedication and sacrifice of your mother. Of your grandmother?"

One stab after another, each statement and question

making me feel smaller and more insignificant than the last.

"You take the offer I made or leave it. As of this moment, Alek will not be permitted inside the Blackmoor residence again until you are pregnant. Any attempt to leave the premises will not be taken lightly. Alek... if you are caught trying to sneak in to—"

"Fuck you, Rose. If you think we can't be in each other's presence without sleeping together, you've got a few marbles loose in that ancient brain of yours. Gretchen and I are friends, first and foremost, and you think you get to just *end* tha—." He coughed and grabbed his throat.

I screamed and threw myself at Rose's feet. "Please. Let him go. Please. I'll do it. I'll do what you want." Tears cascaded down my cheeks.

Rose released him from her magickal grasp, and his choking subsided. "I don't want to have this conversation again." Her voice was thin and pained and tired. "I know what it is like to love. And I know what it is like to lose the one we love. Be thankful for your years of friendship. You were blessed to have so many."

Alek grabbed me by the shoulders, lifting me from the floor in front of Rose. "I love you. I will always love you, no matter what. Remember that...And never bow to her again."

Then he was gone, snarling his way past Rose and between Miles and Diana, who stood speechless in the doorway.

My body shook with the remnants of a sob, and I wiped my eyes, determination filling my soul. I was done being broken. Done being a little girl, crying about her circumstances. Neither my mother nor my grandmother would've begrudged me happiness. They hated being stuck in the House of Lamidae as much as I did. There were others that felt the same and others that didn't. Most said there was no use fighting the status quo, and so they didn't. It wasn't like anyone could win against a woman who considered herself god...at least of our world.

Didn't mean I wasn't going to try.

CHAPTER 15

ALEK

"*A*lek," Miles shouted, sprinting to catch up with me.

Ignoring him, I barreled down the staircase in the foyer and out the giant oak door. I turned to the right, following the path to the left toward the street ahead.

"Alek, you can't give up on her. Not if she's your mate."

I whirled on the Drakonae. Miles was only three or four inches taller than me, but I still had to look up, and in my state of unrest, everything pissed off me and my Gryphon, and not being taller than the alpha-asshole Drakonae calling me out was doing a bang-up job. A growl rumbled from my throat, and I felt my skin tighten and stretch. My beast pushed to come out and rip apart anything it could get its claws into.

"I don't know if she is, Miles. I got thrown out of the Veil as a fucking fifteen-year-old. I don't know my history, or my lore, or anything really about being a Gryphon. I'd barely gone through puberty. My family had just started teaching me. My father had taken me to our family temple once before the Incanti struck our city. There were dozens of us on Earth in ancient times—all teenagers mind you—but I haven't seen a Gryphon in almost two thousand years. As far as I know..." I couldn't say it. I couldn't admit aloud that I was the only one left alive, even though I knew it was most likely the truth.

The big Drakonae fell into stride next to me, and we walked silently down the sidewalk, passing Calliope's shop then the market. We halted in front of the small building Jared and I called the sheriff's office and fire station.

"What do you feel when you are near her? When you touch her?"

I dragged in a ragged breath, staving off the burning rage building in the pit of my stomach. "I want her with a fury I can't explain. My Gryphon wants her. I feel like I'm going to lose control and come out of my skin at the very thought of another man touching her. I want to rip Rose's face off."

Miles chuckled.

"What's so fucking funny?" My voice carried a unique mix of beastly snarl and human annoyance. How could he possibly find humor in my situation?

"I think we've all wanted to rip Rose's face off at one point in time."

Now that I believe. "But you can't. The fight would be over before you could lay a single claw on her." Lamassu weren't gods, but their magick could encompass every-thing around them with a mere thought or flick of their hand to direct the power. I'd seen Rose freeze rooms full of people. I'd felt the chokehold her magick could inflict. I could still feel it around my neck even now, and that small display of power had been just enough to remind me of my place—below her.

"Oh, I know. Believe me, I know."

"At least her magick doesn't work on you when you're shifted."

"It doesn't help as much as you think. I can't shift inside a building without bringing it down on everyone around me. I'm the size of a small gulf stream. At least you can *fit* inside a living room." Miles' tone carried a hint of amusement.

"Touché, though I wonder if it's just your dragon that can block the magick. Have you seen her use her power on other shifted beings?"

"I cannot say that I have, perhaps a wolf? We shift so rarely these days. It's difficult to remember when we fought wars in our beast form. Though I know that even as a Drakonae, if I haven't fully shifted before the Lamassu magick takes hold, I can't complete the shift."

We entered the office, and I gestured for Miles to follow me to the back room. I needed to beat on something, and Jared's reinforced punching bags would have to be my unfortunate victims today.

"Back on the subject of mates..." He stopped, looking at me to see if I wanted him to continue.

I nodded and picked up a couple of boxing gloves from a box against the wall.

"For many supernaturals of the Veil, Magick is how we recognize the connection to our mates."

"Of the Veil? There are no supernaturals native to Earth?"

Miles shrugged. "None that we know of, but that

doesn't mean they don't exist. There are stories in Earth legends that speak of peoples and powers or magick I've never heard of in the Veil."

"I'm betting they all wish they had somewhere else to go now."

"Probably," Miles answered, a frown pulling the corners of his mouth. "Many from the Veil can feel our mates even when we are not near them. We know when they are upset or in pain. Though much of this does happen after sex has occurred or a claiming."

"We haven't had sex, and I do remember my father speaking about a blood bond between himself and my mother. I don't know the ceremony and never witnessed one. They also had these matching glyphs on their bodies. Not sure how those came to be, either."

"That is a start. Blood magick is common for witches. It is possible the Batemans might have some information on your people's practices. I don't know how the glyphs work, but I remember seeing them on your people from time to time."

"I certainly hadn't thought to ask the witches. Probably still won't since Harrison Bateman is Rose's go-to guy. Their family does anything and everything Rose asks. Anything I speak to them about would swiftly find its way to Rose's ears. Not that I blame them, she saved Meredith and Hannah from being stolen by Djinn."

"Saving a child is a debt that is difficult to ever repay."

I took a deep breath, angled my body into a ready-stance, and launched a punch at the bag in the center of the room. Instead of a sand-filled bag, Jared and I had labored to create solid leather bags. They were hard enough to take a beating but soft enough not to tear flesh from our knuckles. The bag dipped nearly to the floor before springing back into place.

Miles moved around to the other side and stood, bracing the bag for my next strike.

I raised a questioning eyebrow, and he crooked a finger, inviting me forward. I struck again.

Left, left, right.

The last punch elicited somewhat of an *oomph* from the dragon shifter.

"Good stance. Lean forward a little more and keep your hands up."

I rolled my neck, followed his advice, and launched my fists at the bag again. This time

Left, right, left, duck.

Left, left, right, knee.

I continued on for the next hour, beating the shit out of the bag until I heard the door at the front of the office open and slam shut.

"Feel better?" Miles stepped away from the bag, grabbing a couple of water bottles from the small fridge in the corner.

"Not really, but at least my Gryphon doesn't feel like it needs to burst out at the moment."

"Alek?" Jared's deep voice called from the front room. "You here, man?"

"In the back," I answered, catching the water bottle Miles tossed across the room. The cold water refreshed my parched throat, but now that I wasn't hitting anything, the anxiety over Gretchen crashed back down around me, filling my brain with frustration and anger and plans that would either get me killed or kicked out of town.

Jared strolled through the hallway, nodding a silent greeting to Miles. "What went down?"

"Rose is a bitch." The words left my mouth like arrows launched from a steel bow.

"We knew that already. All leaders want what promotes their cause over anything and everything else. Some have more morality and integrity, but mostly, they just want their way." He sighed, leaning against the sheet-rocked wall of our training room. "Rose is no different. She has integrity. She doesn't typically lie through her teeth...at least that I've noticed. And she truly seems to be on the side of the supernatural races, but otherwise, yes, she can be bitchy."

"Well said." Miles' voice was low and filled with solemnity. "But back to the basics. Have you ever felt about a woman the way you feel deep in your soul about Gretchen? Finding a mate for a supernatural is a thing that can't be dismissed."

"A mate? Who the fuck said Gretchen was his mate? How can a Sister be...?" Jared's mouth remained open as his words drifted away.

"I don't know if she is..." I started, growling again, and I ran my fingers through my sweaty, spiky hair. "I've spent hours with her every day for over a decade. She was just a child, but I—" *Damn it. I'd wanted to be with her from the very beginning. Needed to be in her presence. Needed to be close by. She brought my weary soul comfort and peace like I'd never had in my life before.*

"You know it, don't you?" Miles asked, his eyebrows raised questioningly. "It's something you can feel. Something palpable in your soul."

"She's a baby."

145

"She's a grown woman in human years, a woman who's been in love with you for a decade. Her pain was as genuine as her desperation to be with you."

"If she sleeps with another man, I might go insane."

"She won't be able to go through with it," Miles said, downing the last bit of his water before tossing it into the garbage can next to the fridge.

"I heard her agree to the terms." My skin crawled like someone was dragging knives along it. My beast wanted out again. It would take her away from this place, but I couldn't let that happen. Not with Xerxes' Lycans and Djinn literally beating at Sanctuary's doors.

"What did she agree to?" Jared asked, concern flashing in his eyes. "Why would she sleep with someone else?"

"Rose said we could be together if she participated in the *joinings* and got pregnant."

Jared fumed, and flames flickered in his irises. His skin illuminated. Fire licked at the edges of his fisted hands.

"Hey, man." I nodded, drawing his attention to his combusting skin.

He inhaled and exhaled several times. The flames disappeared and he sighed. "Sorry, but did you say Rose is going to require her to get pregnant by another before what...you can see her at all? Does she think you're some seventeen-year-old boy who can't control himself?"

"If Manda was in the building across the street, how would you behave?"

"Point taken," Jared said, defeat filling his voice.

"If Gretchen truly is your Gryphon's mate, being alone with her and unable to claim her would be a torture worse than any enemy could devise."

"What do I do? I want Gretchen, but I believe in

Rose's goal of getting us back to the Veil. I want to go home. I need to know if any of my family—my people —survived."

"I want to get home as much as you, man," Jared said, his tone heavy. "But if it came down to saving Manda or going home, I wouldn't be able to leave her."

Miles nodded. "When the choice comes, you will do the right thing. Fate does not make mistakes."

I chucked the sweaty gloves into the plastic crate by the wall. *Fuck.* "Fate sure likes to twist things around."

"The gods have their own agendas. It is not for us to decipher, merely to react in the wisest way possible to stay strong and protect what is ours."

"Our gods aren't even in this dimension."

Miles cracked a half-smile, looking like a man who knew the answer to the riddle everyone was trying to figure out. "Our gods are always with us. Why else do you think the humans around the world struggle to settle on one pantheon?"

"Because they have short lives and are shortsighted," I said, spitting out the words as if they burned my tongue. I'd never liked humans—not until Gretchen. They were frail and easily broken. I was better off not investing time or emotion into a being that wouldn't live more than seven or eight decades.

Technically, Gretchen wasn't *all* human.

It didn't matter. I still wanted her. Loved her. Even if she was completely human. Magick, supernatural, or alien, I would keep every precious day with her and treasure it like a rare diamond. There was no other and would never be another who touched my soul the way she did. In all my thousands of years of life, there had been no one like her.

The roar of a diesel engine vibrated through the air, and my muscles tensed. All the stress I'd released into the punching bag surged back along with even more. My vision reddened, and I forced myself to breathe. In. Out. In. Out. My racing heartbeat slowed a little, and I stalked toward the door.

"Alek, this is not a good idea. You can't do anything. She has to make the choice herself."

"I can kill them all."

"Alek," Jared growled, his tone laced with irritation. He knew I wouldn't kill anyone, but by the gods, I wanted to. I wanted to walk up to Harrison Bateman's bus, climb aboard, and use my claws to eviscerate every single fucking male who'd had the nerve to come *enjoy* one of the Sisters. Any of the Sisters. Not just Gretchen.

The men were worthless human scumbags, paying to fuck and forget. They got to go back to their lives with no memory of their sins. They deserved to feel pain and fear and loss, but then I'd become the monster they feared. I'd be solidifying that they were right, that we were vicious animals to be hunted and killed.

I shoved the front door of our office open and stopped on the sidewalk. Miles exited behind me, but continued walking instead of stopping next to me. "Believe in her, Alek." His voice was barely a whisper over his shoulder. He crossed the street to the green space and flat stone platform in the center of the town circle, and then continued across more street pavement to the front of the bus.

Jared came out to stand next to me while the Protectors escorted each male from the bus to the castle's front door—influencing them to remember nothing of their human lives while inside the castle and then to remember nothing of their experiences outside the castle once they'd left. I'd heard the spiel before. I didn't need to approach to know what was happening or be able to see the gray hairs on several of the human males' heads. My eagle eyesight took care of that, zooming in like a powerful telephoto camera lens.

Most wore nice clothing—they were moneyed. They all looked clean. Of course Rose did a thorough background check and blood tests. Everything was checked and rechecked before they were even allowed onto the bus. Still my beast seethed. My skin tightened, and I felt the Gryphon press outward. They weren't good enough for Gretchen.

None of them deserved to even lay eyes on her.

In Rose's opinion, neither did I.

"I never thought I'd disagree with Rose. Or the plan to—"

"Get us home?"

I dragged in a deep breath. "Yes."

"We've supported her a hundred percent since we joined this crazy caravan of supernaturals in the tenth century."

"I know."

"We wandered before that, never able to stay anywhere longer than a decade or so." Jared's voice held a tone of trepidation. "Should I plan to leave?"

He would leave for me. Abandon everything we'd both grown to love here. I couldn't ask him to do that. I didn't want to do it, either. "I don't want to leave." The answer was honest. Sanctuary was home. The citizens were family. Most of us had been together since Rose had helped the city of Genoa rebuild after it'd burned. It'd been a place we'd been safe from questions, thanks to the vampire Protectors influencing the townspeople by the droves. They were able to keep women from wondering why we never married and men from wondering why we didn't age.

We stayed in Genoa until the 17th century when the French-Savoian army unsuccessfully invaded. Though they didn't take the city down, the plague soon followed, and the House of Lamidae lost nearly half the Sisters before we could flee the city. None of us were susceptible, but the Sisters were...human.

"She's human." I whispered the words, realizing the significance of that fact for the very first time. I'd lose her so quickly.

"I know," Jared answered. "And I know I called you crazy from the start, but if she's your mate, you'll never forgive yourself for letting her go."

"I want to rip their faces off." I curled my fingers into my palms, breathing deeply, willing the talons sprouting from my fingertips to recede. Warmth bathed my hand and I lifted them, opening my bloodied palms to the sky. The wounds healed within moments, but the blood remained. The reminder of what I was. The reminder of the beast I lived with day in and day out, that I knew almost nothing about.

"Removing faces would be a mistake." Jared knocked shoulders with me. "Come on, I need you to go make rounds with me. After that last attack, I've started bringing food to the Batemans." He held up a burlap grocery bag from Bella's market. "Those two girls don't eat enough. The spell they've created with their dad to encompass the town is slowly wearing them down. I know they've told Rose they can keep it up, but I have my doubts."

I glanced toward my friend and nodded. Anything to distract my mind from the dark twisted thoughts about brutally murdering a bus full of horny human males was welcome. "What about Harrison? He doing okay with the stress?"

Shake it off, Alek. It's her choice. Not yours.

Jared shrugged. We walked down sidewalk and turned off on a small side road. The Bateman's house was just a few blocks down. I shifted my eyesight, allowing my beast's supernatural sight to take full control. The magick pouring out of the Bateman house was invisible without supernatural aid, but even without looking, I could feel the waves of power. Amazing what three witches could do. The magick billowed upward from the small house, enveloping the town in an iridescent bubble of magick.

I stopped behind Jared on the porch. He knocked on the door, and Meredith Bateman answered it. Her naturally red hair, usually bright and curly, was dark and twisted sharply back and secured with a pin. Her alabaster skin was yellowish, and dark circles shadowed her tired eyes. Eyes that always had a smile for everyone. Not today. Today she looked like she was doing her best just to be alive.

"Meredith, Bella packed your favorites. She insisted you consume some of the chocolate promptly and in front of me."

Something akin to a smile attempted to tug at the corners of Meredith's mouth. "You guys don't have to fuss so much."

"Sweetheart, if your sister looks anything like you do,

we need to fuss over you more. When was the last time your father pulled a shift?" Jared pulled a small gold box from the bag and opened it. "Eat. Now."

She gave a half-hearted snort of protest, but followed orders anyway, taking a piece of the semi-glowing, pixie-dust-infused treat and popping it into her mouth. The moan that slipped from her throat the next second made Jared blush and my own face heat just slightly.

"By the Mother, that is the best chocolate I've ever eaten." She swiped two more from the box, consuming them quickly. "Where does she keep these in the store?"

Jared smiled at the now-radiant Meredith. Her skin was bright. The circles were gone, and her eyes sparkled with energy again. Even her hair glistened with health.

"They were a special order, just for you and your sister."

"Well, please thank her for me when you leave. Come on in." She waved over her shoulder, beckoning us to follow her inside.

The house was dark and smelled like burnt herbs and spices. I wrinkled my nose and tried to breathe through my mouth.

"It keeps us focused. We trade every three hours. Used to be four or five, but we can't take it for that long anymore. Dad takes a shift anytime he's here. In fact," she glanced at the old grandfather clock against the wall, "he should be here any minute. He can still handle the magick field for eight hours straight. Then we both get a shower and some sleep."

Meredith led us down another hallway and into a small bedroom lit with only a circle of candles. The windows had been boarded up and all the furniture had been removed. The eight-pointed star of Ishtar had been drawn on the hardwood floors in white chalk. A ring of lit candles created the circle around the points. Hannah sat cross-legged in the center of the star. Her eyes were open, but they were white and absent. Words I didn't understand spilled in whispers from her mouth. A certain string over and over, repeated like a drone—no emotion, no consciousness.

Her skin, even in the dim light, was sallow like Meredith's had been. "You can't keep this going much longer, can you?" Even with pixie-dust aiding their energy, there was no way Rose could expect them to keep this up. Maybe a day or two more. Maybe.

"Probably not, Dad will help while he's here for the weekend. Maybe if he stayed, but Rose has him traveling a long way now to find...people." Meredith stepped over the candle ring into the circle and sat down with her back to her sister's back. "She'll wake up in a few minutes. Please wait for her before you leave. She needs some of that chocolate, too."

Jared nodded. "Of course."

Meredith started the chant, and moments later, her eyes turned white and she ceased to be present. We waited. Minutes ticked by and still Hannah hadn't budged. Her eyes were still wide open and as white as snow on a mountaintop. She wasn't chanting anymore, just listing back and forth, like her body was in sync with some sort of music only she could hear.

I nudged Jared toward the circle. "It's been longer than she said."

"I'm not stepping in there. What if I do something wrong?"

"Hannah. Meredith." A deep bass voice boomed from the front of the house. Footsteps thumped as their father made his way to the bedroom where we stood waiting for Hannah to wake up or snap out of it or something.

"What are you two doing here?" Bateman crossed his arms and gave us the body glance, like he was sizing up a couple of teenage boys who wanted to take his daughters to a dance.

Jared held up the bag from Bella, deflecting Harrison's attention from me. "Bella sent energy chocolate and a few other things for them."

"I meant why are you back here?" Bateman's voice deepened further, laced with the protective I'm-their-father-and-you-have-no-business-in-their-bedroom tone.

"First off, I'm not a kid so don't treat me like one. Second of all, Meredith asked us to wait for Hannah to wake up." My tone was angrier than it should've been with a concerned father, but my taking-shit meter was full-up today. Jared gave me a worried glance then turned his attention back to the pissed-off daddy-witch.

"He just meant we were checking on the girls. Bella sends food and stuff to make sure they are getting enough to eat and—"

"You can leave now. I'll take care of anything *my* daughters need."

Jared nodded, putting the grocery bag on the floor next to the wall. "Not a problem, Mr. Bateman."

We backtracked and left faster than I would've liked. Something had Harrison Bateman in a bind, but we didn't have a beef with the witch and we needed them to protect the town.

"I wonder if the barrier is weaker when they change

shifts?" Jared said, turning off the sidewalk toward Main Street Circle. "The attacks are coming more often now. Riley said they've tracked multiple Lycan/Djinn teams moving through the town over the last few days."

"So that last attack wasn't an isolated incident?"

Jared shook his head.

"Why aren't people telling me things?"

"Because you're huge and grumpy and I'm telling you now. After seeing Meredith and Hannah, I don't think the barrier is as strong as it used to be. And—"

"And you think when they switch it's letting them in?"

He nodded, a solemn look casting a shadow of concern across his face. "I think if they figure out there's a pattern to the weakness, we are in deep shit."

"That's assuming they haven't already."

"True."

"At least Harrison will be on guard for the next eight hours or so. Meredith said he took over when he was in town. That'll break up the three hour routine the girls were keeping."

"You go talk to Riley and the other Lycans for an update. I'll meet with Rose."

Worked for me. Rose was the last person I wanted to converse with at the moment. I veered off the sidewalk and headed the back way to Riley's bar.

CHAPTER 16

GRETCHEN

*M*y heart pounded in my chest. The large living space held the fifteen of us who weren't pregnant yet. Only five of the Sisters were pregnant right now, and most of them were close to delivery. The rest of the group had been struggling, even several of the Sister's who'd had children a couple years ago hadn't been able to get pregnant again. There was talk of infertility, but no one had determined a cause or a problem. The pixies had done whole-body healings time and again... There was no explanation, at least none that had yet been found.

Until there were more babies, the visions Astrid had of the next Protector would continue to be unclear. She couldn't see where he or she was. No face. Nothing to help lead the current Protectors to find him or her.

Babies. By the gods, I wanted a baby. My heart and soul longed to hold a bundle of my own in my arms. The men were here for just that reason. We yearned for children. I wasn't any different, except that I wanted a child by the man I'd fallen hopelessly in love with. The man who'd left Miles Blackmoor's office with pain in his eyes that I had felt in the depths of my soul.

I wanted him so profoundly I was actually considering sleeping with another man to achieve that goal. I scanned the line-up. Several of my sisters extended hands to old lovers, men they'd been sleeping with for years, though the men didn't remember them. It was a strange, one-sided relationship my sisters' had carved into their imaginations. I didn't hold it against them. They were fulfilling their duty the only way they could. They'd made sense of something senseless.

Better than me. I'd turned away more men than I could count. Listened to more tongue-lashings than I cared to remember. And now...today...I was going to change everything.

I walked up to a slender middle-aged man with hungry eyes. He noticed me immediately, and a lecherous grin formed on his face. My stomach dropped to my feet, and I felt dirty and disgusted with myself all in the same breath. What was I doing?

This is the sacrifice I have to make. It's the only way to be with Alek. Except I worried that he wouldn't forgive me. That he wouldn't look at me the same way. It was either this or never see him again, Rose had made her ultimatum quite clear.

Several of the Sisters near me were staring, not that I blamed them. I'd been sick or missing from every *joining* since I'd had my first menstruation. Whispers filled the space, and I quickly extended my hand.

He wasn't ugly. His face was nicely proportioned, and his salt and pepper hair was trimmed neatly beneath a bowler hat. His clothing was fine wool and smelled of cigar smoke. He was vintage wine, and I was a freshly brewed pot of iced tea.

"Please won't you join me?" My words were forced and clipped. I pasted on a fake smile, and he took my offered hand. His touch sent an uncomfortable thread of angst through my body.

I wanted Alek to be my first. To be my only.

You can do this. It will be worth it in the end. I kept repeating the mantra as I led him to my chambers, all the while dying on the inside. He was going to see me naked. His body would be in my bed. I'd never be able to forget... any of this.

"You are a gem. May I ask your name? I'm Larson. I know I won't remember you after I leave, but I feel like you should at least know whose name to scream when I make you come until you can't move tonight."

Air froze in my lungs, but I forced myself to keep walking. To not scream and flail and take flight from that spot. I wanted to leave him standing in the hallway and disappear into the bowels of the castle.

They'd never find me. Not in time to guilt me into doing anything. It'd worked for years. It would work again, but then...I'd be making Alek wait and wonder longer. I'd be drawing out my own torture. It was better to get it over with right now.

"I-I'm Gretchen."

"Beautiful name for a beautiful woman."

That sick feeling returned, creeping up from the floor, around my legs, and up my spine until I wanted to hurl. It squeezed and squeezed, determined to rid my body of anything I'd eaten today. I sucked in a quick breath through my mouth, trying to ward off the gagging reflex hard at work in the back of my throat. If I didn't sleep with—Larson—it would just be someone else the next weekend. And then again and again. Possibly months until I conceived. *Oh, gods! I can't do this. I can't do this. I can't do this.*

I pressed my eyes shut and paused. He didn't push or pull. Just stood there, waiting patiently, like the gentleman he was dressed to appear. But a man who led a first inter-action talking about making me scream his name was far from a gentleman.

"Are you well?"

I could say no. All I had to say was no and this whole charade was done, finished, at least for this weekend, but it wouldn't solve my problem. It wouldn't get me what my heart truly desired.

Only sex with a stranger would do that.

Fuck you, Rose.

"I'm good," I said, making sure my voice was soft and sweet. I gestured toward my door, and he released my arm and opened the door for me. I walked through and stepped to the left, wrapping my fingers around the iron candlestick on my desk. "Please close and lock the door behind you."

He closed the door and looked away for just a moment to turn the latch on the deadbolt. In that moment, I swung. The metal thudded against the back of his head, and I closed my eyes. *Please don't be dead. Please don't be dead.* I hadn't hit him that hard, but he dropped to the floor with a thump like a sack of potatoes.

I opened my eyes and jumped away from his sprawled figure. The candlestick in my hand didn't have any blood on it. *Thank the gods.* I set it on my desk and knelt, reaching my hand over his nose and mouth. Warm breath moistened my palm. He was breathing. A quick nudge of his shoulder with my foot said he wasn't waking up anytime soon.

I made short work of undressing him and discarded my own dress, pulling on his pants and dress shirt and jacket. I twisted my hair into a tight bun on top of my head and pushed the bowler into place. Granted I didn't look anything like him, but I certainly didn't look like myself at first glance, either. And most of the Sisters would be locked away in their rooms by now. No one would be patrolling the halls.

At least I hoped they wouldn't.

His shoes wouldn't fit. My feet would clomp about in those like a toddler playing dress-up with her mother's shoes. I'd have to risk it. At least barefoot, I'd be able to move quieter on the stone floors.

I pushed him out of the way of the door and then turned the deadbolt to unlatch it. Turning the doorknob slowly, I inched it open until I could peer through a crack into the dimly lit hallway. No one. Not a sound echoed. I opened the door all the way and slipped out, my shoulders tense and my jaw locked—waiting for someone to call out my name and end this desperate attempt at freedom.

But it didn't come.

I walked slowly down the hallway on my tiptoes, barely breathing for fear that I would make enough noise to be noticed. The dragons could hear everything. Every pin that dropped in this maze of stone somehow made its way to their ears. Male laughter rumbled down the hallway, and I pressed my body into an alcove, praying they would pass by and not turn toward me.

"I can't believe she actually picked a man. We've been trying to get her to participate in the *joinings* for a decade."

"Well, I can't imagine spending the night with anyone but you. Hopefully, your friend made a wise choice."

"You're sweet for saying that, even though I know you don't remember me, but that's why I always choose you, Rawlins." The female voice carried on. "Oh, and she did make a good choice. Karen has slept with that gentleman before. According to her, she's never had better orgasms. Gretchen should be in for a treat."

"Well, well, well. What do you say about me to your sisters? Should I work harder to impress?" The male she'd called Rawlins raised his voice, making a point to sound purposefully hurt.

"You never leave me wanting. Don't you change a thing." The female voice belonged to one of the Sisters who always felt the need to call out Gretchen after she'd avoided a *joining*.

Even though Lina's words shouldn't mean anything, I couldn't help but feel hurt that she would share such personal details with an outsider. With someone who didn't really care about her and who wouldn't remember Lina the second he stepped out of the castle. Everything here was pretense and charade. We had no life. No choices. No free will.

We were no better than slaves to Rose's whim, and no one even seemed to care. They all just helped her, saying it was for the greater good. Their lives were the sacrifice that had to be made.

Well, they were just going to have to sacrifice without me from here on out. I'd find Alek, and if he really wanted to be with me, then we could run. If he didn't want me, I'd leave without him and disappear into some city somewhere. I'm human...human enough anyway. I didn't look or act differently than any other person out in the world—except for the occasional vision.

There was that minor issue, but I could deal with it later. Right now, I just needed to find Alek.

The voices of Lina and her partner faded, and I pushed on, weaving quietly through the stone halls until I reached the foyer. One of the Lycans who frequented the club stood guard at the massive door. A door I probably couldn't budge an inch on my own.

Backing up a few steps, I closed my eyes and took a deep breath. *You can do this. Think.* There had to be another way out. The library had windows, but they were too high from the ground—three floors up. The second level breezeway had windows, too, but even I knew jumping from that level was beyond stupid.

I turned around and headed for the back stairwell. Even though it was higher, the library windows would be easier to go through than the steel bars on the breezeway. It took every scrap of willpower not to run. I couldn't afford to make that much noise. The Blackmoors would hear, especially Diana who rarely left their personal living quarters on the third floor just down the hall from the library.

The stone beneath my bare feet was cold, and a shiver circled my spine. I climbed the dim stairwell. Step after step after step. I continued until the familiar sconces I walked past each day came into view. The third level of the castle was less cold. Large decadent carpets covered the floors. Beautiful tapestries hung on the walls along with paintings I'd been told were from masters all over the world. The Blackmoors enjoyed beauty and art and had salvaged as much as possible since the Riots destroyed a lot of American history. At least that's what Alek had told me.

I passed a Pollock, a Durand, and—one of my favorites —a Leutze depicting a historical figure named Washington crossing a river with his soldiers. He looked strong and brave and like a man someone could trust. Alek had told me that General Washington had led this country to freedom hundreds of years before I was born. Of course Alek also added that it was good Washington was long dead and gone, because he would roll in his grave to see what his country had done with the freedoms he and his men fought so hard to gain.

I took one last look at Washington's face before stopping in front of the open French doors to the library. The lights were out. Better for me. I walked in and closed the doors softly behind me. Anything to dampen the noise I was about to make would help tremendously.

Bee-lining for the floor-to-ceiling curtains on the far side, I scrambled to untie the sashes binding each panel into a perfectly gathered swath. The library sat at a corner in the big castle, so there were two long walls of windows and dozens of curtain panels. As I moved from curtain to curtain, I knotted the sashes together, creating a rope I hoped would get me near enough to the ground to drop without breaking any bones.

Once the last curtain had been relieved of its sash, I went to the farthest window in the corner, the one that looked out over the side of the castle and not the front circle where everyone and anyone might see me. The sun had set while I worked, but true darkness hadn't swallowed the town yet, and from what I could tell, there were only street lamps here and there through the town, unlike the center circle where there were dozens.

I tied the end of my sash rope to the heavy foot of the love seat where Alek and I had spent many afternoons. It looked strong enough to hold my weight. The window screeched a little as I pushed it open, and I winced—each high-pitched wail echoed through the room. *Please don't hear me.* I waited for a moment, but no one came. No one yelled for me to stop.

Tossing the rope through first, I leaned out and looked down the high stone wall. The sashes waved in the soft breeze, and I strained to see where they stopped. Quite close to the ground. It looked like a short jump from the bottom knot. *I can make that. I have to make that.*

"Gretchen." Her voice froze every muscle in my body.

I glanced up through the dark into Diana's cold blue eyes. "Please." The whisper came out before I even thought about it. She must've been in the library when I entered. The door hadn't opened since I came inside.

Diana's head leaned to the left. The decision to let me leave the castle went against everything the Drakonae worked for each day. She was struggling. I could see the shout on her lips forming like a perfect storm. This was my only chance, I'd never get another. Not after what I'd done. No one would ever trust me again.

"It's either this or lock me in a cell for the rest of my life." My voice trembled, fear and longing and desperation poured out of me all at once. "I need to do this. I have to know."

Her eyes widened slightly, realization dawning like a brand new sun welcoming the day. "Alek?" Her tone barely more than a whisper.

I nodded, climbing to the window sill. Turning around, I grabbed the rope and slid one foot down the stone wall until my toes found a small gap and a little leverage.

"Do not leave the town."

"I'm not."

She bit her bottom lip, rubbed her rounded belly, and then whirled, leaving me alone to finish what I'd started. I held still until she disappeared through the large doors in the shadows across the great library. Relief and gratefulness and a good dose of surprise swamped my brain. I'd been an idiot to think I could get out without one of them hearing me. She'd actually been in the library. Had probably been napping and woke up when I opened that damned window.

Still, I'd hadn't expected her to let me go, but I wasn't about to ruin the chance she'd granted.

The wind gusted, sending the hat flying into the air. I watched it sail to the ground and said a prayer for strength. Holding my weight with the rope and one foot, I lowered my other foot to the same stone outcropping and sucked in a quick breath. This was it. I was climbing down the side of the castle. I was leaving the Sisters. I was claiming a new life.

I was slipping.

Oh shit!

My heart lurched in my chest, slamming into my throat. I tightened my fingers over the knot, ignoring the painful cramping in my muscles. My right toes slid off the rock edge of the brick that'd been holding me. Pain sliced through my foot, and I winced, bracing for the impact my shoulders would take. My body *thunked* into the wall, and I waited a moment for everything to settle before I struggled to find footing again. My arms burned from the strain.

The rock I'd been standing on had crumbled, and the edge was gone. I slowly unfolded my arms, lowering myself inch by inch until I found another edge. This time I moved a little faster, not willing to wait and see how long the old rocks would last.

Move hands down a knot, find another toehold, again and again. *Breathe.* In and out. The hot breeze swirled my hair, and sweat trickled from my forehead down my temple, continuing its course until it melted into the heavy dress shirt I was wearing.

I got to the last few knots and looked down at the ground in surprise. It was much farther away than it'd looked from the window above. My rope didn't reach, but I couldn't go back up. My arms shook each time I moved down the rope. One misstep and I'd lose my grip completely. I couldn't take another slip, and I didn't have enough strength to pull myself back up.

I could yell for help. Someone would come. Everyone in this town had super-hearing. I would be off this wall, safe and sound in a matter of seconds. All I had to do was open my mouth...and give up.

"Fuck that." I kept my voice at barely a whisper. This was not the end of my dream. This was just the beginning.

I pushed away from the wall and twisted in the air,

hoping to let my shoulder and legs take the brunt of the concrete below.

Ughffffffff. Air fled my lungs like I'd been hit in the chest with a battering ram. Pain radiated through my whole body, and I lay still on the warm concrete for what had to be several minutes before I managed to roll over and look up at the window I'd come out. The rope barely showed in the dark. The sashes were black. The stones were black and gray. No one would see it until morning. At least I hoped they wouldn't.

I pushed up to my elbows and held in a cry, forcing my unhappy and offended body into a standing position. Alek's house was two streets over on Avenue C. He'd showed me on a map once before, and I'd long since memorized it, hoping one day I'd get to see the town through more than a castle window.

I limped down Avenue A and turned onto First Street, keeping to the shadows. No one seemed to be out, and I made it faster than I thought across to Alek's street. A left turn took me away from the town's center, and I walked slowly along the dimly lit sidewalk, trying to tell one house from another. Few of the houses had lights on, and none of them had lights illuminating the fronts.

Alek had said his house had a blue door, but in this light, everything just looked gray. I had to find it soon. Someone would see me or hear me or smell me. Then I saw the gold emblem of the Gryphon on the door of the house to my right. Body of a lion, head and wings of an eagle. I'd never seen him shift, but he'd explained to me what he was once. What his beast looked like.

I couldn't imagine having a part of myself that could change like that, but I would've given anything to be able to fly. It'd been one of the rare days he'd shared a smile with me. He loved to fly, too, and because of how low-key everyone tried to stay in the town, he was rarely allowed to shift, though he had shared that he snuck out from time to time and would fly at night, circling the town, the empty prairie, and woods that surrounded Sanctuary.

The dark velvet blue sky above beckoned, and I gazed up, wondering if he was up there looking down at me. He wasn't. I knew he wasn't. If he'd seen me, he'd have already come down from the expanse to tell me how dangerous my actions were. I didn't think he'd be mad that I came, just worried about my safety. He was always worried about me. Probably as much as I worried about him each time he left on a mission for Rose. Each time I had to go more than twenty-four hours without seeing him.

I walked up the path to his front door and leaned against the cool wood, tracing the faint gold outline of the Gryphon. Such a wondrous creature. Perhaps one day I'd get to see the other side of the man I loved so desperately.

"Alek." I spoke softly, letting my voice caress the face of the door. "Alek, please let me in." The lever didn't budge when I tried to depress it, but before I could raise my hand to knock, it opened with a swoosh, and I fell into his chest.

CHAPTER 17

ALEK

"Gretchen." I grabbed her around the waist and swept her inside, shutting the door in the same movement. "How?" I didn't even begin to know how to phrase a logical question. How had she gotten out? How did they not see her leave? Did I even want to know what she'd done this evening to end up on my doorstep, in my arms?

"I couldn't do it," she said, her tone thin and weepy. "I want you, Alek, only you."

Cigar smoke and the scent of a human man filled my lungs. The clothes she wore weren't hers. They belonged to a man. A man who'd attempted to have sex with her? My beast roared and pressed against my psyche, stretching against the thin leash of control I possessed.

"What happened?"

"Don't you want me? I came all this way so we could be together, and you only want to know what happened?"

I shook the cloud of confusion from my mind and blinked down at her. *Not want her?* "Of course I want you. By all the gods of the Veil, I want nothing more than you for the rest of eternity, but who let you out?"

"I escaped. I tricked a man, knocked him out, and then came here to be with you. As long as no one sees the rope, no one will even notice I'm gone until Mr. Cigar-man wakes up on the floor of my bedroom."

I rubbed my hand over my mouth and tried not to cringe. I wanted to take Gretchen and run, but everything inside me screamed that I wouldn't be able to protect her. Not with Xerxes and the Djinn pounding at the barrier outside every damn day for the last few weeks. Ever since the Mason lodge in Ada had burned and Charlie had come back with Travis and Garrett and the few Lycans left in her pack, Xerxes had closed ranks. We were his target— Sanctuary, the castle, Gretchen, any and all of the Sisters.

The smell of blood caught my attention. "You're hurt." I said, grabbing her bruised hand and holding it closer. Her skin smelled salty, and her palms were rubbed raw in several places, enough to bring blood to the surface. "What did you do?"

She yanked back her hand and glared, anger flashing in her bright blue-gray eyes. "I'll be fine. I got out. You left me in there and I got out."

Fire stabbed my heart. *Left her?* Rose had all but told me to get the fuck out of town. Didn't she get that? "Was I supposed to take you right there in front of Rose and Miles? Would you rather I be dead? I would be if I'd tried to take you."

"No," she said, her tone rising.

"Shh." I stepped forward and pulled her into an

embrace. The neighbors would hear her if she raised her voice much louder, and I needed to feel her against me. Feel her heart beat. Feel that in this moment she was safe and removed from the greedy hands of the human male who had sought her body.

I breathed in and out, vaguely noticing my pulse syncing to hers. "Gretchen. I'm sorry. You don't know what I went through today when that bus arrived. I wanted to murder all those men. I wanted to tear them apart, pluck their eyeballs from their skulls so they wouldn't even be able to look at you."

"Their eyeballs?" The question came out followed by a giggle and a half-sob.

"Yes. You are mine, Gretchen, but I also want you to be safe. Above everything else, above any claim I lay on you, I want you safe and protected. The castle is where you are safe. Xerxes and his soldiers cross the town boundary every other day. They wait just outside the barrier the Batemans have created. It's not safe for you here."

"One night, Alek, please." Her pleading tone shredded the resolved I'd mustered. "No one will know tonight. Then we can discuss tomorrow."

Discuss? Unless I left—ran like a traitor—we could never be together.

"Alek." Her soft breath whispered across my chest, igniting an overwhelming hunger I'd never before experienced. Her skin sizzled with an energy that pulsed between us. "Please."

"I want all of you, Gretchen." My voice rumbled, deepening as more of my blood rushed south. "I don't know what being with you means for my Gryphon, but I want you in a way I've never experienced before. You are special to me. To my beast."

"You are special to me. You are mine, the beast and the man as one." She ran her palm along my chest, up to my neck, and settled it against my cheek. Her fingers curled, beckoning me closer. The energy flitting between her skin and mine increased, flipping a switch deep inside me. We'd touched so many times before, but it'd always been in innocence. Not until I'd seen her for the woman she was... and then everything had changed.

I slipped an arm around her waist and lifted her from the floor, pressing her luscious body against my hard lines. She submitted, melting into the embrace. I covered her mouth with mine, and she moaned, setting off fireworks in my brain. She tasted like honey and candy and woman. All woman. All mine.

Our tongues tangled inside her mouth, and then she pushed back, moving the dance to my mouth. She tasted me and pressed and took what she desired. She was no meek little girl. If she'd been a paranormal, she'd have growled and dug her claws into my back, and I would've welcomed it. Her fingers kneaded and scraped my shoulders, and her teeth settled on my bottom lip, nipping ever so slightly.

"Hungry, aren't you?" I mumbled and consumed her mouth again, covering it completely and driving my tongue deep inside, claiming what was mine and everything she was offering—giving to me.

"So hungry." Her words spilled out in a gasp for air when I moved my lips to the curve of her neck. I bit gently, basking in the little moans and whimpers of pleasure coming from inside her. Her body was warm against mine, but I couldn't feel her through the thick wool coat and men's dress shirt she wore. The shapeless pants hung low on her slender waist.

I let my talons slide out on my right hand and slipped them inside the hem, shredding them with one downward slice. She made a tiny surprised gasp and took a step back, watching my hand—my claws.

"Do I frighten you?" I dragged the tips of my talons up her bare thigh, watching her shiver from the contact. Her pulse sped in her chest...she met my gaze, but there was no fear.

"No." Her steel blue eyes had darkened to match the color of Texas storm clouds. Desire rumbled and lightning sizzled within us both. There was no fear, only a hunger that matched mine. "Never."

I slid my hand beneath the hem of the dress shirt until I reached her collarbone, being careful to avoid scraping her breasts. Those would feel my mouth before I teased her with anything else. I turned my palm away from her, curling my razor-sharp talons against the fabric of the shirt and yanked down. The fabric barely made a sound as it fell open, allowing my eyes to feast upon the vision of her perfect, petite breasts.

I relaxed my hand, calling the talons back inside me, leaving human fingertips in their place. Stopping myself from reaching for her breasts, I knelt in front of her then slid my hands around her hips and up along the curve of her back, pulling her forward until her breasts swung just in front of my face.

Air puffed in and out of her lungs. She didn't speak. She just waited, her gaze pleading for me to do more. I opened my mouth and latched onto her right breast. She was small enough that I could fit nearly the whole breast into my mouth. It was heaven. She was heaven. I suckled her breast like a man who'd reverently waited his whole life for a pleasure like this—like her.

Her head fell forward, and her knees quivered, straining to hold her upright. She dug her fingers into my shoulders, and I reveled in the slight pain her fingernails inflicted. My beast wanted her to mark me. I wanted it. Between her pants, whimpers slipped out. I lavished one breast and then the other. They pebbled under my tongue, perfect and rosy and pink. Her scent filled my lungs, and I drank it in until I was sure I'd never forget. I never wanted to forget.

I scraped the edges of her nipples with my teeth, and she sucked in a startled breath. Her fingers tensed on my shoulders, and the scent of her arousal filled the room.

"I hurt for you, Alek."

"There is so much more to come before I soothe that ache for us both, my sweet, sweet Gretchen." I followed a path down the curve of her breast to the soft lines of her ribcage. Her abdominal muscles tightened beneath my lips, and I chuckled, taking note of where she was ticklish and storing it away for later.

I rose from my knees to slip an arm under her legs and another around her back. She cuddled against my chest, nuzzling my neck with her lips until a fog inhibited all thought. I stood with her in the center of the living space, just holding her, just letting her press feather-light kisses along my neck and shoulder. I'd never have enough of her. Never be willing to let her go. We would have to leave Sanctuary.

She'd hate me if I sent her back. Fuck, I'd hate myself.

I'd never survive wondering what they might force her to do. They claimed nothing was forced. Rose promised. The Oracle promised, but masters of persuasion could make any man—or woman—believe an idea was their own.

"I'll never let you go again, Gretchen." My voice rumbled from deep within, soothing the anger my beast had held against me earlier that day.

"I'm only yours. I'll only ever be yours." She cupped the back of my head, pulling my mouth to hers, and crushed our lips together. There were no sweeter lips on the face of the Earth. I drove my tongue into her mouth, groaning at the sweetness of her taste.

I moved us quickly through the house, up the stairs to my bedroom, to my bed. Not willing to release her mouth until I absolutely had to, I laid her across the blanket, so ready to taste her I was nearly coming in my pants. Not happening. I was more than four thousand years old, not some over-excited teenager. There would be no rushing tonight, none at all.

She was worth savoring. Every second would be pure bliss, and I wanted to bask in every moment. Savor every kiss and taste and breath she gave.

I spread her on my bed, her long, coffee-colored hair lay across the red blanket in a waterfall of silk, and her skin glowed under the soft lamplight.

"You are exquisite." My words choked in my throat, emotions overwhelming me. I leaned down over her, putting one knee on the edge of the mattress. My heart lurched from the way she looked up at me. Trusting me. She was naked and open, and by the gods, I wanted her to know how much I cared. How much this gift meant. "You are my heart and soul, Gretchen. I couldn't see it until I

175

nearly lost you, and now the idea of ever being without you is unthinkable. Please forgive me for being so blind." The apology stung, but she deserved it. I'd been oblivious. Too caught up in this town and my goal to get home to pay attention to what was right in front of me.

The scent of salt tickled my nose just before tears rolled from the corners of her eyes. *No. No. No. Don't be sad.* "Gretchen?"

"I have waited for this day for so long. I was so scared that I would get to your house, find you, and you would turn me away."

I shook my head. "Never again, I promise. We are in this together, no matter what happens."

A shiver ran through her body and her lips parted. "Make love to me, Alek. Please."

"All night." I whispered, leaning down to kiss her tears away. My mouth traced the line of her jaw to her neck down to her collarbone. Skin like velvet quivered beneath my lips. She put her hands on my head and stroked through my short hair, rubbing it back and forth until every nerve that wasn't already awake woke up.

My teeth grazed one of her nipples, and she hissed, trying desperately to grab a handful of my short hair. I nipped again, this time a little harder, and then soothed the burn with my tongue until she relaxed beneath my mouth. Her other breast received the same treatment before I traced a path down her ribcage with my tongue, circling her navel and working my way down.

Sliding off the edge of the bed, I sank to both knees on the floor and slid my hands up the insides of her thighs, pushing her legs apart until I could see her glistening folds, slick and wet and waiting for my tongue. She tried to close her legs, and my beast growled before I could gain control. "Don't. I want to see all of you. Taste all of you. You are mine." Her legs relaxed, and I gently kissed the inside of one of her thighs. "Say it."

"I'm yours."

"Which part?"

"All of me."

"Good girl." My voice rumbled, my beast soothed that she wouldn't try to hide herself from view. "You should never be ashamed to share yourself with your mate." *She is my mate...* Something deep inside me knew it. Whether I understood my Gryphon side completely or not, I knew Gretchen was mine.

"I'm not ashamed." Her voice hitched, fear stopping her before she finished her thought.

"Tell me." I kissed the inside of her other thigh, a little closer to the goal.

A shiver slid through her, and I smiled.

"I've never done...this, any of this."

Reality hit my face like a right hook from Jared. All the air in my lungs fled. *Virgin.* Of course she was...I knew that, but I hadn't considered how new everything we were doing was to her.

Everything.

"I was your first kiss?" Honor swelled in my chest, and my Gryphon wanted to strut with pleasure. No man had touched her. Not even with a kiss. I straightened between her legs and caught her sideways glance down at me.

"Yes," she answered, her tone unsure. "I know you've probably—"

"Been waiting for you my entire life. No woman I've been with in the past compares to what I feel for you. You

177

are what I've been looking for my whole life, though I didn't even realize."

Her eyes brightened, joy replacing her doubt.

"Trust me."

"I do."

Those two words shattered what remained of the walls I'd erected around my heart. She'd broken every barrier and had my heart in her hands. I'd do anything for her. She was more important to me than any fantasy of going home to avenge my family, family that'd been long dead for millennia. Gretchen was my future.

"Just lie back, relax, and try not to scream."

The wicked smile that flashed across her face only drove me higher and harder. Gods, how had I lived this long without touching her? Fuck Rose's rules. This was bigger than that. One seer in the scheme of things wasn't going to ruin the damn prophecy.

I slid an arm under one of her thighs and sank my face between her legs, letting the sweet scent of her arousal fill my lungs. My body leapt from pleasantly interested to full-hard-on. I wanted to bury myself in her sweet pussy and take her until she cried out my name in desperation, but she deserved better than that for her first time. I wanted it perfect, even if it killed me.

Using my other hand, I traced the silky edges of her folds and slid one finger inside her feminine heat. She gasped and tightened under my grip. I waited, allowing her to adjust to the intrusion. Her body shuddered and finally sighed, releasing the tension that had frozen her at first. Moving my finger unhurriedly in and out, foreshadowing what I would be doing with my dick later brought forth gratifying little mewls of pleasure from her mouth.

I added a second finger, curling them up toward the ceiling and against that extraordinary place inside a woman's body that ignited them. Gretchen's muscled shivered and tightened, and a low moan slipped from her throat. Then I dipped my tongue to her clit, firming my hold on her hip, prepared for the inevitable bucking reaction.

She did. Her hips surged up, her back arcing from the bed, and her hands flailed in the air until they came to rest on my head. Her fingers grasped for a hold in my hair, but it wasn't long enough. Instead, her fingers dug into my scalp, and I growled, both myself and my Gryphon, pleased by her pleasure. Pleased by her sweet taste. Pleased that I had been granted this chance to show her what it meant to be with a man who loved her, even if that man had been an idiot for years and hadn't seen what'd been right in front of him. I was going to make up for it now. She would know how much I loved her, how much I cared.

I slid my fingers from her body and replaced it with my tongue, drinking her deeply as the intoxicating scent and taste permeated my consciousness. I was drunk on her.

"I'm never letting you out of this bed."

"I—ahhh—"

She trembled and quivered with each drive of my tongue. In and out. In and out. Then I circled that soft bud of pleasure several times, bringing her just to the brink of ecstasy before plunging deep again into her body.

"Alek," she said, her voice low and husky and needy. "I need—"

I came up for air, kissing her thighs as I went along.

"Have you ever orgasmed before?" I asked, sliding two fingers inside her slick hot body.

"I-I've p-played with myself, but n-not—" She gasped for air and clutched at the bedcovers, fisting them and pushing her hips farther onto the fingers I was spearing her with. "Gods, it n-never felt this g-good."

I curled my fingers inside her again and covered her clit with my mouth, pulling it slowly between my lips. She was so close, just a little more. I let the edge of my teeth scrape her clit, and she soared.

Her body clamped down hard on my fingers, locking them into place. Had it not been for my arm wrapped around one of her thighs, she would've arced right off the edge of the bed. I held her tight. She dug the heel of her free leg into my back, urging me deeper and closer, and then she screamed.

Not like the loud piercing scream of a banshee, but a strained gasp so completely overwhelmed by pleasure that it'd paralyzed every cell and muscle. She sat up on the bed, my mouth still attached to her clit, and curled over me, trembling.

"Mercy," she said, finally managing to force out a single word.

A chuckle shook my chest. I withdrew my fingers, relishing the whimper she uttered at the loss. "We're only getting started, my sweet, sweet Gretchen."

I got off my knees and scooped her into my arms, moving her to the center of my bed. Then I shucked off my t-shirt and slid off my heavy jeans.

Her gaze lowered to my fully erect cock and her eyebrows rose slightly. I grasped the base of my aching cock and stroked a couple of times, relieving just a bit of frustration. I wanted to be balls deep inside her, but she wasn't ready. Not yet. I wanted her back on the brink of climax before I claimed her fully.

I crawled to her from the foot of the bed, positioning myself between her long, slender legs. Her scent was all I could smell. All I could taste, and I wanted more. "You doing good?" I was on all fours, hovering over her, my hands on either side of her shoulders and knees between her legs. The tip of my cock slid along her mound and then up to her navel. I leaned down to put my mouth on one of her breasts, taking most of it into my mouth, gently kneading it with my lips until she moaned.

She raised her legs from the bed, grazing my hips with her thighs. She arched her body, positioning herself perfectly.

I could've driven straight into her right then, but I held back. It would be better if I waited. The more I could play with her before we joined, the less sore she would be afterward. At least I hoped. At this rate, though, I wasn't going to let her have much sleep.

"Alek, please, I ache for more."

I moved to the other breast, lavishing it with my mouth and the edges of my teeth until she writhed beneath me, begging and pleading and panting all in the same moment. Her skin burned, stoking the fire within me even hotter. My cock stabbed at her soft stomach, but I released her breast and withdrew to feast upon her again.

Her thighs squeezed, trying to hold me in place. I pushed them up to her chest until her calves rested on either of my shoulders. Then plunged my tongue inside her again. She shuddered and moaned and dug her heels into my back. Her fingers raked over my scalp.

The slight pain only edged me further into the need swelling inside me. She wasn't the only one that wanted more. I drew her clit into my mouth and sucked gently, gauging her breaths and the tension in her body, waiting for just that moment before she ignited.

Her legs tightened around me, and I released, dragging in a ragged breath. Then I moved up the bed, shrugging her legs off my shoulders, and pressed the tip of my straining cock against her warm, wet center. I kissed her, loving the taste of her mixed with her arousal.

She wrapped her arms around my neck and pulled me closer. "Please." The word was mumbled into my mouth as our tongues tangled together.

I moved forward another inch, maybe two, giving her time to adjust. It would hurt. I knew it would. There was no way of getting around the initial pain. I just prayed I'd relaxed her enough that it wouldn't last too long.

The torture was all mine now, halfway in, halfway out. I strained against the base need to thrust. Against the instinct hounding me to stroke and join our bodies in a frenzy.

"More." She arched her hips, taking more of me than I'd planned to allow, but she didn't cry out. We hadn't gone far enough yet. It was right there. I could feel the barrier inside her holding me back.

I slipped my arms beneath her shoulders, wrapping my palms up and around, locking her into place, while resting most of my weight on my elbows so I wouldn't crush her. My heart clutched inside my chest. Our gazes met. I raised my head and stared down at her beautiful face. Her bright brown eyes darkened with desire and hunger and an eagerness that made my beast want to roar.

"You are more than I ever could've imagined."

A soft smile curved her lips. "You are everything I always knew you were. Soft and gentle and kind beneath that rough, protective outer armor."

"You're the only one who's called me gentle or soft." I swallowed the emotion bubbling inside me. "I need you." The words came out choked.

"Take me." The trust in her gaze wrenched my gut, and I couldn't hold back another second. The sensation of her warmth and silky heat clenched down as I thrust deep.

A short gasp slipped between her lips.

"I'm sorry." The apology came out instantly along with a moan of pleasure. I fought to remain still. To give her time. I'd hurt her. I'd felt her tense. I knew she was in pain. A slight sheen of sweat coated her from head to foot, coated us both.

She rocked her hips, and I groaned, nearly spiraling straight into an orgasm. She was perfect. This was perfect. We were perfect. "Don't move, or I won't be able to go slow."

"I don't want you to go slow." She rocked her hips again and traced her fingertips along my neck.

Pleasure twisted inside me in a straining knot of antici- pation. Permission granted, I surged forward, pressing deep inside. Her body cinched to mine. I pulled back then thrust again, building from slow methodical strokes to a more desperate, uncontrolled tempo.

Her face flushed pink, and I lowered my mouth to her nipple, taking it deep. She matched my rhythm. Our hearts beat together, also syncing in the moment. She panted and whimpered, and our slick bodies rocked together, the sounds nearly enough to send me cascading

183

into a climax. I reached between us and pressed hard on her clit, moving my mouth from her breast to her lips at the same time.

Her muffled scream came from deep within, filling me with its rawness, and I felt my release surge forward. We flew together in that moment, our bodies burning with the heat of our desire. It felt so perfect.

Too perfect.

Doubt tried pulled me back from bliss, but I banished it from my mind. Nothing would spoil this night, even if it was the only night I ever got with her.

CHAPTER 18

GRETCHEN

I shifted in his grasp, cracking my eyes open at the rays of sunlight stabbing through the dark-ness of Alek's bedroom. His arms tightened around me, and he muttered something about taking me again if I tried to leave his bed.

I snuggled into the embrace and let a slow sigh of contentment slip between my lips. Last night had been...so much...so much more than I'd ever realized. Alek had made love to me and made me come over and over through the night until my body had become a boneless mass of blissful satisfaction.

His mouth had tasted me from head to foot in the most intimate of ways, ways I'd never imagined. Ways none of the Sisters had shared. I was more than happy to exist solely in his bed, between his strong arms for as long as he'd let me stay, although nature's call and my rumbling stomach were determined to force me down a different path.

I wriggled a little, trying to see if he'd relaxed his grip.

"I told you to stay." The rumbling growl at my back gave me goosebumps.

"I need to—" I didn't want to leave, but my body wasn't really going to give me a choice.

His arms relaxed immediately. "Very well, but you must return promptly so that I can ravish you again before breakfast." His voice was playful, but a sad undertone made me wonder what he was thinking.

I scurried to the bathroom to fulfill my body's needs and then returned to the bedroom. He hadn't moved, but my stomach was cramping. The last meal I'd eaten had been breakfast the morning before. So much had happened yesterday...food just hadn't been important.

His eyes opened, brown with flecks of honey-gold. Our gazes met, and then his drifted down to my chest. I was naked and should've felt shy, but I wasn't. I wanted him to see me. I loved the hunger I'd seen last night.

He rose from the bed and walked to where I stood in the doorway, concern or surprise etched into his expression. I couldn't decide which because his naked and fully aroused body was making me forget how hungry I was.

"What's wrong?" I asked, trying not to stare at his...cock.

"The white marks on your collarbone, I don't remember seeing these last night." He traced his finger across my chest, and I gasped. My skin heated under his touch in certain places, and I felt a rush of something I'd never felt before. A cloud of warm energy encircled me, spinning and twirling around my legs and arms and entire body.

"What marks?" I tried to gather my wits and look down to where his fingertips touched my skin. A pattern of glyphs crisscrossed my collarbone like a necklace had been painted on—but each mark glowed as he traced it, like a lamp had been lit beneath my skin, but only when he touched the marks. Once his fingertips passed by, it faded back to white.

I looked up, my gaze stopping at his biceps where the same glyph pattern was etched in a ring around both of his upper arms. "You have them, too." I reached out, touching the marks on one of his arms. They lit, just as mine had, under my touch then faded when I pulled my hand away.

He looked at his arm and brushed at the marks. Nothing happened when he touched them. Then he focused his gaze on me again. He put his hands on my shoulders and turned me away from him. "It's draped around your shoulders like a necklace."

"Do you know what they are?"

He turned me again so that we were facing each other. "I know that my parents had them. I remember seeing them on my father's arms when he would bathe. My mother's were usually covered, but I remember seeing glimpses when she would fall asleep on the couch and the shoulder of her dress would be crooked from turning in her sleep."

"I am proud to wear your mark."

"But I don't know how—" His voice carried even more confusion now. "I don't know what this means for us."

I stretched to cup his face in my hand. "It means we belong together. Don't worry about the rest. We will learn in time, just like you did with your Gryphon's abilities."

He grasped my hand and turned to kiss the palm. "I'm four thousand years old, and I still don't understand everything about being a Gryphon. What if we never understand the link we've created? What if I do something to ruin it?"

I'd never seen him so unsure, so anxious. He was always calm and in control in the library. Like steel, strong and unyielding. This tense and worried Alek was a stranger to me, but the marks didn't bother me, and I didn't have a driving need to understand them at this very moment.

"Nothing is going to happen right now." I kept my voice soft and steady, trying to ignore the small slice of pain that's stabbed my heart at the mention of his age. We would never have that much time. Our relationship would feel like the short season of fall in Texas—so brief you had to be looking for it or you'd miss it.

He drew in a deep breath, and I could see him centering his mind— like he'd taken all the extra thoughts and concerns and filed them away and out of sight. "You're right."

"I think we will both feel better if we eat." My stomach growled loudly, echoing its agreement to my statement. I pushed away my worries and smiled up at him.

A chuckle slipped from Alek, and one of his rare smiles brightened his face. "Very well." He left my side briefly, walking to a dresser across the room, and returned with a large black t-shirt—very much like the one he wore almost every day, steady and predictable. I couldn't remember the last time I'd seen him wear anything other than a pair of jeans and a plain t-shirt. The color of the shirt varied a little, but they were mostly black.

He pulled the soft cotton over my head, and I

smoothed it down my body, not surprised to find the hem at nearly mid-thigh. Alek was a large man, seven feet tall and broader in the shoulders than most doorways. His waist and muscles tapered into this beautiful V-line that made my insides quiver with a very different kind of hunger every time I looked at it. It made me wonder if he had the same reaction when he looked at my breasts...or lower.

"You should put on something, too," I said, licking my lips and taking in the magnificent view below his waist.

A mischievous grin I didn't recognize spread across his face. I'd seen the rare smile on his face—the amusement he usually hid—but this was something else. Something predatory and dangerous that made the skin on my body prickle with excitement.

"I don't think you're as hungry as you claim. On the bed, hands and knees."

I sucked in a quick breath, surprised that those few words turned my knees to jelly. My legs were useless, like my brain had forgotten how to function. Instead, something deep inside my belly throbbed, coiling in anticipation.

He put a hand at the small of my back and guided me toward the torn-apart bed. The coverlet lay on the floor in a heap, and most of the sheets had been shoved to the side from our vigorous activities during the night.

I crawled onto the edge on my hands and knees, fully aware that his shirt wasn't covering most of my bottom. One of his hands cupped my ass while he used the other to push the t-shirt well above my waistline, baring me fully.

"Absolutely gorgeous."

The tip of his cock brushed my slick center, and a

second later, he was all the way inside me. Air rushed from my lungs, and my stomach tightened. My well-used, still-sore muscles took a few seconds to relax into his slow strokes.

He slipped his hands from my hips around to my bobbing breasts inside the t-shirt. The nipples were already stiff, and he immediately rolled and teased them between his thumb and forefinger.

I dropped to my elbows with a moan of tortured bliss... His paced increased, and our bodies slapped together harder and harder. Pleasure swirled inside me, coiling and winding up like a snake getting ready to strike. My breath turned to pants, and my heart thumped hard in my chest like someone going at a wall with a hammer.

"Alek," I half-sobbed, half-begged. The entire lower half of my body thrummed with the need to release. His fingers dug into my hips, just rough enough to give an edge of pain to the pleasure of being filled by him. "Please."

He released one of my breasts and slid his hand down between my legs, halfway bending his body over mine. It was so much. So deep. I buried my mouth in a pillow and came with a half-scream before his fingers even touched the little nub hidden in the folds of my sex.

A growl erupted from his chest, and he drove into me one last time before I felt his warm seed spill into me. My muscles quivered, and I gasped for breath, willing my heart to slow.

He released my body from his grasp and helped me lie on my side while I continued to catch my breath. Then he left the bed and walked into the adjoining bathroom.

I closed my eyes and just breathed, content and sore, though I knew I would be ready for another round in less than an hour. I couldn't get enough of him, and I couldn't help but worry that every second I got with him might be my last.

How long would it take for my sisters to find the man I'd knocked out?

How long before someone saw the rope I'd made from curtain ties flailing in the wind on the side of the castle?

How long before Rose would separate me from the man I loved?

A dark, slimy thread of despair wound through my stomach.

"Gretchen, you are safe with me. Don't be afraid." He'd returned to the bedside and began wiping my thighs and between my legs—cleaning me until every trace of his seed had been removed by the warm washcloth in his hand.

"How did you know I was afraid?" I sat up on the edge of the bed and caught his equally confused stare.

"I don't know." He shook his head and walked away, disappearing into the bathroom again. When he returned, he was wearing a pair of jeans that hung low on his waist, distracting me from my thoughts with the vision of his sculpted torso and the trail of dark hair that led my eyes lower and lower to that delicious V-line.

"Hey." He touched my chin, making me meet his gaze.

"Sorry, you're distracting."

"I know the feeling. Breakfast then shower?"

I nodded. Eating was much higher on my priority list than removing the scent of our lovemaking. In fact, I was perfectly willing to be coerced back into bed after breakfast had been consumed.

We walked down the short hallway to his tidy kitchen,

and he ushered me to a barstool while he moved silently and methodically, gathering the ingredients for an omelet.

"Do you like spinach?" He looked up from the cutting board, his hands full of chopped spinach. "I didn't ask before I started."

"I do." I said, nodding.

"What were you afraid of?" He sprinkled the spinach into the egg mixture already in the frying pan and followed with a little bit of crumbled white cheese. "I don't know how I knew, but I did." The small glass cell phone on the counter buzzed, and he frowned, grabbing it up and typing out something on the screen. I couldn't read it before he pressed send and set it back down. "And I need you to be honest with me."

"I was scared about what happens next." The words were barely audible to me, but he could hear them, just like all his neighbors could hear our conversation right now if they tried. What was even more ridiculous was that the Lycans in town could also read my thoughts. I might be a Sister of the House of Lamidae, but physiologically, I was a human.

"We're leaving, Gretchen. We're going to eat, clean up, and leave. Is that okay with you?"

"Yes."

"Good." He set a half of an omelet in front of me on a white plate. "Eat up. We need to go soon, before the town starts looking for you."

"You weren't okay with leaving Sanctuary before. You want to go back to the Veil. I know you do." I spoke slowly, doing my best to keep from breaking into tears. His words from yesterday in Miles' office still stung. What if he changed his mind again?

"I want you more than I want vengeance. You are mine, and I know in my heart you are the only one who will ever truly be mine. Gretchen, I—"

A loud crash and the sound of scraping metal made him move around the counter, blocking my body from view of whoever had just come crashing through his front door. "Alek Melos, you're not sick. Get your fucking ass out of bed and down to the—" The fire chief's voice died off and I could practically hear the disappointment scrawled across his face. "Fuck me. You could've warned me that we'd need an exit strategy today instead of trying to shove off without a word."

Alek moved aside, his shoulders falling, and I locked gazes with the man Alek considered his best friend—his brother. Out of everyone in the town, Jared MacKay was one of the only people Alek ever spoke about during our visits in the library.

The Phoenix was just as tall as Alek, though not quite as broad. Instead of short dark hair, Jared had long light brown hair that brushed his neck just above his shoulders. His bright steel-blue eyes flashed, but not with anger like I expected. Instead, his gaze carried concern—for me and for his friend.

"I didn't want you in the middle of this. There's no reason for you to leave Sanctuary."

"Dude, you're an idiot. No one can get out of Sanctuary. Are you forgetting the Lamassu-witch powered shield that is failing to keep out the fucking Djinn and traitorous asshole Lycans?"

An angry snarl tore from Alek's mouth. "Fuck." He tossed his uneaten half of the omelet into the sink. The pottery plate smashed into a dozen pieces, and I cringed.

"What barrier?" I whispered. The only barriers I knew of were the blue shields that guarded all the buildings. They prevented Djinn from teleporting in and out, but they didn't keep anyone from walking in or out.

"More got in?" Alek asked, ignoring my question.

"Five are dead. Riley found them this morning. Throats were cut. Not a single one looked like they'd woken up."

"How did they get in the house without waking someone? The teleporting barriers are still functioning."

"Riley can't figure it out. The door was jimmied, but it should've made enough noise to wake at least one person in the house. They murdered the kids, too, Alek."

Bile burned the back of my throat. "Why aren't we told about what's going on outside in the town?" I spit the words out, angry that I'd been kept in the dark. I knew the town worked to keep us safe. I even knew that lives had been risked when Protectors were sought out and people left town, but I didn't know the town itself was under attack or that children were dying... "How could she keep something like this from us?"

"Your Oracle knows." Alek turned to me, his expression stark and cold. "Rose didn't feel it was necessary to burden the rest of the Sisters with the knowledge of the war that has slowly made its way to Sanctuary's door."

Jared released a heavy sigh. "This is why Sanctuary has moved every few decades for as long as long as I can remember. We've been in this town over a hundred years. That's a record. The longest we ever stayed in one place before settling here was the thirty years we spent in the Appalachian Mountains."

"We're all too settled." Alek agreed. "There are so

many people with us now, so many families. It was too hard to keep moving. That's what Miles told me once, so we built the town, built the castle, and then enchanted everything to keep it safe and hidden from spells."

"Even spells can be beaten, and Xerxes is tearing holes in the town barrier one right after another. You know I'm the last person who would tell you to leave your mate's side, but the safest place for her is back inside with the Blackmoors."

"No." I stood abruptly from the barstool and stepped toward Alek. "I'm not leaving you. If I go back, I'll never get out again."

"How did you get out?" Jared narrowed his eyes, scrunching the middle of his forehead, like looking at me funny would solve the riddle.

"I climbed out of a window."

"There aren't any windows except on the—holy fuck." He shook his head. "You're as crazy as he is, and you're human. How are you not black and blue and/or dead?" He stalked toward her, but Alek stepped in between them, blocking his friend.

"Leave her be." Alek's deep voice vibrated through the room.

"We need to go. Once they realize she's missing, your ass is grass, and you know it. We have to fight the enemy at our door. If she doesn't go back now, there's no way you can protect her. Calliope and Rose reported sensing at least three Djinn in town, and that was an hour ago."

"I thought Harrison was powering the spell while he was here. Shouldn't it be stronger?"

"He says there are witches on the outside poking holes

in it faster than he can patch them. The girls are worn out. They've barely slept in weeks."

Alek nodded. "I know." He glanced at me with a look that broke my heart. "Gretchen, I have some shorts in my dresser you can put on. Why don't you get dressed, and then we'll figure out what to do next."

Pain gripped my lungs. I couldn't speak. After everything—after last night—he was going to send me back to my cage. Back to a life dictated by a prophecy that meant nothing to me. We were vessels for the Lamassu to return home, for all supernaturals to get the hell off this planet and go back to the Veil or whatever the hell they called it. Alek cared about me. I knew he did, but when worse came to worse, he was a supernatural, and I was a human. We weren't the same. We'd never be the same.

"Gretchen?" He put a hand on my shoulder, rubbing the marks with his thumb. A prickle of energy skimmed across my skin where he touched, and my whole body shuddered, reminded of the connection between us.

"I'm going. I get it." I pulled away from him and disappeared down the hallway. Alek and Jared continued speaking about the crisis in town. Alek asked who the people were that died, and I took a gulp of air, closing the bedroom door behind me, muffling their conversation.

I found a pair of drawstring shorts in his dresser, slipped them on, and gathered and tied them tightly around my hips. Shoes would be nice, but right now, I just needed to get out and hide, I could worry about my feet later. Once I got out of town, I could hide among other humans. No one would ever be the wiser.

It wasn't a perfect plan, but it was better than going back to the castle. Leaving Alek would rip out my heart.

Still, I couldn't go back. If I did, I'd never get out. They'd never let me in the library again. Probably never let me out of the basement quarters. It would be worse than before.

I couldn't do it.

I wouldn't.

Jared and Alek were arguing about what to do next. They weren't paying attention to me. It would hurt him that I left, but it would be better, easier. We'd had our perfect night. It could be enough. I would survive without him. I hoped.

The window in the bathroom unlatched easily. I pushed it up and jumped to the ground. The dry grass crunch beneath my feet, but there was no thundering voice yelling at me to stop. Neither of them had heard me leave, because they weren't listening for it. I could still hear their stressed voices discussing the dead family of Lycans.

I slipped between the houses and walked quickly down the street. People were rushing here and there—Lycans probably. Most of the town's population were werewolves. At least that's what I'd heard.

Several women passing me with their children stared for a second, but everyone was in a hurry. None of them said a word. None of them made a move to stop my progress down the street...away from the town center.

I got past the neighborhood. Empty lots lay on either side of the street where I walked now. No cover and nothing to hide behind. The open space made me nervous, but I had to get out. I loved him more than anything, but I couldn't survive if he put me back into that stone cage. The Sisters could make do without me. The visions would be weaker for a while, but several of them were ready to

deliver soon. As soon as they did, Astrid would be able to
see her visions clearly again.

Footsteps behind me made the hair on the back of my
neck prickle. I turned, but the street and sidewalks were
empty. When I turned again, I screamed, but the sound
was cut off by a heavy hand over my mouth. One man
grabbed me from behind, and the other removed his hand
long enough to put a white cloth over my mouth and nose.

"We got one. I can't fucking believe they let a Sister
out of that castle."

A strong pungent smell filled my lungs, and my vision
darkened. My arms and legs got heavy, and I sagged. My
knees gave out, but the man behind me held me up,
keeping me from crashing to the asphalt.

"Take her to the house outside the border and then
come back for me. The General will be beyond pleased
with this turn of events."

The General? I fought to stay conscious, but the smell
permeated the air, and darkness pressed my eyelids shut.
Then everything else faded away, too.

CHAPTER 19

XERXES

"Commander Martin has arrived with an update from Sanctuary, Master." Cal stood halfway inside the Oval Office and half in the hallway while he waited to be granted permission to enter.

"Send him in," I said, continuing to stare out the windows onto the outdoor spaces filled with my soldiers near the White House. Vehicles traversed the once-green lawns. Where trees had been, now metal buildings stood— quickly constructed bases of operation for my two Lycan commanders and their growing troops.

The smell of Lycan permeated the room before Martin stepped one foot through the open door. They were a necessary evil and would be disposable once I was through taking over the entire continent. Until then, they were useful and typically got the job done.

Their habit of reading human thoughts had come in

KRYSTAL SHANNAN

handy on more than one occasion. Interrogations were also a comical spectacle. Most humans were unaware of the Lycan ability to mind read, and those that were interrogated and found out about the ability were not left alive long enough to pass along the information to anyone else.

"General Xerxes, Sir." Martin marched into the office, his boots snapped together as he saluted. When I turned, his hand was still at his forehead, waiting to be released to an at-ease position.

"I hear you have an update. Have you taken down the Bateman's barrier?"

"It is starting to crumble, Sir, but it's not down completely. We are able to jump in and out with the help of the witches you send with my units."

I sighed and turned back to look out the window. "Is that all?"

"No, Sir. I've been informed that my men captured one of the Sisters of Lamidae."

My heart skipped a beat, and I whirled on Martin, grabbing him around the neck with my magick and hauling him to within inches of my faces. I could smell the fear on him, but to his credit, he didn't struggle or panic. Even as I squeezed his trachea closed, he merely gagged, waiting for me to decide whether he lived or died.

If he was teasing me, I would kill him...slowly and excruciatingly. I unclenched my fist and released his neck from my magickal chokehold. "Why is she not with you?"

"If she is not what we think, I didn't want to risk bringing someone into your stronghold here. If she's a spy or—"

I raised my hand to silence him. His reasoning was logical, except that his men should've been able to tell that she was a human for damn sure if they could read her thoughts. "Cal."

My Djinn servant stepped through the still-open office door and bowed.

"Take me to the units outside of Sanctuary. Then come back and fetch Commander Martin."

"Yes, Sir."

I stretched my hand to Cal, and he took it, pulling us through a vortex. Moments later, we appeared in the encampment I'd had Martin set up twenty miles from the edge of Sanctuary, far enough that Rose and her minions couldn't sense the movement of my Djinn and close enough that they could get back and forth quickly enough to run effective attacks on the town.

Several Lycans saw me and froze in place, their hands raised in salute. Cal left my side and reappeared moments later with Martin in tow.

"Where is she?"

"This way, Sir." He gestured toward a brown temporary warehouse structure and waited for me to take the lead, which I did.

I yanked open the door and stepped inside. My eyes adjusted rapidly to the dim lighting, and the farther inside the building I walked, the louder the screams became. The kind of screams I liked to hear, but only if I was the one triggering them.

"What are they doing to her? You don't have permission to touch her."

"The men are interrogating her, Sir. She's the only source of information we have from inside the castle. I assure you, no permanent damage has been done."

Imbeciles, all of them. I stormed down the hall toward the sound of the woman's voice. My cock hardened just at the thought of finally having one of the Sisters within reach.

I hadn't been sure the chance would present itself again.

A second chance to begin a race in my image that would rule both the Veil and Earth, a supernatural being more powerful than anything either world had ever seen, and they would be mine, my children. With them at my side, nothing and no one would be able to stand in my way.

I would be invincible.

I would be king.

Shoving the door open, I stepped into a small interrogation room. Two Lycan soldiers had a young woman—naked—and bent over a table with her hands tied behind her back. The man in front of her had his dick nearly in her mouth, and the man behind her had his dick out, about to shove it in her pussy.

She was screaming her head off about someone named Alek killing them slowly by plucking out their eyeballs. A smile tugged at the corners of my mouth. I had to admit her creative threats in the situation amused me. I'd never heard a woman talk about eyeball plucking. But I didn't recognize the name Alek, which bothered me. I knew all of Rose's players. At least I thought I did.

I glared at the men who'd imagined they had the right to sample a prisoner caught at my request. I lifted my hand, directing my magick. Both men gasped and clutched the invisible cords I wrapped around their necks. I squeezed tighter and tighter until the cord of power literally took their heads right off. Blood poured from the decapitation, coating the floor in a slick red pool. Their half-dressed bodies flopped to the floor with pleasant thuds. The scent of Lycan blood in the morning always put me in a good mood. It was a shame I couldn't shed more of it.

Martin stood silently behind me with Cal. Neither spoke. I approached the hysterical woman bent over the narrow table.

Leaning down, I put my face even with hers. "Who is Alek?"

She snapped her gaze to mine and sucked in a surprised breath. "You're going to kill me anyway. I have nothing to say to you."

"I'm not going to kill you right now, little one. I'm going to impregnate you, lock you away in my palace, and have you carry child after child after child until your body gives out or you die. Though once your body gives out, I will have no further use for you and will kill you."

A shudder of energy flickered across her bare shoulders and I bent to look closer at the white marks that flowed from one shoulder blade to another in a gentle upward-facing semi-circle. As I inspected further, I noticed the marks continued over her shoulder and down over the front of her collarbone and chest. It was a Gryphon's mate mark—a necklace of magick that permanently linked them together. *How the fuck? I'd killed off the Gryphons who'd escaped through the portal thousands of years ago.* There were none left.

Unless Rose had gotten her claws into one and hidden him, they'd all been stupid teenagers who barely knew how to shift, much less control the powerful beast that lived inside them.

Easy kills.

"Martin?" I looked over my shoulder at the white-faced Commander.

"Alek is a Gryphon. She loves him, General Xerxes, Sir. She is afraid. I'm not getting a lot more. Her mind is still pretty jumbled from the chloroform...And angry thoughts toward them." He indicated with a nod at the fresh bodies on the floor.

I shrugged. I had no sympathy for men who didn't respect authority. Actually, I had no sympathy for anyone.

"Love, I guess that explains your mate marks. Those don't just pop up after a casual fuck." My tone remained light and energetic. A Sister of Lamidae caught in the open and mated to a fucking Gryphon. Rose must be losing her control over the town.

"You're all going to die." Her voice shot out like the crack of a whip. Even through her pain and torture, she chose to fight. "Alek with kill you all, and Rose will wipe you all off the face of the Earth."

"I'd like to see him try, and I do think this would be much more entertaining if your Alek had to watch what I'm going to do to you. Why don't I just activate these marks so he comes running to get you." I flipped her over, exposing her bruised breasts. Teeth marks showed raw, a stark contrast to her white skin, and a snarl rumbled in my chest.

"Did those men do this to you?" I pointed at the bite marks. She glared, and I turned to Martin. "Who?"

He paused a moment and focused. "The first soldiers who grabbed her, General, before I knew she'd been reported captured."

"How long has she been in your custody?" I narrowed my eyes and roared. "How long?"

"Overnight, General Xerxes, her thoughts say they caught her yesterday morning."

Fucking unacceptable. "You inform your men that no female caught is to be touched by their filthy paws without my express permission or their fate will be worse than the two you already have to clean up off the floor."

"Yes, Sir. General, Sir."

"Take their bodies and put them on spikes in the center of camp."

"Yes, Sir."

He and Cal both grabbed a bloody body and the decapitated head before scrambling to be the first out of the room. Once the door closed behind them, I turned my attention back to the bound woman on the table.

Her eyes opened wide when our gazes met, and she struggled against my hands on her body, on her breasts, then on the white marks decorating her collarbone. I pressed the runes in a particular order, and they glowed bright and hot enough that I felt the magick inside them begin to pulse. It wouldn't stop until her mate's skin touched hers.

She hissed and jerked away from me, but I used my magick to hold her arcing body down and in place, freeing my hands to unzip my pants.

"What's your name?"

"Go to hell, you bastard!" She spit at me, and I leaned down to lick the side of her face, *human, coated in magick.* It'd been so long. I hadn't taken a human woman since Cera. Their bodies were weak and could barely withstand the beatings I preferred to dole out. Even my harem back at the palace were Djinn, not human. Their bodies were resilient and strong, so strong.

This one was different. She was a Sister. She was worth being careful with, gentle even. Worth keeping healthy. She would be the mother of my children. The mother of a new race.

CHAPTER 20

ALEK

I'd lost Gretchen, but we'd been over every inch of the town and couldn't find her. Couldn't catch her scent everywhere. I hadn't slept yesterday all. I could feel her pain, her anger, her fear. Jared was the only one that knew. He'd been there when I realized she was gone. He'd been the one who kept me from telling Rose right away. He'd said we would find her, but we hadn't.

She was nowhere and I could do nothing.

I was useless to her. I'd lost her. I'd failed her. The knowledge ripped through my soul like Jared was burning me alive. His fire would've been preferable to the torture I was living through every moment she was gone.

Now, Djinn were everywhere, and Lycans. Blood slicked the streets. I ran next to Jared. Screams came from a nearby house, and we both turned toward the panic. We weren't fast enough to catch a Djinn unless we surprised him with a sword in the back, but the Lycans we could kill.

We burst through the already shattered front door. A large gray mammoth of a wolf had another wolf's neck in his mouth and two frightened children cornered, shielded only by their mother's bloody wolf form. She was still alive, but barely. Her heart had slowed in the few seconds it took for Jared and me to cross the room.

She snarled at the intruding wolf, but a Djinn kept blinking in and out of the space, stabbing her with a dagger each time he blinked in. Echoes of his laughter filled the room, mixing with the haunting, heartbreaking screams of the children.

Those screams were not unlike the ones I'd heard when my parents had shoved me through the open portal. So many had died that day.

Jared launched himself toward the mother and her children.

I leaped for the monstrous bloody wolf, shifting in midair. My front talons sliced through his mangy hide, and a howl of painful anguish satisfied my bloodlust for at least the present moment. One of these Lycan traitors had taken Gretchen. My mind envisioned her mangled body strewn on a street somewhere in town among all the other dead and wounded. Why couldn't we find her?

Fate had given me one perfect night and then punished me for taking it. It was my fault she'd run. If I hadn't entertained the notion of sending her back to the castle, she wouldn't have left. She'd trusted me, and I'd failed her. In the end, I'd told Jared I was leaving with her anyway, but by then, it was too late. When I'd gone to get her from my bedroom, all I'd found was the memory of her scent and an open bathroom window.

Jared and I had tracked her trail until it'd faded into nothing. I'd wanted to kill myself right there on the spot, but moments later, the entire town had gone on alert. The sirens had gone off in a dozen different areas. The town was screaming in pain around me and I couldn't ignore them. They were my friends, my family, and they were dying.

Screams had torn through the normally quiet streets. Everyone had run for the bunkers or the castle, mostly for the castle. It was the safest place in the town.

"Alek." Jared's voice was a faint call in the distance. "Alek."

I opened my massive beak and screamed at my friend. The sound blasted out the windows in the back of the house, but he barely blinked, flames burning brightly in his eyes.

"He's dead. So is their mother."

I snapped my beak, anger ripping at my soul, and tore my talons through the dead wolf one more time for good measure. Jared had the two Lycan children in his hands. "You take them to the castle courtyard and then get your ass back. I'm going to keep working my way down Avenue B."

I threw my massive head toward the ceiling above us, and he nodded.

I wrapped my wings around the children he'd placed on my back and moved away, waiting for him to open the ceiling so I could fly.

He lifted his arms. Flames soared from his hands, and his entire body was quickly engulfed. The fire was hot enough to singe the feathers on my chest, but the children were safe beneath my wings. A few moments later, the ceiling and roof had disintegrated and the fire had been extinguished.

"You're clear." He turned and disappeared out the front door.

I rotated my neck and peered down at the children on my back. They curled their little fingers into my feathers, instinctively realizing what I was about to do. With a leap, I cleared the charred remains of the house, and two powerful strokes of my wings later we were sailing over the burning town toward the castle.

Two black dragons sat in front of the castle, each of their solid bodies were close to a third of the building's size. Their wings spanned the entire length of the fortress. One of them looked up at me from the ground and then focused back on the figures they were escorting inside. Miles and Eli Blackmoor knew every being in the town. They'd been with Rose for thousands of years. No one was getting inside that castle door unless they personally recognized him or her.

I braced myself for the bite of magick as I cross the threshold of the special barrier that guarded the castle. The children on my back cried out, but to their credit, neither one released their death grip on my feathered neck. I landed softly in the courtyard and was immediately surrounded by several pixies and one of the more recent additions to town—Killían North, an escaped Elf from the Veil.

"Come here, sweet darlings," the Pixies cooed at the children, removing them from my back. "We'll get you somewhere safe. Thank you, Alek, for getting them here." One of the pixies rubbed her hand along my quivering neck, leaving a thin layer of shimmering dust on my feathers.

I pushed the beast back and shifted back to my human form. A white hot pain seared through my body. The runes on my upper arms lit up like someone had set off a nuclear bomb inside my chest.

"Alek, what's wrong?"

I fell to my knees and roared. "Gretchen." I could feel the connection calling to me, surging with life like the dam on a river had been broken. I breathed through the agony of her shared terror. I could find her. The pain shifted to a pulse deep in my chest, and it tugged at the beast inside.

"Rose." The pixies scattered in multiple directions. "Rose."

No. You can't tell her. I opened my mouth to call after them, but another stroke of Gretchen's fear silenced me. Whatever she was going through, we needed the Lamassu and I could weather the Sentinel's wrath, especially if it meant finding Gretchen.

Moments later, the pissed-off Lamassu was stalking toward me.

I tried to stand, but her magick wrapped itself around my body, paralyzing me on the grassy lawn of the castle courtyard.

"Alek Melos, you have betrayed my trust. You have cost the House of Lamidae and every supernatural being waiting to go home. It will take decades and several new children to replace the power of a young Sister in the House. Was I not clear to you when we spoke?" Her voice doubled in size, and her dark brown eyes changed to a bright white. She brought her hand down on my chest, and I felt my heart slow under the burn of her palm.

The burning of the Runes surged again, and between that and the burn of her skin on my chest, I'd just about had enough. My Gryphon cried out from inside me, shaking the ground where we stood and the walls surrounding the courtyard. The marks on my arms burned like hot coals, and the light shined bright enough from them to make me squint my eyes.

"Mate marks." Rose's voice dropped back into the normal human decibel, and her eyes switched back to brown. Her magick receded from my body, and I sucked in a deep breath before rising to face her. My human form was double her size or more, but I knew better than to think I had any advantage over one of the most powerful beings on the planet, no matter how small she appeared as a human.

"You know what they are?" I panted for air, struggling to breathe through the overwhelming desire to shift and take flight. She'd yank me down even if I tried. "I can feel her. I have to go to her."

Her face darkened, and an ache occupied Rose's eyes. She looked at me with sympathy and regret, like she knew something I didn't, but wasn't going to share. "You'll die, Alek. He's called you with her runes. It's a trap."

"If you found Naram was alive, would you go to him, whatever the cost?" Sweat poured from my body, and my Gryphon swelled inside me, building toward another scream that might take down one the castle walls. "I have to go. This is not something I can ignore because you say he'll kill me. If I have to die to save her, I will. It's better than living without her." The last part of the sentence was cruel, but I needed to go. I needed her to let me go.

"If we're going to get her back, we need help." She

turned and shouted Eli's name. The black dragon swung his head over the wall and gazed down at us, steam billowing from his nostrils, his pupils orange with flame.

"Gretchen is alive. She is Alek's mate." Rose's amped-up voice carried through the courtyard above the din of the cries inside and outside the castle.

The dragon's head tipped, and his massive black wings unfurled and pumped, propelling him into the sky.

Rose turned back to me. "Shift and follow the call of your Runes, Alek. They will lead you to her. We will follow you."

I released the magick writhing inside me, and my Gryphon took over, shifting my body into a beast the size of a Clydesdale stallion. My wings unfurled, and I screeched in surprise when Rose took hold of my mane of feathers and leapt to sit on my back just in front of my wing base. I screamed an angry call to the sky above. There would be blood for their actions against my mate. Death would be their only reward.

Leaping into the air, I joined Eli in the sky and turned toward the low pulse tugging my body south. The link to Gretchen got stronger with each pump of my wings in her direction. Desperation spurred me forward, and guilt.

Some of the homes below us were burning. People scrambled left and right. They were being moved to the protected underground bunkers, and some were fleeing all the way to the castle.

If I'd known about what the runes could do earlier, maybe I would've been able to find her immediately. If I'd told Rose what happened, instead of hiding it from her... would Gretchen already be safe? Perhaps not in my arms, perhaps Rose would've killed me or banished me for my betrayal, but Gretchen might be safe. That was all that mattered. What had my ignorance cost her? What had my desire cost her? I could've sent her back the very moment she stumbled onto my porch.

Instead, I'd taken her and loved her, and then everything had changed.

We flew past the edge of town and lines of charred houses. A few people darted through the streets—patrols looking for stragglers. The barrier had been destroyed. Harrison and both his daughters were likely lost. Patrols had been slaughtered. The town was burning beneath us, and all we could do was save as many as we could and hunker down and wait it out.

There were too many. Xerxes had finally come for us, and we were woefully unprepared.

"Most of the town had been secured, Alek. We can't leave Gretchen out there. We have to get her back or she... has to die." The hesitation in her voice reminded me how much she did care for the women. How much had been sacrificed through the years to keep them safe. It didn't make it any easier. "We cannot allow Xerxes to bring forth a race of Lamassu with the ability of Seeing. The world will crumble at his feet if he succeeds." Her voice was quiet, but firm. She spoke the truth, and as much as it hurt, I knew she was right, but I still didn't think I could end Gretchen's life.

In a way, it was my fault. I had been the one who succumbed to temptation. Gretchen was my mate—whatever that really meant in a magick sense, I wasn't sure—but I could've chosen to leave Sanctuary. I could've chosen not to interfere in the destiny intricately wrapped around her life and the lives of every supernatural on the planet.

Rolling hills and grass sped along below us, no roads in sight. Only the pull of the runes called me onward through the clear blue skies. We passed a few groves of wild oaks skirting a streambed. Then the buildings of what looked like a military compound rose on the horizon. Sandbags ringed the parameter of the outpost. Large brown steel bunkers without windows were clumped together.

"He's there," Rose whispered, tightening her grip on my feathered mane. "I can feel him." Her body trembled—the only sign of fear I ever remember her showing in all the time I'd known her.

Rose's terror ripped a hole in my heart the size of the Texas sky. She'd kill Gretchen if it came down to it. I had to get to her first.

Gun shots rang through the empty Texas sky. A growl from the dragon behind me was the only warning I got to bank left and get the hell out of his way. Fire streamed from his mouth like it'd been shot from a science-fiction-style laser gun—men on the ground below us disintegrated into ash. Rose raised her hands, locking the armies into place. Paralyzing their ability to strike. To move. To escape. Eli burned them all, and I continued straight toward the largest building in the center of the compound, two stories of solid tan-colored steel.

She was there. I could feel her heartbeat pulsing with mine.

My claws struck the ground with a soft thud outside the main door.

Rose leapt from my back, keeping her hands raised and taut, channeling her magick to control as much of the camp as she could. "Find her. I can only control what I can see. Be careful."

I rushed the front door, shouldering it in with one lunge. Men—Lycans—came straight at me. Bullets flew and I felt the burn as they struck, digging deep into my body. Djinn blinked in and out, upping the bullet spray, but never staying in one place long enough for me to get a good swipe of my talons into them.

The ground shook. Eli had landed. The Drakonae's scream pierced the silence with a sound that even made my Gryphon shudder with dread. Death and fire would blanket this army. No Djinn or Lycan or witch would survive his fiery judgement.

I slashed my way through several more of Xerxes' Lycan soldiers before bursting into a dimly lit room and shifting into my human form. There were no more guards. Only three hearts beat in this room. Mine, Gretchen's, and the man's I was about to end.

Lights flickered on and off. Eli must've hit one of the compound's generators, but all I could see were Gretchen's glowing marks. The white light illuminated her bruised and bound body. A large man, easily my size, stood over her with a long knife.

"You must be Alek, so good of you to join us." His gaze fell to the matching white glow emanating from the rune marks on my arms.

"Get away from her." Something about him was familiar, but the rage inside me was all I could feel. All I could smell was Gretchen's scent. All I could taste was her fear permeating the air in the room. Pure terror. Pain. Anguish. Hatred.

I lunged, but something invisible stopped me, grabbed my neck, and slammed me into the far wall. *Lamassu magick, this was Xerxes.* I couldn't beat a Lamassu, neither in human form nor beast. His magick, like Rose's, was too powerful.

Two familiar figures barreled into the room after me. I tried to yell a warning, but my vision was waning. His magick choked me harder and harder. Air ceased to pass through my throat. I couldn't fight. Couldn't move. Couldn't help...*Gretchen.*

I could only hear my mate's cries, each one ripping a piece from my dying soul. See her tears. Watch this psychopath destroy everything I cared about.

"Xerxes." Rose's voice took on that special god-like quality and the room shook.

A flash of steel and the sound of metal slicing through the air caught my attention. The lights in the room returned. The dagger was frozen, inches from Rose's chest.

"I'm not that easy to kill."

"No, perhaps not." The tall man narrowed his dark eyes then smiled. Actually fucking smiled. "But your dragon was."

A surprised gasp slipped from Rose's mouth, and I glanced across the room. An identical dagger had pierced Eli's heart. Nothing could pierce a dragon hide—in human or beast form—nothing except dragon steel. There were so few blades on Earth, he probably hadn't thought the blade flying at his chest was a threat. That it would bounce off like a toy made of wood.

Bullets hurt dragons. Artillery pierced their skin because of the speed and the heat behind it, but a simple blade was like hitting them with a loaf of bread. It did nothing. It should've been nothing.

The Drakonae prince met my gaze, and I saw the flame

leave his eyes before he crumpled to the concrete floor. The man I'd known for a thousand years. A brave and strong and powerful friend was gone, and there was nothing either of us could do about it. A man who served and fought at my side as a brother in arms. A man who'd considered me his equal in this world.

"Eli." His name slipped from Rose's lips—a small whisper of the overwhelming grief she felt at his loss. She made no attempt to hide her emotions. Her pheromones spoke to the truth. Her eyes widened with surprise then narrowed with determination.

Eli's blood seeped from his fatal wound and stained the gray floor. My soul wept for a good man, cried for the son and mate and brother he left behind and the babies who would never know him.

I was still captive against the wall, straining to see through the black spots in my vision, watching my friend die to save the woman I loved. The woman fated to be mine. The woman I couldn't have. I wouldn't be conscious more than a few seconds longer.

"Get her now, Alek."

Rose's command tore me from my sorrow, reminded me the fight wasn't over until we'd all breathed our last.

Rose lunged at Xerxes. A white glow surrounded her. Large wings unfurled around her body as it shifted... growing and glowing with her white essence. She'd take the building down with her once she reached her full size. The room couldn't hold her. Hell, the entire building wasn't big enough to hold a shifted Lamassu.

Xerxes magick released me suddenly, his attention completely on Rose now. She was making him choose to fight on her terms or die under her claws. She was giving me a chance.

I leapt across the room, ducking one of Rose's wings before it took out the wall behind me. Xerxes was shifting now, too. So much light filled the room, it was blinding. I couldn't see, but I could smell Gretchen. Her blood. Her sweat. Her tears.

Her heart was beating slower than it should, and her breathing was shallow. I dodged another wing, this time Xerxes's. Rolling over the table, I wrapped an arm around Gretchen's body in the process. My forward momentum carried us both off the table and out from under a stomping foot. The ceiling crumbled above me, and I let my beast come out again. My eagle talons closed carefully around Gretchen, and my lion-clawed hind legs shoved me up the wall, through the falling concrete and steel and other shattering materials. The ceiling above me disintegrated, showing spots of clear blue sky. I pumped my wings, trying to ignore the snarls and the smell of blood behind and below me.

I rose farther and farther until something caught my wing and sent me hurtling toward the floor. Pumping harder, I avoided what would've been a fatal impact for Gretchen and screamed through the burning pain. Rage propelled my Gryphon's cry through the wall of the building, disintegrating it in front of me. I dove through, but not before something took a slice out of my left flank.

The roaring and bellowing and cries of pain continued behind me. I pushed harder and lifted us into the sky again, reaching for the clouds. A bullet struck my side. Then another hit my already injured wing. Pain seared through every nerve. A cry of pain from the small body clutched ever so carefully in my talons tore another piece from my heart. She'd been hit. The scent of her blood burned in my nostrils.

There was nowhere to hide. Speed was our only salvation, and my Gryphon's utter refusal to give up. I wouldn't stop. I pushed for the clouds and struggled to keep a straight path toward Sanctuary.

A painful scream echoed behind me, the unmistakable sound of Death calling another to its door.

Then nothing.

Silence.

No more gunfire.

No more crashing buildings.

I couldn't look back. I couldn't stop.

I had to get Gretchen back to the castle, back to the Protectors. Their blood would save her.

She couldn't die.

She couldn't die.

She couldn't die.

CHAPTER 21

ALEK

"Erick! Help me get them inside," Bailey's voice ran high, urgency spilling from it like a waterfall. "I can't get him to let go of Gretchen."

A whoosh of air brushed along my skin. I was vaguely aware of grass beneath me and the sounds of people yelling instructions from all sides.

"Alek let us help her. You must let her go." Erick's deep voice rumbled into my consciousness.

Let her go? "No. She's been hurt. I'll drop her." My words gurgled in my throat like I was choking. The bitter metallic taste of blood filled my mouth. I could smell it on me, around me. I could smell Gretchen's, too.

"You're on the ground. You made it back." Bailey's voice was soft and encouraging and pleading. "Please, let us help her. She's been shot, Alek, and so have you."

Shot? It was starting to come back now, the fight, seeing Eli die. Watching Rose... What had I seen? Had she made it out of there? I couldn't remember. Blackness swallowed me again.

I OPENED my eyes and groaned. Pain burned like fire in my side, and I struggled to breath. Gretchen's heart beat slowly against my chest. So weak, her life was slipping away as she lay in my arms. *No. I couldn't lose her. Not after everything that'd happened.* Not much time had passed, maybe a minute.

"Let me have her. Please, Alek," Bailey asked again. Her small hands tugged at my arm with the strength of ten men, but I still didn't relax my grip.

"Xerxes hurt her." My voice still wasn't right. It gurgled and rasped, the words barely discernible. Was I dying? My heart still beat in my chest, but all my other senses were so foggy. My vision blurred in and out.

"I know. Let go." Bailey touched my arm again, determination mixed with desperation. "I can help her."

Finally, my brain was able to get through to my tightly clenched muscles. I relaxed my grip and released my precious cargo into Bailey's waiting arms. Erick's mate was so small, but as a vampire, she rivaled even the strength my Gryphon allowed me. She hadn't used it for fear of hurting Gretchen, or perhaps in fear of startling me into another shift.

"I'm sorry." My voice was foggy, and my mind kept flashing back and forth from the present to the fight with Xerxes, the fight where Eli had died. Rose had been there, too. She'd shifted and fought Xerxes by herself. "Rose. Where is Rose?"

Erick placed his wrist over my mouth. "Drink before I dig these bullets out."

His blood seeped between my lips just before his fingers slipped inside the wound in my side. "Damn you, vampire!" I gritted my teeth and dug my fingers into the sod beneath me, willing them not to clench into a fist and slam Erick's solid body, but the desire to rip the vampire's head off flashed through my mind anyway.

"Damn me later, once you don't have lead scattered through your body like shrapnel from a bomb. You're lucky they didn't hit you with anything bigger than a rifle." My mind faded to black again. Pain seared my nerve endings, and I lost consciousness again.

MY EYES FLUTTERED open to the bright afternoon sunlight. I was still on the grass. *How much time had passed? Where was Gretchen?* Her scent had faded, and I couldn't hear her heartbeat. I vaguely remembered holding her when I'd landed. I'd made sure I took the brunt of the fall, cradling her in my wings as the ground had rushed toward us. Tired, so tired, but I needed her. I needed to know she was safe.

"Where's Gretchen?" My voice rumbled deep and gruff, like a drunk who hadn't spoken in days. Everything hurt. My body felt like it'd been run through a meat grinder.

"Bailey took her inside the castle. Bella is removing the bullet from her abdomen. Then Bailey will give her some blood to heal her. Don't worry. She will be fine. It didn't look too bad."

"Rose didn't come back." The words came out slowly,

223

not a question, just a realization. I'd already asked him once, and he'd ignored me. That could only mean she hadn't returned from Xerxes compound.

"Eli?"

I closed my eyes and took a deep breath, visualizing his bleeding, lifeless body. "No."

"I guessed as much. I'm surprised you didn't hear Diana's scream all the way out where you were. I've heard pain in my years, but never like that. Miles had to shift and go inside to keep her from leaving the castle. Brace yourself." Erick put an arm beneath my shoulders and lifted me into a sitting position.

Pain sliced through me, and I fought back the urge to vomit. *Brace yourself.* That was it, and then his damn fingers were digging between my ribs. "Fuck." I shuddered, breathing through the convulsions once Erick had removed the last bullet.

"Five." Erick licked his fingers, making noises like he'd just eaten a T-bone steak. "I got three out while you were in and out."

"Enjoying it?"

"While you do taste amazing, my friend, I was just trying to spare you some pain by hurrying to get the others out when you weren't present to enjoy it."

I nodded, appreciating the kindness. Having his fingers digging around inside my guts wasn't exactly pleasant. "Bailey better not be digging in Gretchen's body with her hands." The snarl came out like the lash of a bull whip, mostly because my whole body still burned from the gunshot wounds.

"I could've used a knife, but it's faster with my hands, and no, Bella is using pixie dust to get Gretchen's bullets out. The Lycan doctor in town was killed, and we don't have anyone else who is capable. The pixie dust is the safest method. I suppose I could've left the bullets in you and waited for Bella—"

"Shut up, Erick. Help me stand."

Erick jumped to his feet and extended a hand. My wounds were already knitting back together—thanks to the infusion of his blood. "Thank you."

He nodded. "What happened to Eli and Rose? Do you know?"

A heavy sigh slipped from my chest. "Xerxes was there. He threw a dagger at Rose and one at Eli. Rose only saw the one. It was a distraction and—"

"It worked." Erick's voice took on a pained tone. His face tightened, and his bright blue eyes flashed red for a split second. "Fucking bastard."

"Yes." *Totally agree.* I took a deeper breath as the pain in my lung faded to a dull ache. "Rose fought Xerxes, giving me a chance to get Gretchen out. Before we'd entered the compound, I heard her tell Eli that Gretchen had to be saved...or—" I couldn't say it. I still couldn't believe she would've done it, or that Eli should kill her. *He wouldn't have done it. Would he?*

"Or be killed?" Erick put a soft hand on my shoulder. "Rose was many things. She was a strong leader who made a lot of hard decisions that many of us did not understand. She was also a caring woman who lived with a broken heart. She knew you'd never be able kill the woman you loved. When it comes down to it, none of us probably could have. If it'd been Naram, she wouldn't have been able to do the noble thing, either. Mates are part of us. We're bonded at a cellular level."

"Rose is probably dead. To save Gretchen from Xerxes. I can never repay that debt, but now that she's gone and we can't continue this." I waved my hand in the air. "What are we supposed to do now? How do we finish what she started?"

"I'm not sure we can, but we have to fight or run. Xerxes will leave us no choice." He motioned toward an open set of French doors. "Come. Let's go check on your mate. Most of the fighting outside in the town has died off."

"Is everyone inside the castle?"

"Most." Erick walked ahead of me a few paces. "Some of the pixies returned to the river outside of town. Some people are here. Some are in the bunkers beneath Riley's bar or the bunker beneath the cafe. Calliope is upstairs pacing the halls with Eira, helping Miles keep Diana contained. Those are the ones I know for sure."

"What's keeping the Djinn out of the castle?"

"The four-foot-thick stone walls and the original tele-porting barrier. We're hoping they don't have any heavier artillery than we've already seen. Otherwise, the castle is coming down soon. We had a couple of Lycans jump the walls, but they were ended quickly." Erick turned to wait for me to catch up. "Did you see any artillery with that capacity where Xerxes was?"

"Yes, but Eli destroyed most of it. Everything there was ash within seconds, and if it wasn't burnt, it was running with its tail between its legs."

"Nothing in the world quite like Dragonfire, still, that couldn't have been Xerxes' entire force. How many men?"

I fell into step and continued with Erick down the open corridor to the fortified basement entrance. "There were at least a hundred, perhaps more. Not even close to the armies I imagine he's amassed by now. Perhaps one regiment."

A defeated sigh slipped from Erick's lips. "I was afraid of that."

"Did any of the Batemans survive?"

"Hannah did. Finn and Teagan got to her before that neighborhood was overrun. Harrison and Meredith were both killed. They had to knock Hannah unconscious to get her to leave them." His tone deepened, and his speech slowed, each word more painful than the last.

So many friends.

Bile rose in my throat, and I inhaled deeply. I'd known Meredith since she was a little girl, begging for piggyback rides from every giant of a man who lived in Sanctuary. She'd never been afraid of any of us, even me. A smile tugged at the corner of my mouth. After she saw me shift once, she'd called me *pretty bird* when no one else was around to hear. It had always made me laugh. She said she did it because I didn't laugh enough.

Gretchen had mentioned that, too—that I didn't laugh or smile. She was constantly trying to coax me into a *better mood.* That's what she called it, saying I was too serious.

She was right.

They both were.

I spent my life preparing for the worst, waiting for the day when I would get my vengeance, but life was more than that. Now I wanted more. I wanted to live. I would never have a chance to show Meredith I'd found someone who made me happy, but I had a chance with Gretchen, and I didn't intend to waste it.

Erick spoke several words softly and knocked on the

steel covered oak door—much like the one barring the entrance to the castle. This one was also set deep into rock and opened from the inside only. No hinges or hardware showed on the outside. There was no way to pry it open. Steel beams were used to barricade it, and I heard them being removed before the door creaked open, allowing us entrance.

Javier's blue eyes flashed, the afternoon light glinting off them in the dark. "Good to see you alive, Alek."

"You, too." I nodded to the lanky Protector.

"Nobody else?" He peered over my shoulder into the empty hallway.

Erick shook his head. "We're not positive. Rose is either dead or captured by Xerxes. She hasn't returned and—"

"We can't afford to send anyone out looking for her."

"No," Erick said, his voice soft, but laced with anger. He'd been with Rose for thousands of years. She was his leader and a friend. Her loss and the loss of the Drakonae were blows to Sanctuary that might tear it apart forever.

We walked past Javier into the dark tunnel. He shoved the heavy door closed behind us and put the three steel bars in place before turning to walk with us into the open play area of the *club* part of the castle. The play areas were filled with families huddled together—crying children and broken-hearted husbands and wives who'd lost their spouses.

The pain in their cries threatened to bring tears to my eyes. We hadn't been ready for this. It'd been a small attack. Xerxes' men had been feeling us out, and we'd been vulnerable. There were too many families, too many people to protect. Over the years, Rose had continued to take in more and more and more.

How could I have turned on her? I'd helped put them all in danger. The battle started because Xerxes had gotten his hands on Gretchen. Because Rose had chosen to once again protect the House of Lamidae against all odds and left the town. She'd made herself vulnerable to save one woman. That's how important each of the Sisters were to her, how important they should've been to me.

Instead, I'd put one above the others. I had put myself above the others.

"Quit beating yourself up, asshole," Javier said, his tone more growl than speech. "This would've happened regardless of who you decided to fuck last night."

"Javier." Erick's tone struck at Javier like a shot from a rifle.

It bounced right off the vampire sadist, though. Javier had no boundaries. He always said what he thought and did what he wanted. How Rose had convinced him to take on the Protector mantle baffled me.

"He's right, Alek. The Djinn teams had been poking holes in the town boundary for days before—"

"Does everyone in the town fucking know my personal business?"

A wicked chuckle shook Javier's chest. "Pretty much."

"Not that it wasn't easy to predict for those of us that paid attention to your routine. I'm surprised Rose didn't interfere sooner than she did. Perhaps because she knew you weren't really an obstacle until you realized how much Gretchen meant to you."

"I don't need a session with a psychologist, Erick. Where is Gretchen?" All I needed at that moment was to feel her presence. Smell her scent. Touch her. By the gods, I needed to touch her and know she was alive and well.

My memory consisted of somehow half-climbing half-flying my way out of Xerxes and Rose's Lamassu smack down before the whole building had come down around them. My wounds had weakened me, but my Gryphon made it back the twenty or so miles to Sanctuary—to the castle, and from there, my memory faded in and out.

The three of us passed by the private play rooms and then through another steel door into the living space of the Sisters. It really was like a prison down here. I'd never noticed it before, having only visited the castle club once or twice and then at night, but now, at the height of the day, it still felt heavy and dark and damp.

They lived in a dungeon. Granted, the space had brightly colored rugs, furniture, and art, but it was still windowless and cold. The fluorescent lights glared and gave of a persistent hum that probably would've driven me crazy in no time.

No wonder Gretchen spent every hour she could manage outside of the Sister's designated quarters and as high off the ground as possible. The library was on the top floor of the Castle. The only parts higher were the towers, and those weren't accessible to the Sisters.

Door after door after door. How far into this place had they taken Gretchen? "Where is she?"

"We're almost there. I can feel Bailey close now."

We swung around another corner, and Erick knocked on a closed wooden door that'd been painted bright red.

"Come in." Bailey's voice was soft on the other side of the door.

Erick turned the knob and opened the door, stepping aside so I could enter first.

"I'm headed back to the entrance. See you two later." Javier gave a half-salute and disappeared around the bend in the hallway.

I hurried through the door into a small room, furnished with a double bed, an armoire with a mirror, and a small desk in the corner. That was it. This was what her room consisted of. A few drawings had been attached to the walls and I recognized Gretchen's handiwork. She had a good eye for capturing the life below the surface. She'd drawn portraits of all three of the Blackmoors. Some of the pixies who visited the castle regularly were also among her collection. The black-and-white pencil drawings were realistic, each showing a part of the subject's character so deeply it was like she'd trapped emotions on the paper. Over her desk was a large sketch of me...reading alone in the library. It was a side portrait. My eyes were trained on the book, my faced relaxed, and just the corner of my mouth showed the beginning of a smile that I'd caught and held back.

Like I always did.

"You always fight being happy." Gretchen's voice carried softly through the room from the bed ahead of me. "I wanted to draw you with a smile, but you don't laugh enough. I couldn't see—"

"It's an amazing piece of art, Gretchen. People would give you their fortunes to have you do their portrait. Kings would woo you to their courts for your talent. You drew the truth and captured it. There is nothing to explain." I moved to the side of the bed and sat on the edge beside her, sliding my hand over hers.

She started to jerk it away, caught herself, and left her hand tensely quivering beneath mine.

I removed my hand, swallowing the dread that'd been climbing in my throat from the second I'd know Xerxes had taken her. He'd stolen her from me in more ways than one. The fireball of energy that usually exuded from her presence was missing. In its place were glazed-over sapphire eyes that barely made contact with mine.

The bruises that'd covered her face and arms and probably every inch of her were fading before my eyes. Bailey's blood was working quickly. Gretchen's clothes had already been changed, unlike mine that still showed where the bullets had torn their way through.

"You're very strong, sweet girl." Bella leaned forward and pressed a soft kiss to Gretchen's forehead. "Between the magick in Bailey's blood and my dust, you should be in tip-top shape in a matter of hours."

"Thank you." Gretchen's words were barely more than a whisper.

"I don't have to say take good care of her." The pixie met my gaze. "But I need to speak with you in the hall for just a few moments."

My body tensed. Gretchen didn't want me to touch her, but I sure as hell wasn't leaving her side again this soon.

"We'll stay until you come back, Alek." Erick's words of assurance didn't help to alleviate my irritation, but Bella wasn't backing down. She'd crossed her arms resolutely and was tapping her index finger on her bicep. Patience was not one of her gifts.

"I'll be fine, Alek." Gretchen's tone tore at my heart. She was healed on the outside, but *he* had ripped out her joy, and I didn't know what to do to even begin to put it back.

"I don't want to leave you. I never wanted to leave you." She needed to know that, that I wouldn't leave her. I'd thought I'd made it clear before, but she'd left my house hurt and betrayed by the discussion Jared and I had so stupidly had where she could overhear. It had been thoughtless, careless, and I'd nearly lost the only thing in this world I cared about.

She was right in front of me now, but I still felt the distance. The pain she'd incurred was life a knife to my gut. I knew what Bella was going to tell me.

Gretchen met my gaze and nodded.

Did she believe me? Did she still think I would choose going home over keeping her? I'd only considered sending her back temporarily, until we had the situation with Xerxes' soldiers breathing down our necks under control.

That's not going to happen. Ever. And now without Rose... I wasn't sure how we'd be able to keep him at bay at all.

I rose from the bed and followed Bella and her long blue hair through the bedroom door. She closed it gently behind us, her face long and drawn and tired.

"Do you need food?" Her naturally blue eyes were duller than they should've been, and her skin didn't glow like it always did. Instead of alabaster and healthy pink, she was white and gray and...flat. "What's wrong?"

"I need light. It's difficult to be down here for so long. I've been healing and patching up people with Bailey for hours. I'm nearly out of dust, and I need the sun like a meth addict needs their next fix." She let a soft sigh slip between her lips. "That's not why I need to talk to you."

"I know." My gut twisted again, and bile found its way into the back of my mouth.

"It was bad, Alek. She's been..." Her tone dropped, the words cracking as she tried to get them out. "She's been raped multiple times. Bailey said she scented both Lycan and Lamassu...on her."

My Gryphon raged inside me. It was my fault. If I had been listening better, she would never have gotten out of my house. They would never have found her, never have taken her. "I had her. She was safe, and then...I lost her."

Bella placed a gentle hand on my arm, and I jerked away. I didn't deserve comfort. I deserved nothing.

"She chose to run, Alek. You can't blame yourself any more than you can blame her."

"It was my fault."

Bella shook her head and lifted her hands to cup my face. Warmth. Peace. Love. Forgiveness. I couldn't describe it, but she imparted all those through her hands, magick in a touch. I pulled her hand down.

"I don't deserve any of your reserve magick, Bella. Save it for someone who really needs it."

Her eyes brightened, and she pushed her hands back up to my face—apparently, she had a little more power left than she appeared to. "I give when I see fit, and you, Alek, are in desperate need of a little peace. You won't be able to *fix* Gretchen. She will never be the same person she was before this happened. You need to be okay with that and support her as she learns to deal with the scars she carries."

"I will always love her."

"That was not what I said. I said *support*."

"Anything, Bella, she is my mate...at least—"

"She is, Alek. You wear your kind's marks. She is part of you now, but men typically try to fix. That's not what she needs."

"I will be what she needs. Rose called them mate marks, too. Do you know what they are? Or how—" I clammed up, not sure how to finish that question. The marks had appeared when Gretchen and I slept together. She'd been a virgin, but I hadn't.

Bella sighed. "I know they are unique to Gryphons. I know that they appear when a Gryphon gives his heart, and I know they will link her to you for as long as you live. It's a soul bond. That's why you can feel things when the marks are activated."

"Do you know how..."

"No. I'm afraid the intricacies of the marks were known specifically to your people."

Of course they were.

"I used to think the prophecy was all that mattered." My shoulders slumped. "Learning about my kind, taking revenge for the atrocities done to my family, but in the end, Rose sacrificed herself to save Gretchen. We can't finish the prophecy without Rose to cast the spell to open the portal." My chest tightened. The contradiction made my head pound. *Why?* "There are still two Protectors that need to be located."

A frown darkened the pixie's face, making my hands clench. There was so much about Rose no one had questioned. She took in all supernaturals who needed a home, and she gave them sanctuary. No one had ever thought to ask why...

"Above everything, even the prophecy, keeping the Sisters out of Xerxes' hands was Rose's first goal. She was truly afraid of what might happen if he succeeded in taking any of them. That is why she fought. That is why she traded herself for Gretchen."

"What if she's dead?"

"It is likely. Though I think she must've wounded him as well or our town would be overrun by now. Instead, we have quiet streets, and Calliope has said there are perhaps only two or three Djinn still hanging around."

"What do you think they are they looking for?"

"Weakness."

The Pixie's words echoed in my mind, a haunting warning of what was coming. Our fight had just started.

CHAPTER 22

XERXES

I stood silently, grimacing as my girls bandaged my abdomen. The slash marks from Rose's talons were an inch deep and stung like a bitch. Any other wound would've already healed, but these would take weeks. They would bleed and seep and burn. I could take the pain. I'd had worse.

What I couldn't comprehend was Rose's carelessness. She'd shown up to save that slip of a woman. In the overall scheme, one Sister wouldn't have slowed her little prophecy down by more than a few decades. Instead, she'd thrown herself into the fray so that fucking Gryphon could steal my prize right out from under me, literally. Even if I did get the wench pregnant, it would be years before the child would be a threat to this precious world or any other, but Rose had always been a big-picture kind of girl.

Tension twisted in the back of my neck. I rubbed it

and winced. Roshanna's talented mouth on my dick was distracting me from most of the pain as Lily was taping over one of the especially deep gashes.

"Forgive me, Master," Lily said, bowing her head. "I caused you discomfort. Should I fetch a whip?"

I caught her chin between my thumb and forefinger and raised her face until I could see her dilated eyes. My little half-masochistic-half-sadist wanted to be punished, needed it. She'd thumped my wound on purpose, hoping for some attention from my whip.

"Go to the play mat and kneel there until I return."

"Yes, Master."

"Do you want us to bandage her, too, Master?" Iris glanced up at me hesitantly from the floor at Rose's side. My brother's wife was equally carved. Her clothing hung in long, torn strips around her bloodied body. I'd gotten the upper hand in the compound, and Cal had teleported in and out, slicing up her legs with the dragon steel blade until she'd shifted back to her human form, unable to stand upright with so many wounds incapacitating her.

Plus, there was the poison. I hadn't told Cal, but the dagger he'd been given was coated in a film of dragon fire. The chemicals or magick or whatever anyone wanted to call what happened inside a fire-breather Drakonae were deadly to Lamassu. Dragon steel—the hardest steel on earth or Veil—was melted and purified for the first time beneath the heat of a dragon's breath, but during the later smelting and shaping, most of the residual poison was removed. To truly have a poisonous weapon, a finished steel sword had to be held in the fire of a Drakonae for a few seconds.

"No, don't touch her."

"What about the dagger in her chest?"

I smiled and shook my head. "If you pull it out, she'll bleed to death in a few minutes. I need her to last longer than that." Rose's heart still beat, slowly, but it continued to do my work for me— pumping the poison through her body. Every *thump thump* weakened her more. Finally I had the great Rose Hilah in the palm of my hand. She hadn't told me where the portal dagger was. In fact, she'd seemed surprised that I thought it was in Sanctuary. *Imagine that.* Her good little soldiers weren't sharing everything with their great leader. I'd stabbed her, slowly and carefully, making sure the tip of the knife nicked her heart before shoving it the rest of the way in at an angle I knew wouldn't kill her right away, knowing the blade of the knife itself was slowing the leak inside her chest.

Lamassu were resilient. Her self-healing abilities would keep her alive long enough to give me the pleasure I'd been cheated out of so many thousands of years ago.

Iris bowed and backed away from Rose's still body.

Then she helped me into a fresh shirt, and buttoned it, leaving the top one undone just the way I preferred.

I ran my hand through my damp-from-a-shower hair and shuddered, feeling my balls tighten as my body prepared to climax. I reached down and grabbed a handful of Roshanna's long, silky black hair and pounded her mouth, shoving my dick halfway down her throat. She gagged softly, but continued to massage my balls with her talented fingers as I shot my cum straight down her well-trained throat.

Once I finished, she licked my dick clean and tucked it carefully behind the zipper of my slacks. She pulled the zipper up and fastened the buckle on my leather belt, all the while licking her lips. When she finished, she bowed her head.

"Thank you, Master."

"You did well and pleased me. You're dismissed, Iris, you too."

Roshanna rose from her position on the floor at my feet, and she and Iris scurried through the side door of my suite into the small adjoining room they slept and lived in.

"Cal." I spoke loudly, making sure the Djinn on the other side of my suite door heard me. "Enter."

The tall Djinn appeared a moment later. He also had bathed and changed clothes. His cream colored tunic and pants were free from the bloodstains that'd covered us both from the fight outside Sanctuary.

"Report?"

"The camp was all but destroyed, Master. The remaining Djinn are patrolling the town, looking for an entrance to the vault you said would be within the city limits, but as of the last update I received, there has been no success locating it or the portal dagger." Cal kept his voice even and calm. A difficult task when he knew the news he delivered was not what I wanted to hear. Rose hadn't given me anything, regardless of the cutting and stabbing and torture. The bitch was tougher than she looked.

"Fetch Rahim to carry her. We're going to the tomb."

"Yes, Master." His reply carried the slightest sigh of relief.

The dagger wasn't going to walk out of Sanctuary on its own. There was time. Their barrier was down and many had died, for nothing. Their leader was bleeding to death on my floor. Soon the town would descend into chaos. It was only a matter of time before they revealed the location of the vault, and with it, the dagger she was determined to keep from my grasp.

Cal blinked away, returning a few seconds later with younger version of himself. Rahim was Cal's brother. Both men stood at an intimidating six-and-a-half feet tall with dark hair and shoulders that could carry grown men without a second thought. They were strong and quick and loyal to a fault. Though that probably had everything to do with the fact that I had their sister and youngest brother locked away safely in a *quppa* box.

I did love a tightly knit family. Emotions made people weak. Family made them even weaker and easier to manipulate.

"Master." Rahim bowed low.

"You take her, and be careful not to jostle the dagger next to her heart." I waved at Rose's body.

"Yes, Master."

Cal stepped forward and extended his hand, waiting for me to clasp his wrist before we would teleport to the tomb where I kept my own brother chained and wasting away, one millennia at a time.

I wrapped my fingers around his wrist, and then we blinked. Space folded around us in a rush of color and speed that made my stomach jump. Then we were there, in the dark tomb beneath what used to be the grandest city on this fucking planet—Babylon.

It had truly been one of the greatest wonders of the world. I'd felt the smallest splinter of remorse when I'd betrayed the city to the Horde. The poison I'd provided them had killed my entire race, except for Rose and Naram. Those two crafty Sentinels had evaded the barbarian soldiers and stolen the Sisters out of the temple without a sound.

Cal lit several torches on the wall, pulling one down to light the way. I crossed to the half of the palatial room that housed my dying brother. Rahim followed silently, blinking with Rose closer and closer and closer, working hard to keep her body steady in its precarious position.

"There." I spoke clearly, allowing my voice to carry through the large room. Walking to them, I knelt down and wrapped my fingers around the hilt of the dagger in her chest.

Rahim stepped back to stand next to Cal a few feet away.

"Naram, you should drag your decrepit body out here to say goodbye to your mate."

"Fuck you, brother." Naram's shout was more forceful than I'd expected after seeing him last time. The food from my last visit must've really helped raise his energy level.

"She's the one that's fucked." I pulled the dagger from her chest, and Rose moaned softly, opening her eyes to meet my gaze directly. "You will die beneath the city you loved so dearly and with the man you loved more than anyone else on the Earth, but he will live on, seeing you rot and decay until only your bones remain to remind him of what he lost. Of what he could not save."

"You're a bastard," she whispered, fighting for breath, fighting against the blood that would slowly drown her. The poison from the dagger would hinder her natural healing abilities.

Chains scraped the floor across the room, and Naram's beastly form advanced slowly, each step a painful effort.

242

The shackles had long since created sores on his ankles and paws. His head hung low, also chaffed and bloody from the dragon steel collar around what used to be a well-muscled neck. Now, he was thin and weak, hollowed from malnutrition and atrophied from limited movement.

"Rose." He strained against his chains, leaning into the shackles and re-opening old wounds. Desperation strained his gaunt face in his futile effort to reach his mate.

I'd had Rahim place her just out of reach. The need to touch her, comfort his mate, hold his wife—everything inside him was driving him further over the edge of madness.

"I couldn't feel you." Rose's voice broke with emotion. "Why couldn't I feel you? I felt the connection between us die thousands of years ago." A sob tore through her chest, rattling through her liquid-filled lungs like a pinball in an arcade game. She coughed, spewing blood onto the floor. "I would've kept looking. I'm so sorry."

"Shh, it doesn't matter now." Naram knelt on the floor, stretching his lion's neck as far as he could. Not far enough. She still remained at least three feet from even feeling his breath on her face. He shifted to his bedraggled human form and stretched his arm toward her—still unable to breach the distance between them. "I love you, Rose. You are mine."

"And you are mine."

I rolled my neck back and forth, enjoying the show of pathetic emotion. The torture on both their faces had been well worth the wait and effort of keeping Naram chained and on the edge of life for all these years. He'd died on the inside the day I told him I'd killed Rose, and now he would die a little more each day. Every time he looked at her body, he would blame himself for not being enough.

My brother's downfall had been hoping he could get through to me, but Rose...Rose had been a worthy adversary, and a frustrating one. This was my reward, and I reveled in it. In the smell of her blood staining the floor. In the scent of death hanging over her like a shroud from Tartarus, waiting to carry her to the afterlife.

She would trouble me no longer. My vengeance was complete. What they'd taken from me was irreplaceable, and now Rose was balancing the scale with her death. Once Naram joined her in the underworld, I would focus solely on conquering the humans, one pathetic country at a time.

All would bow to me on Earth.

Then all would bow to me on Veil.

Even those fucking Drakonae pricks who thought they were invincible. Just because they'd taken down the Blackmoor dynasty didn't mean they would have a shot in hell against me and my army.

Once the time arrived.

Once my children were born.

CHAPTER 23

GRETCHEN

*N*othing hurt. My body was healed. Bailey's blood and Bella's pixie dust had done their work. I should be fine. I felt fine. I felt like I could jump off my bed at any moment and run from the room.

But I didn't.

I just stared uncomfortably at Bailey and her mate Erick. Pulling the covers up to my neck, I shifted to my side and stared at the wall instead. Bailey looked like she wanted to talk. I didn't want to talk. I just wanted to forget.

Forget the pain. Forget the terror. Forget how stupid I'd been for leaving Alek's house. Forget how stupid I'd been for not listening to Rose's warnings, to all of their warnings. Even Alek had said it was dangerous, but I hadn't listened. I'd ignored them all, and I'd paid the price.

Those men, that man. Everyone who'd touched me had

hacked a piece of my soul away. I didn't hurt because I couldn't feel anything anymore.

And I didn't want to.

I'd pulled away from Alek like he was diseased. I'd seen the pain and hurt in his eyes, but I didn't care. I couldn't care. He couldn't fix me. No one could fix me. No one could take away this sick feeling in the pit of my stomach, this ball of blackness and guilt that twisted and rolled and threatened to overtake me.

"Give it time," Bailey said, her voice soft and tender in the silence of the room.

She didn't know anything about me. *Time? Really? Time would erase the memory of those men's hands on my body, of them using me and hurting me and torturing me for their pleasure and amusement? Really? Time. That's all.*

"Leave me alone."

"I promised Alek we'd stay till he returned."

I threw the covers off my body and sat up. "Get. Out." My voice sliced through the small room, surprising even me with its ferocity.

"If you ever want to talk, I've been there." Bailey continued like I hadn't just shouted at the top of my lungs. Like my outburst meant nothing.

"You don't know what I went through." Tears burned at the corners of my eyes. *No. No. No.* I didn't want to feel it. I couldn't. It was too hard. It was better to be still and silent and feel nothing. Why wouldn't she just let me feel nothing?

"I was raped, too. Tortured, beaten, hunted. The list goes on, Gretchen. So yes, I do know a little about what you are going through." She whispered something to Erick, and he left Bailey's side and slipped out my bedroom door, leaving just the two of us...alone.

"I don't want to talk about it. I want to forget it. Tell me how to forget it. How to not feel their hands sliding up and down my skin. How not to feel where they slapped me. How not to feel the—" My throat closed up, and I couldn't finish the sentence. "I deserved what I got. I ignored everyone's warning."

"Don't you dare." Bailey's voice struck like a whip.

I flinched and turned away from her again. Tears poured uncontrollably down my cheeks again. "I snuck out. I left Alek's house. I left the safety of the castle. I didn't believe that it could be as bad as they said."

Bailey moved to sit beside me, careful to keep her body from touching mine. "No one deserves what happened to you. Don't ever think that. Not for a single moment."

"You could make me forget." I turned to meet her intense gaze. "I just need to forget. I can't live like this, with this."

"You can't heal if you forget."

"I don't want to heal. I want to forget. The Protectors make the men forget us when they leave here after the *joinings*. How is this different?"

Bailey's mouth tightened, and her gaze dropped to the floor. "Influencing someone takes something away. Magick always comes with a price. Erasing trauma could erase more than you want to part with. It's not worth the risk."

"That's my choice."

"No." Bailey's voice firmed again, becoming harsher, less comforting and more insistent. "I can't do it anyway. I'm not strong enough, and I haven't learned how." She stood from my bedside and walked to the door. "Plus, you have something I didn't have for a really long time."

I scoffed, flopping back onto my pillow.

"You're not alone."

My breath caught in my throat, and I choked on the angry words I wanted to spit back at her. *Alone.* I might not be alone in this exact moment, but I would be. Another crisis would come and what happened to me would be old news. Unimportant. Irrelevant. But I didn't yell or scream. I just let the deadness inside me swell and quiet the pain.

Just because she wouldn't help me—couldn't help me—didn't mean the other Protectors would refuse me as well.

The door opened and closed. I could smell him before he rounded the foot of the bed and stepped into my line of sight. "Can I get you another blanket?"

"No."

"I want to hold you." His brown eyes begged for permission, but I couldn't. The thought of anyone touching me sent a sliver of terror down my spine like the sharp tip of a blade being dragged slowly from my neck to the curve of my lower back. I could still feel the blade. I *had* felt it, but it hadn't been steel. It'd been the tip of a talon or claw, and it'd reminded me of Alek and our night —that one wonderfully perfect night, forever trapped and locked away in the back of my mind—but now...now I couldn't...I couldn't let him touch me.

I didn't want him to see my fear. I didn't fear him, but I was terrified of what my memories would do to him. How they would hurt him. Make him feel guilty. He didn't deserve to feel guilty. No matter what Bailey said, I knew what'd happened to me was my fault.

Not his.

Only mine.

And I would have to live with it, at least for now.

"Gretchen?"

I glanced up, meeting his pained expression. His shoulders were slumped forward, and his hands were clenched at his sides. The tendons in his neck strained, and his cheek twitched, stress showing in the muscles of his jaw.

"No." I couldn't explain past that, not without letting it all out, and I wasn't ready to do that.

He sank into the chair at my desk and ran his hand over the worn fabric cover of *Little Women*. Without a word, he picked it up and turned to the first page. His voice rumbled softly. " 'Christmas won't be Christmas without any presents,' grumbled Jo, lying on the rug.'"

Anger surged through my chest, burning across my ribcage like a firestorm. I wanted to scream and tell him to put it away. That book was my safe place. It had been my favorite story since the very first year I'd met him in the library when I was eleven. He'd placed it in my hands after returning from a mission that had kept him from Sanctuary for over two weeks—a mission that had made him miss my birthday and our annual reading of the story. Now he was reading it while I was broken and angry and scared. He was ruining it.

"Stop." My voice broke. I climbed from the bed and ripped the book from his hands. "You can't fix this with a story." I hugged the book to my chest, tears burning trails of fire down my cheeks.

"I don't want to fix you. I just want you to feel safe. This book has so many good mem—"

"And I don't want them tainted with this." I waved my

hands in the air. "I'm ruined, broken, dirty, and I won't let you destroy the memory of this book by mixing it into...this."

His cheek flexed, and I saw his arms move, but I couldn't react. Not fast enough. Those big strong limbs of his wrapped around my shaking, angry body, and I screamed, terror overwhelming everything inside me that wanted him to touch me. That wanted his comfort. I couldn't. Not yet, maybe not ever.

He released me instantly, and his voice shook as he spoke. "You are strong, and I love you, and you are mine."

I backed away from him, shaking my head. "It hurts too much. I can't live this way."

"I will do anything to help you, Gretchen. I would die right here, right now to save you from another second of agony. Please don't call yourself ruined or dirty. You aren't those things. You are my beautiful mate with sunshine in her heart and a smile on her lips. You are everything to me and always will be. No matter what you choose to do, I support you."

"You heard me." I climbed to the center of my bed, wrapping myself in my blanket like the cocoon of fleece would somehow insulate me from anything outside of my bedroom.

"I did, and I want you to know it is your choice. I want you to feel safe and whole. I don't want you to suffer a moment longer than you have to, and if what you want is to forget, then I'll find someone who will do that for you, but if *you* make the choice to heal on your own, I am with you. You are brave, even if you don't believe it. You are strong, even if you feel weak. Bailey was right about one thing."

"What?"

"You are not alone."

I curled into my bed, contemplating his words. Exhaustion claimed me a few minutes later, and I drifted to sleep, knowing he was watching over me from across the room.

WHEN I WOKE AGAIN, my room was once again inhabited by a Protector. This time it was Javier.

His blue eyes glinted at me, cold and discerning. He had no affection for me. No affection for anyone. All the Sisters called him an asshole and a sadist. One of the Sisters was into that kind of masochism, but mostly, he played with a few of the unattached Lycan females in town. I'd seen a few of his scenes over the years. For a fleeting moment, I wondered if the pain of his lash would erase the pain in my heart. Maybe Bailey was right, maybe there was a way to heal without erasing anything.

"It won't." He crossed his arms and frowned. "Hiding from pain with more pain is like slapping a Band-Aid on a stab wound. It might cover the hole, but the wound beneath will rot and kill you all the same."

"How did you know what I was thinking?"

"Everyone who goes through trauma thinks about it. I made the mistake of using a woman once who wanted to hide from emotional pain by burying herself in physical pain, but I'll not be making it again."

"What happened to her?"

"She had to face her shit."

"You're an ass." The words tumbled out before I could stop them. I'd never been so purposefully ugly. I wanted to hurt him.

"So I've been told." He chewed on the inside of his cheek and cocked his head toward the hallway. "Still doesn't change the fact that you tried to talk Bailey into whitewashing your brain, which she can't do, by the way."

"I know. Will you do it?"

He nodded, and a strange fluttering of excitement made my hands tremble. "Alek sent me in here to talk to you. First, do you care about Alek at all?"

My chest clenched, and I turned from Javier's hard gaze. My heart pounded in my chest. Of course I did. I loved Alek more than anything in the entire world, but I was so scared that I couldn't think straight. It was irrational, but it was my reality. I didn't want to be scared, but I was. That's why I was trying to get my brain reset. "I'm so scared."

"Of him?"

"Of how his Gryphon reminds me of—" I couldn't say it. I couldn't compare him to that monster. They both had talons the size of my fingers, though Alek would never hurt me. I knew that. Deep down in my soul, I knew he would never...but I couldn't shake the memory of Xerxes. Of the way he'd used that against me. The way he'd compared himself to Alek. He'd purposefully planted the similarity in my mind, and now I couldn't shake it.

"I'll take that as a yes." He crossed to the door and opened it. "There are some things we need to discuss before you make this choice. Bailey didn't lie when she said magick comes with a price."

Alek walked in, his face somber and etched with pain. "Please give us a moment." Alek's tone was soft, beaten.

"No, don't leave." Each word a struggle. Another man.

I was surrounded by men, but I needed him to help me. I needed him to fix me.

I winced, pulling my comforter tighter around my shoulders. Javier's words stung with truth, but this was the best option. I didn't see an end to the pain or the fear. I couldn't live and be afraid of the man I loved. Everything had been perfect, was perfect, until it wasn't.

I'd ruined it with my stupid choices.

Now when I looked at Alek, I saw the beast first instead of the man. A scary beast, not the beast that I'd found amazing and strong and wondrous, and now I didn't want to be touched.

"I'm sorry." Alek knelt at the side of my bed, setting down a fresh glass of water.

"I need you to move away from me." My voice shook with each word. I trembled from the tips of my fingers to the end of my toes. Every few seconds I would steal a glance at his hands, waiting for them to change into the deadly talons I knew existed beneath his human facade. My mind had created a monster where my heart knew it didn't exist. It wasn't fair.

He nodded and backed away from the bed, taking up residence once more in my desk chair. "I'm sorry about earlier. I shouldn't have. I'm so sorry. I just needed to touch you, and I thought if you could just feel our connection—"

"I want to forget. I can't live like this. When I think someone is going to touch me, I freak out. I feel them, Alek. I feel their hands and...everything. I'm not strong enough to heal on my own."

"Javier."

The vampire stepped toward the bed again.

Alek turned back to me. "I told you I would die to save you from another moment of suffering. I meant what I said. You are more important than anything to me in this entire world. This can heal you. This can take away your pain. This can give you back your life, your spirit, everything. If this is what you need, I want it for you with my whole heart."

Relief flooded through me. We could just go back to that night, to when the world was perfect and right. There were no monsters behind my closed eyelids, behind every sound, in every touch.

Javier took a seat on the other edge of the bed. "I have to touch your head to do this."

I swallowed my fear and nodded, inching closer until I was within arms-length of him. This would be worth it. I could do this. I could handle his touch long enough to give me a second chance to be in love with Alek, to belong to him the way I'd wanted for so long.

Javier placed his fingertips on my scalp and temple. "Look directly into my eyes."

"Okay."

"Before I start, I have to warn you. This is not an exact science. There's always a chance that more will be taken than what you might want to lose."

"What do you mean?" A new fear shot through my body. I'd lost so much. Losing this pain felt like the answer, but the tone in Javier's voice stilled my heart.

"You might not feel the same way about Alek after this. You might not love him. You might not remember things about him. Memories are tricky, and taking them away is one of the most challenging things a vampire can attempt. We don't really worry about the men who come back and forth to the castle. They're expendable to some extent."

I glanced at Alek, expecting him to call the whole thing off. Part of me wanted him to make that choice for me. On one hand, I wanted nothing more than to forget all that had happened to me since I crawled out his bathroom window. On the other, I didn't want to lose him. What if I forgot him and was left with this aching hole in my heart that I couldn't explain or fix?

"You won't lose me, Gretchen, no matter what. Even if we have to fall in love all over again, you have my heart. Rose said that's why the marks came. Part of my soul is inside you, and part of yours is in me. That's the light that shines when the marks glow. We are forever bound. Memories or not, I will always love you."

My stomach twisted, and my fingers shook in my lap. He was right...we could fall in love again, would fall in love again. Like he said, we were bonded. These marks on my collarbone linked us at a level I didn't even pretend to understand.

"Look into my eyes." Javier's voice cut through my whirling thoughts.

I snapped my gaze to his and then jerked away from his hands. *No.* "No. I can't. I won't risk losing you, Alek." Tears welled in my eyes. "I don't know how I'm going to get through this. I don't know when I'll be ready to touch you or anyone else again...ever."

"Are you sure?" He came out of the chair and squatted beside the bed. "Javier can make it so you don't have to live with any of it. Even if you lose some of our memories, we can start fresh. It will be okay."

"No. I can't lose you, too. They took my dignity and

my confidence and most of my sanity. The only thing I still have in my life that's good is you. If this magick backfires and steals that good away along with the bad, then I'll lose the only thing that ever mattered to me." I backed away from Javier and wrapped myself into my comforter again. "As scared and confused as I am, I'm still not willing to live *without* our memories."

"I'll let you guys talk." Javier stood and left the room, closing the door behind him.

"I'm going to need time. I can't even begin to guess, but I—"

"It doesn't matter, Gretchen. Anything you need, for as long as you need, no matter what."

"What if I'm always scared? What if I can't get past it? Ever?"

"It doesn't matter. I will love you forever."

I nodded, trying to make myself believe the promise he'd declared more than once, but my head was swimming, and I needed to be alone, at least for now. "I need to sleep. I'm so tired."

He stood and started to reach for me, but stopped his hand halfway. "Do you want me to stay? Or send someone else to sit with you?"

"I just want to be alone for a while."

He nodded. "Of course." His words were soft, but I could still hear the worry lacing the edge of his tone. "I'll check on you in a little while."

I lay down, buried my face in my pillow, closed my eyes, and waited for him to leave. When the door opened and shut, I opened them again and glanced around the room. He had left. Just as he'd said he would.

Relief and sadness swelled in my body at the same

time. Nothing about the choice I'd made was going to be easy. I had to be okay with that. I had to be okay with taking it slow. I had to trust that he was telling the truth. That he was okay with slow, too. My gut said he wasn't lying, but I still worried. I couldn't help it.

I was broken. Even if I managed to glue all the pieces back together, the cracks would always show. They would be part of me.

Forever.

CHAPTER 24

ALEK

I opened the door onto the main club area of the castle basement floor and nearly collided with Bella.

"How is she?"

"She chose not to erase the memories." My chest tightened painfully, and my heart pounded behind my ribs, reminding me how much I'd wanted her to choose what I'd thought would be the easiest way for her to heal, to move on. To somehow be okay with something that would never be okay.

I gritted my teeth against the tears welling in my eyes and the overwhelming urge to fall apart. How was I going to handle never touching Gretchen? I'd almost reached for her when I left. I knew I'd do it again. I needed her, craved her touch. "I told her that no matter what she needed, no matter how long it takes, I will be there for her."

Bella tipped her head to the side and met my gaze, her blue eyes filled with compassion and understanding. The pixie said it would be hard. She'd warned me this could happen.

"You need to let it out. Go fly, Alek. For a few minutes at least. You're no good to Gretchen or yourself or anyone here depending on you in this state."

My body shivered from head to foot. My Gryphon wanted to scream, wanted to weep, but I couldn't show weakness. I didn't want those damn soldiers to report back to Xerxes that he'd won.

He hadn't won.

We were still here, and we were still capable of fighting. That bastard wasn't going to get away with this, with any of this.

"I won't be gone long."

Bella nodded.

I hurried through the rest of the club area, up through the ground level entrance, and out into the green space and courtyard of the castle.

"Alek." Jared's voice carried across the open space.

I turned toward my friend. Calliope stood at his side along with Bailey and Erick. Her eyes were red from tears, but her mouth was hard and the tips of her fingers were blackened from her claws straining to get out.

"What?" I asked, crossing the lawn to join them.

"We're going to get Eli's body," Calliope said, her voice tight and drawn like the string on a crossbow.

We were all on edge. I only needed the smallest excuse, and I knew I'd explode.

"And Rose's, we need to bury them. They shouldn't be left in the open."

259

"Let's go." I leaned forward, putting my hands on the grass, and called my Gryphon forward. I shifted over the span of a few moments then shook my head, ruffling the feathers along my neck.

I leapt into the air, pumping my wings, and watched the others jump the wall. Erick grabbed Jared around the waist, and Bailey looped an arm around Calliope's waist, following Erick's lead. Both vampires cleared the high stone walls with their passengers in fluid movements that appeared effortless. Once clear, they moved swiftly through the town with the unnatural speed only a vampire possessed. I flew hard, but wouldn't have had a chance in hell of keeping up had they not been purposefully running at a slower pace I could match.

There were no signs of any remaining Djinn or Lycan soldiers, not in Sanctuary or the surrounding areas. For the time being, they'd pulled away.

About ten minutes later, we reached the scarred and burnt encampment where Xerxes had been holding Gretchen. There were no signs of any soldiers, a blessing and a curse. I was glad not to have to fight, but I wanted to rip them to shreds. Not today.

Today was for our fallen comrades. Today was for mourning what we'd lost.

Swooping low, I landed in front of the collapsed building where I'd seen Eli die, his body lay beneath the rubble. I opened my beak and shrieked, the sound waves barreling through the broken bits of concrete and wood and steel. It moved slightly, and I loosed another cry, this time with enough sonic force to blow half the rubble a dozen yards backward.

Bailey and Erick rushed forward, moving the smaller

pieces of concrete and steel beams like they were made of plastic. A few moments later, Erick climbed out of the center of the destroyed building with Eli's body in his arms.

"What about Rose?" Calliope asked, climbing over a large piece of crumbled concrete.

"Her body isn't here. I found traces of her blood everywhere, but he must've taken her body," Erick said, his tone angry. "Bastard won't even let us bury our dead."

"Maybe she's not dead." Bailey crossed the rubble to stand next to Erick. "We don't know for sure. Alek left when she was still alive."

I nodded my large head, affirming her statement, and then pawed the ground, motioning to Eli's body.

Erick laid the mangled, beaten body of my friend on the ground in front of me, and I pumped my wings just enough to lift myself a few inches from the ground. I scooped up Eli's body with my front legs and tucked him tightly against my chest. Then I rose into the air, hovering long enough to make sure the rest of the group was headed back with me.

Erick and Bailey each grabbed their respective passengers and blurred across the landscape, though not going as quickly as they could have. They matched my flight speed, and we returned to the castle courtyard with haste.

Diana and Miles were waiting. The Drakonae female's cries for her fallen husband gave voice to the pain and anger still raging inside me. No matter what I told myself, I continued to blame myself for not moving faster, seeing more, or realizing what Xerxes was doing before it happened.

Rose and Eli were monumental losses to the town.

Eli left behind a brother, a pregnant mate, children who would never know their father.

Rose left behind a town. Without her direction and magick, I wondered how we would survive. She was the glue that'd held us all together. Now that she was gone—though without a body, there was hope—what was the next step? The Sisters' visions had been spotty at best before Gretchen left. Now without our leader, there was no way they'd be able to find the last two Protectors. Not that finding them would do any good. Rose was the only one who could enchant the tattoo that would link them to the other Protectors.

I laid Eli's body gently on the grass and backed away, giving Diana and Miles as much space as they needed. Pushing my Gryphon back, I stood in human form again.

Miles glanced over his shoulder and mouthed a 'thank you', his face dark and his cheeks wet from tears. Diana was hunched over Eli's body sobbing while Miles kept a hand on the small of her back. She worked frantically, using the fabric of her skirt to clean away the dirt and blood and bits of rubble sticking to him.

The air around us was icy, and frost had crept across the green lawn, tipping each blade of grass with white. Within a few minutes, the castle walls had turned white, and ice continued to form and grow and expand above the walls, closing over the courtyard like a frosted glass dome.

I shivered, and rubbed my bare arms, but remained still along with all who had come outside to pay their respects. Diana wasn't the only one crying over the loss we'd just been dealt. A few more minutes dragged by before Miles pulled Diana off Eli and lifted his brother from the ground.

"Thank you for bringing him back to us." Diana's words choked in the back of her throat. Her pain bled from her like sweat on a hot summer day. She rotated her hands in the air, and ice rose from the ground, creating an altar between us and her. It grew to waist height with a hollow in the center large enough to put...

I sucked in a quick breath, surprised when Miles placed his brother's body in the hollow.

She didn't stop. Ice continued to form and grow and cover Eli's body until he was expertly encased in a thick brick of crystal clear ice—safe from the elements and anything else that might disturb him.

Eira stepped forward and embraced her friend. She and Diana had bonded on the journey to Sanctuary and were never far apart. Had it not been for Eira finding her Killían —her mate—she would've lived in the castle with the dragon queen.

Miles stepped forward and spoke aloud. "This will protect his body until we are able to take him home."

To Veil? My eyebrows weren't the only ones in the group that shot up to full mast.

"When...how..." Eira asked the question all of us wanted to know.

"Soon."

The raven-haired vampire turned to her Elvin mate with a question on her lips, but no words spilled from them. The Elf didn't respond, either, but there was a mutual understanding that passed between them. They all shared a secret.

The only way home right now was with one of the daggers of Orin, which meant they'd gotten their hands on the one that had opened the portal and allowed Diana to pass through to the world of Earth.

"Miles, you can't leave us," Jared said, his voice rough and gravelly. "We've fought side by side with you for centuries. We owe Rose and Eli more than a cowardly retreat."

"Eira, Killían," Miles said, his voice calm and less emotional than it had been only moments before. "Please take Diana inside. I don't want her in the open." He kissed Diana on the top of her white-blond hair and sent her inside with the Eira and her Elvin mate. Both women had rounded bellies, and every male in the castle would die before they allowed a single blow from the battle coming to darken the door where the two mothers-to-be were staying.

"We will not leave you, Jared, but we are leaving. Rose is gone, and this fight has already taken my brother."

"A lot of us have died." A male Lycan I didn't know by name stepped forward. "I've lost two brothers and several cousins. Loss is not yours solely to claim."

Heat flared from Miles, and his eyes showed the Drakonae fire burning within them. "Will your loss turn you into a raging murderous beast with no soul that lives only to kill everything in its path? That is what will happen if I or Diana falls. You will be saddled with a full-sized Dragon that hates all living things on the face of the Earth."

The Lycan didn't respond, but he did step back into the quiet ranks where his kind had gathered in the corner. Mikjáll stepped up to the altar of ice and laid a hand on the cold tomb.

"We can't stay here. We're trapped and cornered. This

castle will be a tomb for us all if we do." Mikjáll pressed his forehead to the ice and then moved to stand at his father's side, his tone solemn and filled with finality. "There are too many to carry to the portal. Not enough of them fly. We're not like Xerxes, aided by an army of teleporting psychopaths."

"Not all the Djinn are evil. I'm not leaving without Manda," Jared spoke again, breaking the uncomfortable silence. "She deserves a chance."

"Because she didn't die in your fire?" Mikjáll shot back, a flash of anger bright in his gaze. "That shouldn't earn her anything. According to what I've heard, she has enough betrayals under her belt to deserve anything coming her way."

Jared snarled and his eyes burned. The ice surrounding him melted to water, and the frost on the closest walls turned liquid and ran into puddles on the stones of the courtyard floor.

"Enough," I growled. "Even now, he's winning, turning us against each other. Getting you to abandon people you've spent centuries protecting—"

"What about Sochi's child? That monster still has her. You promised to help us." A small slip of a woman, holding a sleeping baby in her own arms, stepped forward, Riza— the Kitsune who'd been rescued during our mission to save Charlie. Her dark eyes flashed. "Like the Gryphon says, how can you just leave? There are so many who still need your help. Without Drakonae, how do we stand a chance against that madman? You would abandon us all to die, one slow death at a time."

"One mistake," Miles said, his tone soft but sharp. "One more mistake. One slip turns my mate into a homi-

cidal killer. You and everyone in this castle would die. She
would either eat you or encase you in an icy tomb. Xerxes
has already shown his hand. He possesses dragon steel and
was crafty enough to surprise my brother. Do you really
want me to take that chance with your life, with the lives
of everyone seeking sanctuary in this fortress?" He waved
his hand at the large group of Lycans standing next to a
huddled group of Sisters. "What choices do I have? Leave
now and pray that you survive, or risk being Xerxes next
target and die knowing my mate will kill all of my closest
friends?"

"Diana, stop. Please." Eira's voice cut across the
courtyard.

Diana returned to Miles' side. Her tall, silvery figure
cut a breathtaking view against the snow and ice back-
drop. Her hair was the color of the snow, and her silver
dress shimmered with iridescence. Calliope had made it
especially for her, and it was stunning. Fit for the queen
she had been and the queen I knew she would be again
one day.

Her bright blue eyes blazed with a white fire exclusive
to Drakonae born as ice-breathers. "We can't leave *our*
friends, Miles," Diana said, standing next to her mate.
"There's no way we can get them all out. So that option is
invalid, and I know we said we'd leave if Rose was ever
lost, but we can't." She shook her head. "They are all right.
Perhaps our home is Veil, but your heart belongs here in
this town. I haven't been here long, but I already love
these people." Diana waved her had across the
mismatched crowd. "These are our people, our family. If
we can't take them home when we go, who will stand with
us against the Incanti? I know better than to believe an

army is waiting for our return, to help us storm the city of Orin and take back what belongs to us."

Miles slipped an arm around his mate and stared at her round belly for several long, silent moments before looking up and meeting my gaze then, and the waiting hopefulness of everyone in the courtyard. He rubbed his hand over the stubble on his chin and sighed—still not convinced. Still at war over protecting his mate versus risking everything to save the town and the people of Sanctuary.

The soft crunch of shoes on fresh snow drew my focus from Miles' battle of indecision. My chest heaved, pain twisted through my gut. I wanted to rush to her side, but I didn't. My skin itched, and my Gryphon paced, groaning and growling with anger. She shouldn't be out here. She should be safe beneath the surface of this stone fortress. Hell, we all should. We shouldn't be standing beneath a dome of ice, discussing our plans like we had a chance, Drakonae or not. I'd seen what Xerxes had. We didn't have a shot in fucking hell if he came at us with his full force.

Gretchen moved slowly from behind the group of Sisters with Javier walking a few paces after her. Astrid stepped forward to stop her, but Javier threw the Oracle a snarl that stopped her dead in her tracks. He might be known as the asshole Protector, but he was an asshole on our side, and I was damn glad.

"Gretchen?"

She straightened and turned to face the group, standing at my shoulder but not touching. It would've taken so little effort to lean an inch to the right and brush my arm against hers. She was so close I could feel the warmth from her skin. Our hearts synced up in seconds, and I breathed a small sigh of gratitude. I could be what she needed. I'd promised to be what she needed, no matter what.

"We have to fight. We can't let him win. If you go to your world, he will follow you. Maybe not today, maybe not for a hundred years, but he will come, and he will use us to create a race of Lamassu that will help him achieve that goal. He will be stronger than ever before."

"We have the only key on this side of the portal. He'll have no way to get through once we go and take it with us."

"You don't think he has Djinn guarding the portal? Lycans? Witches? What else does he have that you don't know about?"

Miles' mouth gaped open for a split second and then snapped shut.

"Your mate is wise beyond her years, Alek." Diana offered a compassionate glance toward Gretchen. The Drakonae queen turned to Miles. "She's right. This fight isn't over until he's dead. We already have one war waiting for us on the other side of that portal. Do you want to always be waiting for a war to follow us through as well?"

Gretchen slipped her hand into mine and squeezed.

The smallest gesture meant the most. I could feel her fear, her hesitation, but she reached for me. It was more than I deserved. I'd failed her, and she'd still chosen me. After everything she'd endured, she chose not to endanger her memory of me even if it meant forgetting all the pain and suffering *he'd* caused. Through all the darkness, she'd reached for the light. My heart bloomed with hope that hadn't existed moments ago.

The marks on my arms glowed beneath my thin t-shirt.

Hers glowed brightly beneath her dress, some shining from her exposed collarbone. Strength unlike anything I'd felt radiated from her, from the love that we shared. From the love we would rebuild even stronger than it'd been at the start.

She glanced to Miles then Diana, then let her gaze pass over everyone in the courtyard. Murmurs of support echoed through the quiet space.

"We fight together. And we take him down once and for all. Together." Gretchen's voice rang like a trumpet through the courtyard and echoed back at us from the dome overhead.

Everyone nodded. Everyone echoed their determination. "Together."

We fight.

CHAPTER 25

GRETCHEN

I'd touched his hand, and the world hadn't shattered around me. He hadn't turned into a clawed monster. His hand had been warm and soothing to my tired nerves. The town had quieted for the night. *The calm before the storm.*

People were everywhere in the castle. Sleeping bags lined the hallways. Even the Sister's quarters and the club space in the secure lower floor were filled with displaced families from throughout Sanctuary. Footsteps were a constant on the stone floors. The patrols never ended.

Alek had squeezed my hand and gone with Miles, Diana, and several others who made up Rose's trusted circle. They'd disappeared into Miles' office, and I'd retreated to the farthest corner of the library, our favorite couch. The fabric held just enough of Alek's scent to make it seem as though he were there.

The cushions dipped next to me and I startled, not realizing until that moment that I must've been drifting in and out of sleep. I drew my legs beneath me and hugged the afghan tighter to my chest. The temperature of the castle had plummeted since Diana had covered the fortress in a dome of ice. The supernaturals didn't seem to care, but I could see each breath as I exhaled. The two pairs of socks, jeans, two sweatshirts I'd grabbed before giving my room to a displaced family of five were just barely cutting the chill in the air. The heavy blanket helped, but the second he sat down, warmth enveloped me.

I opened my eyes and squinted in the dim light. Night had fallen and only the soft yellow glow of the wall sconces broke through the dark shadows of the great room.

Alek's presence was like a magnet, pulling us together each time we came close. Our glyphs glowed bright for a few seconds, reminding me that we were bonded. We were one, and I could *feel* everything...including the fact that his body ran at least ten degrees hotter at the core than mine.

Along with that warmth, there was a cocktail of pain, regret, and hope.

"I can move," his deep voice rumbled, agony stressed in each word.

Part of me wanted to climb onto his lap and bury my face in shirt. Feel the power beneath his strong muscles cradling me, caring for me, loving me. Alek loved me. I could see it each time those beautiful brown eyes glanced my direction—the way they were looking at me now, glinting with possession in the flickering lamplight. His was an all-consuming passion reserved only for me, but tethered, waiting patiently. He didn't push, didn't ask for anything. Just offered exactly what I needed.

I wanted to take his offering.

But the other part of me was still so raw. I'd showered, but I still felt their hands. Still heard their voices and vulgar comments. Still felt where the bruises and aches from the assaults had been. Still felt how *he'd* reveled in my pain, the cruelty in his touch.

They were phantom pains erased with magick, but the memory of their touch, *that* I still remembered. I hoped one day I wouldn't. I hoped one day all of the bad memories would be erased by good ones. One day at a time. One stroke of Alek's fingers would replace one in my memory from my attackers.

"I don't want you to leave me."

A heavy sigh of relief slipped from his chest, and he let his body sink more completely into the cushions. "I will never leave you, Gretchen. You are my heart and soul."

"You are mine, Alek." By the gods, I needed to touch him, to feel the connection between us course through my body. I scooted from my protected corner and burrowed against his side, pulling the blanket along with me.

He wrapped his arm tentatively around me, waiting... but I didn't start or jerk or recoil. All I felt was peace, acceptance, support, and warmth, so much warmth.

"Would it be okay if I read a little?" He lifted his other hand, and I peered up, recognizing the cover of *Antony and Cleopatra*. "I thought it might help us both." Alek's voice dipped lower, gravelly and choked with emotion. "I love you."

My heart began to thaw.

He hurt for me, with me. And he loved me. He'd never

give up on me. We would get through this together, and I would be able to stand at his side and be able to claim that I had experienced a great love the way only Shakespeare could describe.

I turned my head and looked up at his face. "And I love you, my guardian Gryphon."

His eyes darkened at the moniker, and a single tear rolled down his cheek. He leaned his head down, pressing the softest kiss to my hair. Then he flipped open the volume to where we'd left off. His voice rose and fell, rocking me into a peaceful sleep. I was safe. No matter what came next. As long as we were together, we would overcome.

* * *

I hope you enjoyed MY GUARDIAN GRYPHON! Thank you for spending time with me in my world. Please consider leaving a short review. Each one helps tremendously.
XOXO
Krystal Shannan

Turn the page to read part of the Sanctuary series conclusion in book 7, MY VAMPIRE KNIGHT!

CHAPTER ONE

"It is the secret of the world that all things subsist and do not die, but retire a little from sight and afterwards return again."
—Ralph Waldo Emerson, *Essays: Second Series*

CALLIOPE

THE WARMTH WAS GONE.

The light was gone.

The protection spell was gone.

Everyone stood in the courtyard hoping beyond all hopes that Rose somehow still lived. That Xerxes hadn't killed her. But he had. I was sure. And I couldn't tell them, because the only way I knew was the damn charm in my hand. The small white crystal Rose had linked to my soul hid me from *him*. And if the spell on mine had broken, my sisters already had a target squarely on their backs.

Fear snaked its way through me like the cold fingers of Death himself, choking and suffocating and painfully reminding me of the fate that waited if I didn't find a way to hide again. If I didn't find someone else to protect me. Someone else to rebuild the charm.

My sisters and I would all die. Over. And over. And over.

These people in Sanctuary thought Xerxes was the only bad thing out there. The only monster. But he wasn't. I closed my fingers around the small white crystal and took a deep breath. I couldn't show emotion. Certainly not fear. Not the earth-shattering-soul-stealing terror filling me now like water filling a sealed grave with me locked inside.

No.

No one could see me like that. I was better than that. Stronger. I had survived this long. Survived so much. There had to be a way for me to save myself and my sisters from *him*.

He was coming.

He would torture them first, though.

He always did. They were my weakness. The way he could punish me most efficiently. The way he took advantage of what remained of my heart.

"Calliope?" Erick's mate, Bailey—also one of the town's vampire Protectors—stepped to my side and touched my shoulder. "What's wrong? Do you feel something?"

Something? I'd felt too many things since coming to this town. It'd made me soft. Made me forget. Made me think I deserved things I knew I didn't. Tricked me into caring about people when I should've stayed focused. I glanced down at my hand. My fingernails were long black claws, which meant my eyes had morphed too. *By the Gods!* Attention was not what I needed right now.

"Just feeling the loss," I replied, willing the proper emotion into my voice and forcing my body to transform from its agitated, ready-for-battle state.

"We don't know that she's dead yet," Bailey whispered. "There's still hope. There was no body." They'd only found Eli's body in Xerxes destroyed camp. While his death had been a painful blow to the town, everyone hoped their precious Rose had survived.

I nodded and patted her hand. There wasn't any hope, body or not. I knew Rose Hilah was dead, but I couldn't tell Bailey that. I couldn't tell any of them. They would want to know *how* I knew and I wouldn't tell them...I hadn't even told Rose all of it.

I glanced around the frozen stone courtyard then up at the distorted clouds overhead. Diana had sealed us inside. The entire castle was encased in a fucking snow-globe of ice. Not that I begrudged her grief over her lost mate, but at least she still had another. She would survive. She should be grateful. In a world like ours, survival was everything. The quicker they *all* remembered that, the better off everyone would be. Rose had made us feel too safe. Too protected from things outside Sanctuary. We all had our reasons for hiding here.

Mine was gone now. Missing and dead.

"Stay close to Erick." I glanced into the sapphire blue eyes of a woman who considered me a friend. I liked Bailey. I didn't want her to die. But friends weren't a luxury I'd ever been able to afford. This town and its inhabitants thought I was their friend—their ally. That I would help because I'd always helped. And I would've because of my arrangement with Rose, but now...now I was on my own. They had their problems, and I had mine.

Rose was gone.

My gaze drifted to one of the other vampire Protectors —Eira. She and her Elvin mate, Killían, stood next to the Drakonae, Miles and Diana. The dragonfire swords on Eira and Killían's backs gleamed in the morning sunlight. Their weapons could hurt Xerxes, though they had no way to get close enough to use them. And Eira was nearly as pregnant as Diana, so that knocked out two very powerful warriors on Sanctuary's side. Diana and Eira's mates would be unfocused and more vulnerable because of their concern.

The odds for the upcoming fight were not promising.

My gaze darted to the other individuals circling the casket of ice Diana had built around her dead husband Eli. Seeing Eli's body—the death of one of the most powerful supernaturals in town—should've made everyone run for the hills. Instead, Gretchen, the young Sister of Lamidae who'd been tortured by Xerxes, had come out slinging words around like *fight* and *win* and *conquer*, and everyone had bought the speech. Alek, her Gryphon mate, stood beside her, holding her hand. It was all so sickly sweet and made me want to hurl. Not because I begrudged the woman her happiness, but because I didn't get to have that. No one had or would ever look at me the way Alek looked at Gretchen.

The pixies huddled together, trying to look tough, but mostly pulled off looking like a group of terrified My Little Pony wannabes. Their ponytails incorporated every color on the spectrum. Pixies were powerful, but they weren't fighters. Sooner than later, they'd all leave and go back to their grove of oak trees outside the town and disappear.

Jared stood off to one side, near Alek and Gretchen, flames licking at his fingertips, a thirst for blood on each whisper of breath he exhaled. The warmth of his Phoenix's fire had melted Diana's frost in a ring around his body that extended out several feet. He was a wild card and wouldn't help me. His only thought was for Manda—the traitorous Djinn held captive by Xerxes himself. Even if Jared managed to get to her, she'd never be welcomed in Sanctuary.

Then there were the wolves—Lycans. A large group had gathered with us in the courtyard, at least fifty or sixty. Charlie, Travis, and Garrett at the forefront, their two children in their arms.

All the Lycans had agreed to throw their fucking hat into the ring, too. Given the opportunity, they would die for those they loved. I wasn't on that list. Not even Rose had truly cared. I was a means to an end. They were all a means to Rose's end.

They were all stupid.

We should be leaving, not preparing to make a stand.

ABOUT THE AUTHOR

Krystal Shannan lives in a sprawling ranch style home with her husband, daughter, and a pack of rescue Basset Hounds. She is an advocate for Autism Awareness and shares the experiences and adventures she's been through with her daughter whenever she can.

Needless to say, life is never boring when you have an elementary-aged special needs child you are home-schooling and half a dozen 4-legged friends roaming the house. They keep her and her husband busy, smiling, and laughing.

If you are looking for leisurely-paced sweet romance, her books are probably not for you. However, for those looking for a story filled with adventure, passion, and just enough humor to make you laugh out loud. Welcome home!

www.krystalshannan.com

Other Books By Krystal Shannan

<u>Vegas Mates</u>
Completed Series

Chasing Sam

Saving Margaret
Waking Sarah
Taking Nicole
Unwrapping Tess
Loving Hallie

Sanctuary, Texas
Completed Series

My Viking Vampire
My Dragon Masters
My Eternal Soldier
Mastered: Teagan
My Warrior Wolves
My Guardian Gryphon
My Vampire Knight

VonBrandt Family Pack
Part of the Somewhere, TX Saga

To Save A Mate
To Love A Mate
To Win A Mate
To Find A Mate
To Plan For A Mate (coming next)

MoonBound
Completed Series
Part of the Somewhere, TX Saga

The Werewolf Cowboy #1
The Werewolf Bodyguard #2